SO
MUCH
MORE

Books by Dana Wilkerson

Throwback RomComs
More Than Pen Pals
So Much More

Books by D.A. Wilkerson

Totally 80s Mysteries
A Totally Killer Wedding
Most Likely to Kill
Of Heist and Men
A Totally 80s Christmas

Mystery Journals
Mysterious Musings
My Totally Suspect Notebook

SO MUCH MORE

A Throwback RomCom

DANA WILKERSON

So Much More
A Throwback RomCom – Book 2
by Dana Wilkerson

© 2023 Dana Wilkerson

Designed in the USA
Published by Dana Wilkerson, LLC
Edmond, OK
danawilkerson.com

First Edition: September 2023

Paperback ISBN: 978-1-948148-52-8
eBook ISBN: 978-1-948148-53-5

Dedicated to anyone who has ever been able to relate to REO Speedwagon's "Can't Fight This Feeling"

prologue

. . .

Chicago, May 1988

Wendy

"Can we do this again?" Randall asks, his cheek resting against my head as I sit curled up on his lap on his couch.

I pull slightly away from him so I can look him in the eye. "Do what again?"

"*This.*" He points to me and them himself. "You and me. Here. Doing this. Talking. Whatever."

My eyes widen as my heart pounds. "But earlier you said …"

Panic flits across his face before he tamps it down, but I catch it.

"I said I'm not going to kiss you, and I'm definitely not ready to date anyone right now," he says. "It hasn't even been a week since Colleen and I broke up. But we're friends, right? I trust you, and I've enjoyed being here with you and talking to you. I needed this. I want to do it again. Do you?"

I search his eyes as I consider what I want. I want him, I know that. But do I want what he proposed? Can I handle it? Can I let him hold me like this, be emotionally vulnerable with him, and keep it from going beyond that? Externally, I think I can. But internally, it'll kill me to keep my feelings to myself and not fall for him even more than I already have.

This is a terrible idea, my brain says.

"Yeah, I want to do it again," my mouth says.

"Promise me you won't tell Leslie," he says as he tucks my

hair behind my ear. "She and Ash need to focus on each other right now, not on us."

My friend Leslie and Randall's brother Ash are currently on their first official date. I haven't known Leslie all that long, but we've become close very quickly. I don't want to keep something like this from her, but I also don't look forward to her interrogating me about it, which she'll undoubtedly do. She'll be shocked beyond belief that I'm interested in spending time with Randall, and I can't imagine she'll think what he's proposing is a good idea, either. Because it's not.

"Okay," I agree. "And if we don't want them to know, we should probably hang out at my place instead of yours, since Ash has a key to your apartment."

"Great plan," he says. "Ash doesn't always warn me before he stops by." He gently pushes my head back against his shoulder and folds his arms around me. "Now, tell me all the reasons you think I'm amazing."

I giggle. "You're a mess."

"Come on, don't get shy on me now." He squeezes me. "I need a boost after the way Colleen treated me. Tell me why you like me. And if the reasons are good enough, I might also tell you why I like you."

My heart rate increases, and I try to will it back to normal as I admit, "I like that you can act goofy and not be ashamed of it. I like how you make everyone around you feel like they're important. And sometimes I like your cockiness."

"Only sometimes?" He pokes my side, and I giggle again.

"Yes, only sometimes. I like that you're confident in yourself. But you don't always have the best judgment about when to rein it in."

He's quiet for a moment before saying, "I can't argue with that. And that's one thing I like about you—you're not afraid to tell people what you really think. Although ..."

I lean away so I can look at him again. "Although what?"

He smirks at me. "You don't always have the best judgment about when to rein it in."

I swat his chest. "Hey!"

"It's true, though. You can't deny it."

"Okay, fine. You're right. Sometimes I should keep my mouth shut."

"You have the cutest little mouth, though."

His hand moves to my cheek as his gaze lingers on my lips, and I grasp his wrist.

"Don't do that," I whisper.

"Right." He moves his hand back to my hip, which isn't much better. "Sorry. We're friends. Friends don't say or do things like that."

Friends don't sit on each other's laps, either, but for once I don't say what I think, even though this is one time I definitely should.

one

. . .

June 1988

Randall

My obituary will read, "Randall Hamilton was a loving son, brother, and friend. He died a slow, agonizing death due to Wendy O'Halloran's indifference to his charms."

Currently, the woman in question is lying on her couch, her head in my lap, chattering about one of her PR clients who has been more than a handful. However, I'm paying more attention to my fingers sliding through her long, silky, red hair than to what she's saying.

It's weird to have a close, platonic female friend. I've never had one before. It turns out I like having a woman to talk to without romantic complications—someone who can help me put my life into perspective. But the more time I spend with Wendy, the more I want to crush her to me and find out how her lips would feel against mine. She seems perfectly content not to kiss me, though, so I've kept myself in check. I respect her and value her friendship too much to try to take this to a level she doesn't seem to want. Cuddles and conversation are what we agreed to, and I'm going to stick to that, no matter how difficult it may be and how idiotic that idea was in the first place.

When I truly think about it, I'm not sure I'm ready for another relationship so soon after Colleen, anyway. And if I ever do take things to the next level with Wendy, it will be for a real relationship, not a friends-with-benefits situation. Wendy deserves better than that. In fact, she needs a man who's much better than me, so I should put any notions of a potential relationship with her out of my head right now.

"Randall?" Wendy pokes my leg.

I snap to attention. "Hmm?"

"Are you listening to me?"

"Yep." I nod to emphasize my semi-lie, even though she's lying on her side and not looking at me.

"What did I just say?"

"You were telling me all about Pamela Sanders and how she's driving you bananas."

"But what exactly was I saying about Pamela?"

Wendy rolls onto her back so she can look up at me. I brush some hair out of her face as I gaze down into her emerald eyes.

"You were saying she's going to marry her German Shepherd while juggling knives and roller skating around Buckingham Fountain. Which sounds like an amazing PR opportunity to me, though you might want to steer clear of the flying knives." I grin at her.

"Well, I tried to convince her to juggle puppies instead, but she simply wouldn't listen."

"That's probably a good idea," I say. "It's all fun and games until a puppy gets a finger to the eye."

"Or worse," she adds.

I chuckle. "I'm not sure I want to know what's running through your mind right now."

She smiles, but then a confused look crosses her face. "I should be mad you weren't paying attention."

"But you're not?" I'm running my fingers through her hair again.

"Nope."

"I'm sorry I wasn't focused on you." Actually, I *was* focused on her, but not in a way I want to tell her about.

"You have good reason not to be." She sits up.

"Hey." I take her by the shoulders to try to move her back where she was. "Come back here. I'll pay attention now. Scout's honor."

"No." She removes my hands. "It's not you. I promise. I've been rambling way too long. I should let you get home. Ash is probably wondering where you are."

My brother, who moved in with me a few weeks ago, couldn't care less where I am. "He and Leslie are out tonight. He won't be in until late, if at all."

"Still," she says, "I've kept you here way too long. You were the one who came over to talk, and I've monopolized the conversation. Will you be okay? Do we need to talk about Colleen any more?"

I ran into my ex-girlfriend and her new boyfriend—my former friend—when I was picking up takeout on my way home from work. I drove home in a daze, parked my car in the garage, and decided I didn't want to head up to my empty apartment. Instead, I walked to Wendy's and shared my food with her, and then we ended up talking on the couch together, like always.

"I'll be fine," I say. "I'm over her. I truly am." I mostly am. And that's due in no small part to all the time I've been spending with Wendy. "But it was still a sucker punch to see them together."

She nods and rests a hand on my thigh. "I'm sorry for what she put you through."

I stare at her hand for too long before I look back at her face and respond, "You don't need to be sorry. She's the one who hurt me."

"I know. But you're my friend, and when you hurt, I hurt. I hope someday you'll be able to see her without any kind of reaction other than being glad she showed you her true colors before it was too late."

See? This is why Wendy is good for me. And it's why I want to kiss her so badly right now. Well, it's one of many reasons.

I need distance from her, so I stand. As I'm about to move toward the door, Wendy also stands, wraps her arms around my waist, and rests her cheek against my chest.

"You deserve so much better than Colleen," she says.

I loop my arms around her and hope she didn't register the stutter in my heartbeat at her unexpected hug and words.

"Thank you."

"You're welcome."

Wendy pats me on the back and then pulls away. I reluctantly let her go.

"I'll see you at work tomorrow," I say as I head out the door.

"As always." She smiles as she closes the door behind me.

I slump against the elevator wall as I ride down to the ground floor. I don't know how much longer I can do this with Wendy. I don't want to lose her friendship, but keeping my feelings to myself is one of the hardest things I've ever done.

As I reach the conference room at Carter-Jenkins PR the next morning, Wendy is headed my way from the opposite direction, so I wait for her. She's wearing a stunning dress, which isn't typical, as she usually wears skirt suits that look like they were specifically created to mold to her curves. This dress looks even better on her, and I struggle to keep my eyes focused on her face. I shake my head in a vain attempt to rid myself of thoughts I shouldn't be having about her.

"What's that head shake for?" she asks as she stops in front of me. "Thinking about how you need to stop singing Debbie Gibson songs in the shower?"

I laugh. "Have you been hiding under my bathroom sink again? I told you to stop that."

She shrugs. "I can't help it. It's so cozy under there, and it has such great acoustics for my private concerts."

"You're a nut," I say with a fond smile.

"As long as I can be a macadamia nut, I'm good with that."

"Macadamias are my favorite, so that works perfectly." To be more specific, chocolate-covered macadamias are my favorite. I shake my head again before I start thinking about Wendy covered in chocolate. "Anyway, I was thinking about how I need to behave myself."

"Please don't," she says. "Your jokes and witty comments are what make all-staff meetings bearable. Before you were here, they were torture."

I've been working at Carter-Jenkins for only a few weeks as in-house legal counsel. But I've known Wendy much longer than that, because Ash used to be the PR firm's general counsel on a contract basis, and our previous law office is located around the corner. Wendy was in our offices much more often than she needed to be. I used to think that was because she had a thing for my brother, but she recently assured me that wasn't the case. Now I'm wondering why she was there so much.

"Randall!" Wendy snaps her fingers in front of my face.

"Sorry." I shake my head again. "I'm a little distracted today."

She cocks her hip and plants a fist on it. "Oh, yeah? What's distracting you?"

I can't help raking my eyes up and down her body. The calf-length bright blue dress isn't inappropriate for the office, but there's something about it that makes me want to—

Wendy snaps her fingers again as she sighs. "It's the dress, isn't it?"

"What? No." I stick my hands in my pockets and try to look nonchalant.

"This," she sweeps her hands up and down her body, "makes you not pay much attention to what I'm saying, doesn't it? Please be honest with me."

I snag her wrist and pull her farther away from the doorway. I wait for our co-worker Brian to pass by us on his way into the room before I say in a low voice, "I'm sorry if I made you uncomfortable. I shouldn't have looked at you like that—not in the office. Well, not anywhere, actually, since we're friends and all. It's disrespectful."

She briefly closes her eyes. "It's fine. I know you respect me. It's that I don't want the other guys looking at me like that."

"They'd better not be looking at you like that," I growl out. But I wonder if she wants *me* looking at her like that.

Wendy huffs out a laugh. "As if you can stop them. You couldn't even stop yourself. But anyway, now I know not to wear this dress to the office again."

"It's not the dress." I cringe, wishing I can take the statement back as soon as I say it.

She tilts her head and gives me a curious look. "No? Then what is it?"

It's her, no matter what she's wearing. I want so badly to say it, but this is neither the time nor the place. In fact, I'm not sure there is a time or place for me to say that to her.

"Hey, you two," Leslie says, her head peeking out the conference room door, "get in here. We need to get started."

two

. . .

Wendy

"What in the world is going on between you and Randall?" Leslie demands from across my office desk mere minutes after I return from the all-staff meeting.

I lean back in my cushy pink leather chair, look her in the eye, and lie through my teeth. "Absolutely nothing. And close the door if you're going to talk about personal matters at the office."

She spins around and swings the door shut before planting her hands on top of my desk and narrowing her eyes at me. "I don't believe you."

"Why would I lie to you?"

"That's yet another thing I don't know. If there's something romantic happening between you and Randall, I'll be ecstatic. I know you've had thing for him for as long as you've known him, and he's a great guy. So for the life of me I can't fathom why you're not telling me."

I force myself not to cross my arms over my chest as I ask, "Why do you think something's going on between us?"

Leslie jabs her finger onto my desk. "Because before the all-staff meeting, you were holding hands. And then during the meeting, the two of you kept giving each other sly little smiles when you were talking about Pamela Sanders. What was that about?"

"We weren't holding hands." He was holding my wrist—those

are two completely different things. "And those looks you think you saw? They were nothing."

They weren't nothing. They were Randall and me acknowledging he knows how much Sandra drives me batty. I usually don't complain about my clients to anyone, or at least I didn't until Randall. I feel like I can tell him anything. Well, anything other than I dream about him every night and am dying to know if he tastes as good as he smells. And oh, does he smell heavenly.

"They weren't nothing," Leslie says. "And I'm not the only one who noticed."

My heart beats faster as I try not to panic. Since there's nothing of substance happening between Randall and me, I'd rather not be the subject of office gossip.

"Who else noticed?" I ask.

"Aha!" She jabs a finger into the air. "So you admit there's something to notice!"

I rest my forehead on my desk and lightly bang it a few times before looking back up at her. "We'll talk about that in a minute. Who noticed?"

"Brian asked me about you two as soon as you left the conference room. I told him nothing's happening, which I now know is wrong. Just admit you're having a torrid affair with Randall Hamilton that for some inexplicable reason you don't want your best friend to know about."

"We're not having an affair. Not that it would be an affair anyway, since we're both single. We can do whatever we want."

She crosses her arms over her chest. "Then what is it?"

I shrug and take the easy way out. "I promised him I wouldn't tell you."

"Wouldn't tell me what?"

"Nope. You're not getting me to trip up again."

Leslie holds up a finger. "Wait a second. I'll be back." She's out the door before I can ask where she's going.

Two minutes later she reappears with Randall on her heels. As soon as the door clicks shut behind him, she says, "Now that you're both here, you can decide together whether Wendy is allowed to break her promise to not tell me about what's happening here." She points her finger back and forth between the two of us.

Randall's eyes widen and he shoots me a beseeching look.

"Sorry," I say. "She figured out something's going on. I didn't say a word."

With quick flicks of his long, slender fingers, Randall unbuttons his suit jacket, drops his tall frame down onto the lavender couch in the corner of my office, and rests his elbows on his knees. I take a second to admire the forearms peeking out from his sleeves and the way his charcoal-gray pants stretch over the thighs I've curled up on so many times.

"Go ahead and tell her." His words draw my attention up to his mouth, which doesn't help me be any less distracted by him. "Now that she knows something, you know she's not going to let it go."

I tear my eyes from Randall and focus on Leslie. "We cuddle."

"You c-cuddle." She looks between the two of us in disbelief. "Is this a joke?"

"Nope." Randall pops the "p" in the word as he props one ankle on the other knee and makes himself comfortable on the couch. The sight, unsurprisingly, makes me want to rush over, plant myself on his lap, and snuggle up against him. I'm as predictable as Pavlov's dog.

"We cuddle," he says. "That's it. She's my cuddle buddy."

Leslie is speechless.

"No, that's not completely accurate," I say. "We also talk."

Randall bobs his head up and down like a plastic dog on a dashboard. "True. We sometimes talk. While we cuddle. Other times we just cuddle."

"Stop saying 'cuddle.' It's weird," Leslie says. "What do you talk about?"

"Life," I say.

"Family stuff," Randall adds.

"Work."

"Our feelings," he states matter-of-factly.

Leslie's jaw drops. "Your *feelings*? About what?"

"Colleen," he says.

"Life," I repeat.

"You and Ash," Randall says to her.

"Really?" I ask him. "You're telling her that?"

He shrugs. "Why not?"

"You don't tell people you talk about them behind their backs!"

Leslie's hands go to her hips. "And exactly what are you saying about us behind our backs?"

"That you're perfect for each other," Randall explains, "and seeing you together makes us both want what you have."

"Seriously?" I ask him.

He spreads his hands wide. "What's wrong with admitting that? It's true, and there's no shame in it."

"He's not wrong," Leslie tells me.

I huff out a breath. "Fine. It's true. I want what you and Ash have. Are you happy?"

"I'm not happy you've been hiding this from us."

"It wasn't hard." Randall runs a hand through his dark hair. "You and my brother have been a little wrapped up in each other lately." He quickly adds, "Not that there's anything wrong with that. I'd be the same in your shoes."

"So that's all you do when you're together?" Leslie asks.

Randall and I nod.

"You don't kiss?"

We shake our heads.

"You don't … do other things?"

We shake our heads again, but then Randall says, "Sometimes I give her a foot rub."

If I were next to him, I'd elbow him in the ribs.

Leslie's gaze bounces between us a few more times. "I'm not sure what you mean by … that word I don't want to hear from you again."

"Does it matter?" I ask, as Randall says, "We can show you."

I gasp. "We're not showing her!"

"Get over here so I can cuddle the heck out of you, Wendy O'Halloran." His demanding tone sends a shiver through me.

"Go on, then," Leslie says with a grin, clearly having noticed my physical response to him. "Show me how you do it."

"No, I'm not doing that in my office!"

"Then cuddle Leslie," the man himself says. "There's room right here next to me." He has the gall to pat the couch cushion.

"No!"

"I guess I'll have to explain it to her then," Randall says.

My, "Please don't," is completely ignored.

"It's not always the same," he begins, as I bang my head on my desk again. "But usually we start out with her sitting sideways on my lap, like this." I can imagine he's gesturing with his arms, but I refuse to look up. "Then she lays her head on my shoulder, which is easy for her to do since she's such a tiny little thing and I'm not, and then I put my arms around her, doing my best to cop a feel without seeming to do so."

My head pops up. "You do not!" Though I can't say I'd mind if he did.

He chuckles. "No, I was checking that you're listening and not giving yourself brain damage over there." He continues the torment with, "Sometimes we spoon on the couch," and I groan. "I'm always the big spoon, obviously, since I'm twice her size. We tried it the other way one time, but that was a colossal failure. Her nose poked my back, which was ticklish."

I cross my arms over my chest. "Are you done?"

"No, I haven't told her about—"

"Enough!" I cut him off. Although I have no idea what he's about to say, I know I don't want Leslie to hear it. "Let's keep at least some things sacred here, all right?"

Randall holds his hands up. "Got it. The rest is sacred."

"Thank you."

Leslie says, "You two realize you're playing with fire here, right? One of these days one of you might want more, and what if the other person doesn't want that? What happens to your friendship? What happens to your working relationship?"

It all falls apart.

"The way I see it," Randall says, "one of us might want more whether I'm hanging out on Wendy's couch or I'm playing third-wheel to you and Ash at home. It doesn't matter how much time we spend together."

My stomach clenches. "Is that why you come over?" I ask him. "To avoid being the third wheel?" I think I might be sick.

"No!" he practically shouts. "This started before Ash moved in with me, remember?"

"Hold on," Leslie says. "When exactly did this thing begin?"

I sigh. "That night I took you over to Randall's place so you could tell Ash you were ready to date him."

Leslie's eyes widen. "This has been going on for a *month*? How often do you see each other?"

"A couple times a week," I say. "I'm sorry I didn't tell you. I wanted to so many times."

Randall says to me, "I shouldn't have asked you not to tell her. That wasn't fair to either of you. I'm sorry."

"No, I'm the one who should be sorry," Leslie says. "This wasn't the time or the place to confront you about this. I apologize, and I'm going to let everyone get back to work."

She leaves my office and closes the door behind her. Randall and I look at each other.

"Are we going to keep doing what we've been doing?" I ask.

"I don't know. I need to think about it. But we shouldn't continue this conversation here."

I swallow the lump in my throat and nod at him. "Why don't you come over tonight so we can talk about it?"

three

. . .

Randall

"**W**hat is *wrong* with you?" Ash asks from the love seat across from me.

I drop my head into my hands. "I don't know," I mumble.

"How did you think this wasn't going to come back to bite you?"

When I glance up at him, he looks so high-and-mighty sitting with his arms crossed over his chest, I want to smack him.

"Stop it, will you? I know I screwed up. I shouldn't have let this go so far with her, but I couldn't help myself. She's … ugh, I don't know. It feels so *right* when she's in my arms."

Ash gives me a thoughtful look. "Is it her in particular, or do you feel that way any time you hold an attractive woman?"

I sigh and close my eyes as I try to compare how it feels to hold Wendy compared to any other woman. I honestly can't remember. All I can think about is how her tiny but curvy frame fits exactly right against mine, how her hair tickles my neck when she's curled onto my lap, how our heartbeats and breathing start out erratic yet eventually sync up when I'm spooning her from behind with my hand splayed possessively across her belly.

"I'm a terrible, horrible person," I say.

"That wasn't a direct answer to my question, yet somehow you answered it. And the fact that you're not your usual cocky self about this tells me you care a lot more about Wendy than you're letting on to me or maybe even to yourself."

I throw myself onto my back on the couch, staring at the ceiling. After a minute of silence, I turn my head to look at him. "Is she going to hate me?"

"I don't know." He narrows his eyes at me. "What are you planning to do that might make her hate you?"

"It's not so much what I'm going to do as what I've done— starting this thing with her that I can't finish. Because I did start it, and even if she doesn't want to be with me, it's going to make things weird between us when I end it."

"Is ending it what you want?"

"No, it's not what I want!" I punch the back of the couch. "I like her, man. I like her a lot, and I didn't realize how much until the last week or so. But I have to put an end to it. I'm an absolute disaster. I screw up every relationship I'm in, and I won't do that to her. *I won't.*"

"What do you mean, you screw up every relationship? Colleen's the one who jacked up this last one."

"She might have cheated, but I drove her to it," I explain.

"No. There's never a good excuse for cheating. I don't care what you did. If she wanted to sleep with someone else, she should have broken up with you first. That's not on you. But what is it you think you did that drove her to it?"

"I wasn't …," I search for the right word, "… enough. She always wanted me to do more, to *be* more, and I couldn't. I tried for a while, but it didn't take long for me to realize I didn't like her enough to want to try. I should have broken up with her then, but I was too chicken to do it. I didn't want to end up alone. I figured being with her was better than being with nobody, and I've never been good at picking women who are good for me anyway."

Ash sighs. "Colleen never accepted you for who you are. She expected you to be someone you're not, but a person who truly loves you won't try to mold you into who they want you to be. You need a woman who will not only let you be you, but also encourage you to be the best version of yourself you can be. And yes, you probably should've broken up with Colleen, but that still doesn't make it okay that she cheated on you."

I stare at him.

"What?" he demands.

"Look at you giving relationship advice. It's a new side of you. I'm not sure if I like it or not."

Ash rolls his eyes. "Well, get used to it. You're going to need it if you want to survive Wendy."

I can't help the smile that overtakes my face as I look back at the ceiling. "She's a little spitfire, isn't she?"

"Yes, and if you stupidly try to break things off with her, and she doesn't want you to, she'll go down swinging."

"She doesn't want more from me. If she did, she would've told me, or she would've kissed me, or something. Wendy speaks her mind and goes after what she wants. You know that."

"I'm not so sure."

My head turns toward him so fast I get dizzy. "Not so sure about what?"

"That she doesn't want more."

"Why aren't you sure?" I demand, sitting up.

He shrugs. "Just a vibe I get."

I laugh. "A vibe? You get vibes?"

"Sometimes. Shut up."

"You shut up." I flop back down and stare at the ceiling yet again. "If she wants more, why hasn't she done anything about it?"

"Maybe for the same reason you haven't done anything about it—she thinks you don't want more. You're never shy when it comes to women. If you want to be with someone, you let her know. But you haven't let Wendy know. Instead, you're …," he waves his hand in my general direction, "… all weird and stuff. You're never like this."

He's right.

"I didn't tell Wendy I want her because *I* didn't know at first. And here lately I've been afraid to do anything about it for fear of losing her."

"Well, now that you know, do something about it. You said

you were too much of a chicken to do the right thing with Colleen. Don't be a chicken with Wendy. Tell her how you feel, and then let her decide if she wants to put up with you or not."

"But what if she doesn't want to put up with me?" I throw my arm over my eyes. "Not that it matters, if I'm not going to let anything happen between us. *Ugh.* I'm so mixed up about this whole thing. I never get this worked up over a woman. But I think I need to learn who I am on my own. I haven't been single for more than a month or two at a time since I was in high school. I've got to figure myself out."

"It's hard to argue with that, but you'd better tell Wendy that's what you need instead of just telling her it's over. I'm pretty sure she'd understand. How long do you think it'll take you to figure yourself out?"

I take a minute to consider my answer, since I've not really thought about this until now. "A few months? A year? I don't know. I'm grateful for my job at Carter-Jenkins, but you know I only became a lawyer because Dad practically forced me into it. I need to decide what I want to do next and make a plan for how I can afford to make that happen."

"You don't have to do that alone. Wendy can help you."

I shake my head. "She shouldn't have to."

"Maybe she wants to," he counters. "I think you need to give her the chance to make that decision instead of making it for her."

My chest grows tight at the thought she might want to do that, but I say, "You know how I get when I start dating someone. I fall fast and hard and I get so wrapped up in her I forget the rest of the world exists. I can't do that right now. I've got to straighten my life out, and I want to spend as much time with the girls this summer as I can."

Our younger sisters, Tonya and Sonya, are eighteen and seventeen, and Tonya leaves for Duke University in the fall. When I left home for prep school at fourteen, the girls were six and five. I don't know who they are now as almost-adults, and I'm about to lose my chance with Tonya.

I add, "I'm so angry I wasted this last year on Colleen instead of getting to know our sisters better."

"I get that. I get all of it. But Wendy can't wait forever."

"What does that mean?"

"She'll be thirty-one in a couple months."

I freeze. "She'll be what, now?" I had no idea Wendy is more than four years older than me.

"I was surprised, too, when Leslie told me, but it's true. And I know she wants a family."

This new information complicates matters. Wendy might not want to wait until I get my life figured out—if she wants to wait for me at all. And it wouldn't be fair of me to ask her to.

"Do you care that she's older than you?" Ash asks.

"No. I don't care how old she is."

"She may also make more money than you do. Do you care about that?"

Do I? "I don't think so." I grin at him. "Might be nice to have a sugar mama."

He picks up the copy of *GQ* on the coffee table and hurls it at me.

I bat the magazine away as I chuckle. "I'm kidding."

Brrring!

Ash reaches over and grabs the phone off the end table. "Hello? … She is? … Okay. I'll tell him. … Love you, too. Bye." He hangs up. "Leslie and Wendy went to McConnell's for a drink after work, and they're both home now if you're ready to go talk to Wendy. Are you?"

"Not really, but I'm not going to be any more ready later tonight … or tomorrow … or next week, so I might as well get it over with."

"Be honest with her and listen to her. Those are the two best things you can do."

"Yes, sir."

four

. . .

Wendy

I'm pacing the floor in my living room when the phone rings, and I pounce on it.

"Hello?" I say breathlessly.

"Hi. It's me."

My pulse goes into overdrive at the sound of Randall's voice. "Hi. You want to come over?"

"Yes, I'll be there in five."

I continue to pace as I think over the conversation I just had with Leslie at the pub. She seems to think he'll be open to being more than friends, but I'm not so sure. But I'm determined to tell him exactly how I feel and that I want more than what we've been doing, although the idea that he might not feel the same has my stomach tied up in knots.

When he buzzes up on the intercom, I press the button to unlock the building's front door, crack my door open, and perch on the edge of the easy chair across from my couch. My knees bounce up and down as I wait the interminable amount of time it takes Randall to reach my apartment on the eighth floor. I sit on my hands so I won't chew my fingernails.

He knocks instead of coming on in like usual, and my heart drops. "Come in," I call out.

Randall enters, and when he spots me in the chair, he stops in his tracks. "What are you doing over there?"

"Um, sitting?"

A look of determination crosses his face. "That's not where we sit."

My heart leaps into my throat, and I force myself to say, "It's where I'm sitting today." While I'm dying to have his arms around me, I can't touch him until I know what he wants.

He takes his usual seat on the couch. *"No."*

My eyes widen at his resolute tone.

"No, what?" I ask.

"No, you're not sitting over there. Get over here with me." He pats his lap.

"I can't."

"And I can't have this conversation with you sitting all the way over there. I need you right here."

I rub my temples. "Randall …"

"Please."

Considering this might be the last time I get the chance to be that close to him, I give in.

Once I'm settled sideways on his lap with my hand pressed against his wildly beating heart and his arms wrapped securely around me, he says, "I don't want to stop doing this."

All the breath whooshes out of my lungs. When I'm able to pull some air back in, I say, "You don't?"

"No. Do you?"

I shake my head vigorously, and I'm about to tell him I need more than what we've been doing when he interrupts me.

"Good. But …"

I can't breathe again while I wait for him to finish his thought. When I think he's not going to, I whisper, "But what?"

"But I want more."

Now I'm afraid I might hyperventilate. "Me, too."

He shifts me so he can look me in the eye, and he tucks an errant strand of hair behind my ear. His hand then slides to the side of my neck with his thumb resting beneath my chin, absolutely searing my skin. "You do?"

I swallow and nod and then snake my own hand up to slide into the short hair at the nape of his neck. "I want so much more."

His gaze focuses on my lips, and I close my eyes as I anticipate the kiss that's about to rock my world, but then he says, "I'm not going to kiss you."

My eyes pop open and my face heats. "What?! Why? Why don't you want to kiss me? You said you want more!"

I try to push away from him, but he holds me in place.

"I want to kiss you—you can't imagine how much—and I do want more, but if we're going to do this, I need us to take things slowly. So slowly it'll undoubtedly be painful."

I study his eyes, which are as serious as I've ever seen them. "So you want to date me … but you don't want to kiss me? That's what you're telling me?"

"No. I want to date you, *and* I want to kiss you, but I'm not going to kiss you. Not yet."

"But why?" I know I'm whining, but goodness gracious I want this man's mouth on mine.

"We'll talk about that—and more—in a little bit. First, I want to make sure *you* want to date *me.*"

"Yes, I want to date you. And I want to kiss you. Right now." I poke his chest on each of the final two words.

He chuckles and shifts my head back to his shoulder. "You're cute when you're fired up."

"I'm not cute," I grumble. He'd better think I'm more than cute if he wants to date me.

"You're ridiculously cute, you gorgeous woman."

I allow myself a small smile. "Okay, I can deal with gorgeous."

Randall lets out a belly laugh that vibrates all the way through me. "Dang, I love you."

My heart pounds as I slowly angle my head to look at him. Did he mean it, or was he saying it flippantly?

"Excuse me?" I say. "That's not taking things slowly."

His eyes widen when he realizes what he said. "I mean I love you as a friend!" Those baby blues open even wider at that proclamation. "I mean … oh man, am I messing this up."

"Please continue." I'm not sure what I want him to say, but I do know I want the truth about how he feels. "Let's see how much farther you can stick your giant foot into your mouth."

Randall takes a long breath. "Wendy O'Halloran."

"Yes, Randall Hamilton?"

"We've been friends for a while, right?"

"Right."

"And I love you like I love a friend."

My entire body tenses.

He adds, "But …"

"But …"

"… I'd like to see if maybe someday I might love you as more than a friend."

My heart beats frantically as I pat his cheek and attempt to appear calm and collected. "You finally came around to it there in the end. But you might need to kiss me to make up for declaring your love for me prematurely."

He cocks his head to the side. "Okay, one kiss."

I perk up. "Really?"

Before I have time to prepare, he rapidly closes the few inches between our faces and pecks me on the nose.

"There. Done." He gives me a silly grin.

"Ugh, I hate you!" I swat his chest, and he presses his hand against mine to hold it in place.

"No, you don't. You love … I mean you *like* me. A lot, I hope."

"The jury's still out on that," I lie.

"That's a little concerning. As a lawyer, I know how fickle juries can be."

He tickles my side, and I shriek as my body automatically jerks away from his touch, but he keeps a firm hold on me and continues tickling me as I flail around trying to get away from him while not really wanting to get away from him.

When we settle down again, I ask, "If we can't kiss, can we still cuddle?"

"I think so."

I raise an eyebrow. "You think so? Why don't you know so?"

"Because I don't know if I can keep holding you like this without kissing you. I've been teetering on the edge of control, and I don't know if I can hang on anymore."

"Oh, I'm definitely cuddling you then." I poke his belly. "And you can't stop me."

"You really think so? I'm more than a foot taller than you and weigh at least twice as much as you do, my little Munchkin."

The possessive nickname sends a thrill through me, yet I give him a mock glare. "Are you threatening me, Randall Hamilton?"

"No!" He cups my shoulders and looks me dead in the eye. "I will never threaten you or touch you in any way that will hurt you. I swear to you."

I match his tone so he'll know I'm as serious as he is. "I know. I was kidding."

He nods. "Good."

"And I'm not a Munchkin." I sit up as tall as I can. "I'm at least six inches taller than they are."

Randall grins at me with a gleam in his eye.

"Why are you looking at me like that, you weirdo?" I ask.

"You want to know what I call you when you're not around?"

"No," I shake my head, "I don't."

"Well, I'm going to tell you anyway. I call you Glinda."

"Glinda?" I can feel my forehead wrinkling. "Why?"

"Because you remind me of Glinda the Good Witch in *The Wizard of Oz.* Just like her, you're kind and you're beautiful and you love to help people."

My heart melts. "That's so sweet. I love it." I remove his hand from where it's resting on my hip and kiss his palm, since he won't let me kiss his mouth. "You're a real smooth talker."

"Not trying to be smooth—only honest," he says.

"I appreciate that. Can I call you the Wizard?"

He chuckles. "Why? You think he and Glinda had a little something-something going on?" He wiggles his eyebrows.

"No, but neither will we, apparently."

"Touché, my good witch."

five

. . .

Randall

How I'm going to keep from kissing the woman in my arms, I don't know. I didn't plan to implement the no-kissing rule, but when her mouth was inches from mine, begging me to taste it, I knew if I gave in, I wouldn't be able to stop, and that would lead to other things, and … well, then I'd be right where I always am at this point in a relationship, and I want to do things differently this time.

I also didn't intend to come right out and tell Wendy I wanted more with her. In fact, when I arrived at her apartment, I was certain I was going to tell her I needed time on my own to get my life together. But then I walked through the door and she was sitting alone in that chair looking so anxious, and my heart nearly shattered. Breaking things off with her or putting a potential relationship on hold were no longer options. I'm now all in.

"Have you eaten dinner?" I ask her.

"Nope. You?"

"Not really. Let's go get something." I loop one arm under her knees and stand with her still in my arms.

She giggles and wraps her arms around my neck, her mouth hovering dangerously close to mine. "You going to carry me there?"

"Do you want me to?"

She gives me a quick kiss on the cheek. "I do, but you'd better put me down. You're going to need to preserve your strength in order to keep up this no-kissing nonsense."

"It's not nonsense, and I recall you kissing me about ten seconds ago."

"Cheek kisses don't count," she declares.

"No?"

"No. Or nose kisses or forehead kisses or palm kisses."

"Or top-of-the-head kisses," I add.

"Neck kisses?" she asks hopefully.

"Definitely not. That's like second base—maybe third."

"Nope, it's only first-and-a-half. But I do love a good necking session." She shudders in my arms, and my resolve wavers precariously.

"No." I shake my head firmly. "No necking. And I didn't know anyone actually said that word outside of movies set in the 50s."

"I say it. If I can't kiss your neck, can I lick it?"

It takes every bit of my strength to set her down on her feet to get her tongue away from the vicinity of my neck.

"I think maybe you're an evil witch," I say as I take her hand in mine. "Or a vampire, considering your neck fetish. Are you a vampire?"

"You tell me." She bares her teeth at me and hisses.

"Do vampires hiss? I don't think they hiss."

"Shut up and take me on a date."

"Yes, ma'am."

She cocks an eyebrow at me. "You like me telling you what to do?"

"It's oddly exciting." Yet I hated it when Colleen ordered me around.

"Good to know. I'm storing that little nugget of info away for future reference." She licks her lips, and I can't tell if she did it on purpose or not.

I pull her toward the door and try not to think about what she intends to order me to do in the future. "I'm starving. Let's get out of here."

"Hold up," she says. "I need to grab my purse."

"No, you don't. I'm paying."

Wendy yanks her hand out of mine and plants both hands on her waist. "I'm perfectly capable of paying for my own meal."

I hold my hands up. "I didn't say you weren't. I only said I'd pay."

"If you do, then I'm paying next time."

"We'll see." I don't intend to let her pay for anything ever.

She steps right up to me and shakes her finger in my face. "We will not see. We'll take turns paying on our dates. This is the 80s, and I'm a modern woman. I can afford to pay, and I will. Got it?"

I grab her hand and kiss the tip of her finger. "Got it."

"Finger kissing is okay?"

"Yes, but no finger licking."

"Ooo, now I want fried chicken."

She gets a dreamy look in her eye, and I laugh.

"And fried chicken you will get, my lady. Let's go." I start toward the door again, but she resists.

"I still need to get my purse, because that's where my keys are. You want me to be able to lock up, don't you?"

"Of course. Safety first."

She disappears into her bedroom to grab her purse, slips her shoes on, locks the door behind us, and finally takes my hand again.

As the elevator descends to the lobby, she asks, "Can I lick my own fingers?"

I groan. "Wendy ..."

"I'm talking about when I'm eating my fried chicken." She pokes me in the ribs. "Get your mind out of the gutter."

"You put it there, you evil vampire Munchkin witch."

She giggles. "I'm loving all the nicknames. Now I need some good ones for you."

"So, Ponyboy," Wendy says, "are you ready to explain why you won't kiss me?"

"Really? You're going with Ponyboy?"

As we walked to the diner and while we perused the menu, Wendy tried out a host of potential nicknames, from guttersnipe to chickadee to lip-hater and more. I nixed them all.

"Yep. You look like an older, handsomer version of C. Thomas Howell."

"I appreciate the compliment, but I hope I don't remind you of his character in *The Outsiders*. And aren't you a little …" I trail off when I realize what I was about to say.

"Aren't I a little what?" Wendy's jaw is set, and I don't like the look in her eyes.

"A little … beautiful, good, vampire witch?"

"A little *what*, Randall?"

Why did I hint at her age? "I'm not going to say it. I shouldn't have thought it."

"How old do you think I am?"

"Twenty-three?"

She glares at me, and I sigh. I might as well admit the truth. "I know you're thirty."

Her eyebrows shoot up. "How do you know that?"

"Ash told me."

She closes her eyes and inhales through her nose. "I'm going to kill Leslie."

"No, you're not," I say. "Look at me."

She reluctantly opens her eyes.

"I don't care how old you are. It does not now nor will it ever bother me that you're older than me. Okay?"

She nods.

"I'm also not bothered by your sixth toe," I tease.

"I don't have six toes!"

"I'm actually hoping you have ten."

When she rolls her eyes, I know we've gotten past the age hurdle.

The waitress brings our drinks, and we spend a few minutes discussing the finer points of *The Outsiders*.

Then Wendy prompts, "Back to the lack of kissing and what had better be an excellent reason for it."

"I have this pattern," I explain, "where I fall fast and hard and get so caught up in the physical side of a relationship that I don't learn anything important about the woman I'm with, and I lose track of who I am in the process. I don't want to do that again. I don't want to do that with *you*. I want to take plenty of time to get to know you, and I need to know who I can be in a real, adult relationship that exists primarily outside the bedroom.

"In my past relationships, kissing tended to lead to more, which is why I can't kiss you yet. This might be overkill, and it might make us feel a little like we're in high school again, but I honestly don't know how much control I can exert, since it's been such a long time since I've tried, so I need to take things slowly on the physical side.

"What's happening here," I wave my hand back and forth between us, "I want this to be about so much more than a kiss— more than a night or a weekend or even a lifetime of physical passion. I want to know your heart, your mind, your *soul* before I learn everything there is to know about your body."

Wendy fans her face with her hand. "Holy smokes, that was sexy. You're starting off with a bang." She claps a hand over her mouth and giggles. "Or not, as the case may be."

I can't help but chuckle.

"I'm sorry," she says. "I don't mean to make light of what you said. I feel honored that you shared that with me and that you want to do this in the way that feels right to you. It also feels right to me, even though I didn't realize that until now, and I couldn't have stated it nearly so well. I've had similar issues in past relationships. I also fall too hard, too fast, and without any real commitment involved on the guy's part, so I feel like I'm constantly in a state of limbo, kind of like how I've felt the last month with you. I'm too old to keep living that way. And I want to get to know the real Randall Hamilton—the one behind all the cockiness and the witty banter."

One corner of my mouth quirks up. "You don't appreciate my banter?"

"I adore the banter. I *live* for it. But I know there's so much more to you, and I can't wait to discover it."

A lump forms in my throat. "And I can't wait to learn everything there is to know about Wendy O'Halloran." I reach across the table and take her hand in mine. "I'm sorry I put you in a state of limbo. I took advantage of your heart that first night, and that was wrong. I should have thought about what I was doing to you."

"I was a willing participant," she says. "You took advantage of nothing. Don't put that blame on yourself. But I'm glad we're now getting it all out in the open. There's one thing I'm confused about, though. You said you don't know how much control you can exert with me, but it seems you've been controlling yourself just fine for the past month."

She's not wrong, but neither am I. "I controlled myself because I thought you didn't want more. I'm not one to kiss someone unless I know they want it. But since I now know you want to kiss me, it makes things considerably more difficult."

Wendy nods. "I understand that. I also kept myself under control because I didn't think you wanted more with me. It wasn't easy, but it was easier than now, when it's all I can do to keep myself from climbing across this table and letting everyone in this restaurant know you're mine."

I suck in a breath at that visual and her possessiveness. "I'm going to need you to not say things like that."

"You didn't like it?" She shoots me a flirtatious grin.

"That's not the problem, and you know it."

She giggles. "I do. And I'll try to control my words as much as my actions. For now." She tilts her head to the side. "Speaking of words, what did you mean this morning when you said, 'It's not the dress'?"

I force myself not to smile. "What do you think I meant?"

"That it was me, not the dress?"

"Precisely. You look incredible no matter what you're wearing. But I'll admit I was a tiny bit disappointed when I got to your apartment and you'd changed out of that little number." I grin at her.

"I thought about leaving it on, since I thought I might need some help convincing you to date me, but then I realized it would be harder to curl up on your lap in that dress than in shorts and a T-shirt, so I changed."

"Wise decision," I say, my eyes tracking over the parts of her I can see. "Though like I said, it doesn't matter what you wear, you always look great to me."

She blushes and then says, "Thanks. Back to the conversation from earlier, is there anything else you need to tell me, when it comes to us dating?"

I nod and admit something I've never said out loud before, but I completely trust Wendy with the information. "I also have this problem where I become who others want me to be. It started with my father, and it has transferred to pretty much every friendship and relationship I've ever had. And I'm tired of it. I don't want to do it anymore. I want to be *me.*"

Wendy squeezes my hand. "That's who I want you to be, too." Then she laughs. "Though that might not be the right thing to say after you told me you don't want to be what others want you to be."

"That was the exact right thing to say." I stroke the back of her hand with my thumb. "Will you promise to tell me if you feel like you're in limbo with me again? If you ever wonder how I'm feeling about you—about *us*—I need you to tell me."

She gives me a sweet smile. "I promise."

six

. . .

Wendy

"**Y**ou were like a piranha with that fried chicken," Randall says as we walk back to my apartment hand-in-hand after wearing out our welcome at the diner. "There wasn't a scrap of meat left on those bones."

I swing our arms between us. "I get serious about my food."

"Obviously."

"What's one thing you get serious about?" I ask.

He suddenly stops, raises our linked hands high, and then twirls me around a few times. When I finally stop, I wobble a bit, giggle, and fall into him. He folds me into an embrace and leans down to kiss the top of my head. I slip my arms around his waist and look up into his grinning face.

"I get serious about making you giggle," he says, "and I was pretty sure that would do the trick."

"It did."

"What else makes you giggle?"

I tap my lips as I think. "Puppies. Weird Al songs. *Tom and Jerry.* Old people holding hands."

"I think old people holding hands is sweet." He kisses my forehead, sending goosebumps all the way to my toes. "I want to still be holding hands with my lady when I'm eighty."

"Hey, that rhymed. And I think it's sweet, too. Would you still hold my hand if it was wrinkled and crooked and had warts all over it?"

"For sure. Would you still hold my hand if I only had two fingers?"

I cock my head to the side. "That would depend on which fingers you still have left. Pointer and middle? Definitely. Thumb and pinky? That might be stretching the bounds of my acceptance," I tease.

"Hmm." He runs his hands up and down my back, touching me with only his thumbs and pinky fingers, and my entire torso fills with heat. "You're positive about that?"

"Actually, I'm positive I'd hold your hand even if all your fingers were nubs." I pull one of his hands up to my mouth and kiss the tip of each finger.

We smile at each other for a few seconds before he tucks me into his side and we continue on our way toward my apartment. We don't speak again until we exit the elevator on my floor and he stops outside it.

"You're not walking me all the way to my door?" I ask.

"Nope. There's a tiny bit less temptation if we say goodnight here. But you better believe I'm going to watch you sashay all the way down this hall."

"Okay, then," I say. "Good night."

"Okay, then? All I get is an 'okay, then'? No, 'Thank you for the fried chicken,' or, 'You're the sexiest man I've ever laid my gorgeous green eyes on,' or, 'I'm sorry I tried to nickname you chickadee'?"

I smirk up at him. "You get all three of those."

"Okay, then," he mocks and then throws his arms out wide. "Give me a quick hallway hug, and then skedaddle so I can watch you walk away."

I fling my arms around him and squeeze him as tightly as I can.

"*Oof.*" His arms close around me. "Can't ... breathe. Need ... air ... to ... live."

I giggle and ease up on him the slightest bit.

"I'm not the biggest fan of the standing cuddle," he says. "Your face is too far away from mine, Munchkin."

"It's not my fault you're taller than the Tin Man. Plus, you can't do anything to my face anyway."

"I beg to differ." He peels me off him, cups my face with his hands, and then leans down and kisses both cheeks, my forehead, my nose, both temples, and my forehead again. Finally, he tilts my head down and kisses the top of it, and then he turns me away from him and gives me a nudge. "Off you go."

It takes me a few moments to steady my wobbly legs after his onslaught, but then I sway my hips as widely as possible as I walk down the hall. When he laughs and wolf whistles at me, I toss a saucy grin over my shoulder at him. As I unlock my door, he's still watching me, and I blow him a kiss. He pretends to catch it and throw it into his mouth. I'm giggling again when I step into my apartment.

"Leslieeeee, where are you?" I say to her answering machine. "Call me the instant you get this!"

After I walked through my door, the first thing I did was curl up on my couch in the spot where Randall always sits, and I grinned at absolutely nothing for several minutes. Then I leapt up, changed into my pajamas, and settled into the easy chair to call Leslie, who has the audacity to not be home.

She's probably with her boyfriend—*kissing* him. Which I wish I was currently doing to mine, although I'm also fully on board with the decision not to. I need a relationship where the man is focused on spending time getting to know me and caring about me as a friend and respecting me a person, instead of my usual nothing-but-physical relationships. It'll take some getting used to, but it's what I want and, frankly, what I've craved my entire adult life.

Leave it to Randall Hamilton to finally be the man to give me that. I thought—and hoped—he'd be all over me the second we decided to be more than friends, but he surprised me with his decision to hold off on the physical side of our relationship. In a way, I'm jealous of all the women who came before me who didn't have to wait. But at the same time, I feel special that he wants more with me than he ever has with any other woman and that he's willing to make sacrifices in order for that happen.

Brrring!

I snatch up the phone. "Leslie?"

"No, it's your mother."

"Oh. Hi, Mom."

"Try not to sound so excited to talk to me," she teases.

"Sorry. I was expecting a call from Leslie. And I'm sorry I didn't call you back last night. I didn't get your message until it was too late to call, and today has been a little crazy. What's up? Is everything okay?"

"Not exactly. I got a call from your father two nights ago. To clarify, I'm talking about Jack—the father you haven't heard from in ten years, not your dad who loves you more than life itself. Jack would have called you, but he didn't have your number. I refused to give it to him, which meant he was forced to tell me why he wanted to talk to you after all these years. He has some news, but this isn't anything I want to tell you over the phone. Can I drive down tomorrow and see you? Or do you have plans after work?"

"You can always come visit, but I'm not going to be able to focus on anything until I know what you're going to say. Please tell me now."

"Okay." She takes an audible breath. "Jack recently found out he has another daughter who's twenty-eight, and he wanted you to know you have a sister."

If I weren't already sitting down, I'd be falling down in shock. A swirl of emotions rushes through me: rage that my father obviously cheated on my mom during the short time they were married, elation that I have a sister, anxiety about what I'm supposed to do with this information, and disappointment that I didn't know about her until now.

"Wendy, honey, are you still there?"

"Yeah, Mom, I'm here. I'm trying to process."

"I know it's a lot to take in, and it would have been so much better to tell you this in person. I should have just driven down and surprised you."

"That's all right."

"It's really not. I'm sorry I messed this up and now you're down there all alone to try to deal with this."

"I've got Leslie." And Randall, but this isn't the best time to tell her about him.

"Yes, but I still wish I was there. I also need to tell you that this sister is going to be in Chicago this weekend and would like to meet you."

"Oh, wow." It's Wednesday, so the weekend isn't very far away.

"You don't have to meet her."

"I think I'll want to, but that's really soon. Where does she live?" Maybe she's close enough I could drive to see her in a few weeks or months after I fully get used to the idea.

"Little Rock."

"Arkansas?"

"Yes."

"What's her name?"

Mom pauses. "Andrea."

I suck in a breath.

"I know," Mom says. "What a coincidence."

When I was three, a little after my father left and it was just me and Mom, I had an imaginary sister named Andrea. I have two half-brothers now, and I love them dearly, but they're teenagers. I've always wondered what it would be like to have a sister or a sibling my own age.

I ask her, "Are you saying you want me to meet her? You're not upset by this?"

"I'll admit I was shocked when Jack told me, but I knew he wasn't faithful to me."

My jaw drops. "You did?"

"Yes, it's why I kicked him out."

My heart lurches into my throat. "What? I thought he left us."

"I know, because that's what I told you. I thought that would be easier on you. You were so little. There was no way I could tell you the truth. I know I should have done so later on, and your dad has always told me I needed tell you what really happened, but I just couldn't. I was embarrassed and ashamed. I'm sorry I lied to you, honey."

"Mom …" I grip the phone so tightly my hand hurts almost as much as my heart does from the knowledge my mom has lied to me my entire life about why my father left.

She sighs. "I'm so sorry. I shouldn't have sprung that on you like this."

"No," I say in a small voice, "you shouldn't have."

"I can come down there now to be there with you, if you need me to. Your dad can't come because he's in the middle of a big trial, but I can be there in a few hours."

"No, I don't want you driving here from Milwaukee late at night." I might be angry with her, but I love her and don't want her driving alone in the dark, especially when she's upset because she knows I'm upset. "I'll be fine."

"Are you sure?"

No. "Yes."

"All right. Call me tomorrow?"

No. "Maybe."

"Honey, I love you so much, and I'm so sorry. I truly am." I can tell she is by the sound of her voice. And I'll forgive her, but I'm not quite ready yet. "But if you want to meet your sister, I need to tell you how to make that happen."

I sigh. "I'll call you, Mom. I promise."

seven

. . .

Randall

"So is there a chance I'll be an uncle in nine months?" Ash asks when I walk back into our apartment.

I ignore him and head into the kitchen to grab a Budweiser from the fridge. I take a long drink and then steel myself before going back into the living room. I don't know how Ash is going to respond to my decisions. Not that he gets a say in them, but he'll have a definite opinion.

When I re-enter the room, he mutes the TV.

"That's the first thing you're going to ask me?" I drop onto the couch and kick my feet up on the coffee table.

"You were gone several hours. That's a lot longer than it takes to break up with someone. I simply assumed. Maybe I shouldn't have."

I hate that he assumed, but until today, that would have been an accurate assumption to make of me, so I can't justifiably be annoyed with him.

I take a long drink of my beer. "I didn't sleep with her."

"Good, because I like her, and I don't want you to break her."

I narrow my eyes at him. "I like her, too. And I also want to keep her heart in one piece, which is part of the reason I'm holding off on the physical stuff."

One of his eyebrows raises. "This is new."

I spread my arms wide. "This is the new Randall Hamilton—

the *real* Randall Hamilton. I hope you're prepared to get to know me."

"I already know the real Randall Hamilton," my brother says, "and I like him. I just haven't seen him in a long time. Welcome back."

"It still blows me away when you know the perfect thing to say." Ash has never been much of a talker or dispenser of life wisdom, but he's changed over the past month or so since Leslie came back into his life. "I like the new Ashley Hamilton, too."

"Look at us being adults," he says.

"It's weird." I grin at him.

"It truly is. Now, tell me what happened with Wendy."

I tell him most of it.

"You really didn't kiss her?" he asks.

"It took the strength of a small army, but no."

"How long do you think you can keep that up?"

I sip my beer as I think about the answer, but mostly I think about Wendy's full pink lips, which gives me my answer. "I don't know, but I'll admit it adds an interesting element to the relationship."

"That's one way of looking at it."

"You don't agree with my decision?"

"I think it's a great decision, because you'll have much more time to talk to each other if your mouths aren't otherwise engaged. Holding off can be a good thing, but it's going to be a challenge."

I groan. "Tell me about it."

"Did you talk about how often you're going to see or talk to each other, since you don't want this relationship to take over your entire life?"

"No."

"You'd better do it soon."

"I will the next time we talk." I pause. "Do you and Leslie limit your time together?"

"We do."

"Really?" I'm surprised by his answer, because it seems they're always together.

"Yep. Three nights a week, we do our own thing—spend time with friends, chill out at home, do a hobby, whatever."

"How did I not notice that?"

"Because you've been off … cuddling … with Wendy."

I laugh at the look of distaste on his face. "Have you ever said the word 'cuddling' before?"

"Never. It felt strange coming out of my mouth. I don't want to say it again."

I grin at him. "But *do* you cuddle?" If he says no, we'll need to have a talk. My brother doesn't have much experience with women, so I might have to teach him a thing or two about the fine art of cuddling.

His face turns red. "Yes. And I haven't gotten any complaints."

"Well, I haven't gotten any complaints about the way I comb my hair, but that doesn't mean I do it right."

Ash taps a finger on his lips. "I've been meaning to tell you—"

"Shut your fat mouth. My hair looks amazing. I was trying to make a point."

"Which is?"

"Ask Leslie if you're doing it right."

He looks uncertain. "Are you sure there's a right way and a wrong way?"

"Absolutely, and it differs from woman to woman. That's why you gotta ask."

"You asked Wendy?"

"You better believe I did—especially because I'm so much bigger than her. I could easily hurt her and not realize it."

Brrring!

Ash picks up the phone. "Hello." He raises his eyebrows at me. "Hi, Wendy."

I leap up and try to grab the phone out of his hand, but he twists away and thrusts an arm out to block me.

"Yes, he's here. Hold on a sec." He turns back toward me, mouths, "Calm down," and finally hands me the phone.

My pulse is racing when I say hello.

"Hi," she says. "I don't know if this is okay to ask, because we didn't talk about how often we'll see each other, but can you come back over here?"

By the time she's finished speaking, I can hear the anxiety in her voice, and my heart inches up into my throat. "Yes. What's wrong?"

"I got some weird news a little bit ago, and I need you to hold me. Can you do that? Can we still do that?"

"Of course we can. You can always ask me for that—always. I'll be there before you know it."

I hang up and make a beeline for the door.

"Is she okay?" Ash asks.

"Doesn't sound like it. Don't wait up."

I don't allow myself to run until I'm out on the sidewalk, but then I sprint. Since it's late, I don't encounter many people, which is good, because I just terrified a woman who's out walking her dog.

"Sorry," I call over my shoulder to her. "Girlfriend emergency!" I smile at the reality that Wendy is now my girlfriend.

When Wendy opens her door, I take one look at her distraught face and then grip her waist and haul her up against my chest. Her arms and legs wrap around me, and she clings to me like a monkey with her face buried in my neck. With a jolt I realize I've never held a woman like this when we weren't on our way to the bedroom, but there's nothing sexual about what we're doing. Instead, I'm providing Wendy with the comfort and protection she needs, and my heart swells with emotion as I kick the door shut and carry her to the couch.

I rock her for a minute while smoothing a hand up and down her back. When her breathing finally evens out, I say, "You want to tell me what happened?"

She nods and then resettles herself into her favorite sideways position on my lap.

"I have a sister," she says.

I don't remember her mentioning a sister before, but I wait for her to tell me what this sister did to hurt her, so I can figure out how to give the woman a piece of my mind.

"I didn't know I had a sister," she finally says.

"Oh," I reply automatically, before realizing the importance of what she said. "Oh!" I slide a hand up to cradle the back of her head, drawing her closer into me. "That's big news."

She nods.

I say, "I don't know much about your family, so can you tell me about them and what this means?"

eight

. . .

Wendy

"My father, Jack, moved out when I was two," I explain to Randall. "He and Mom were teenagers when she got pregnant, and they immediately got married, as people did back then. I always believed he walked out on us, because that's what Mom told me." I take a deep breath. "But she told me tonight that's not what happened."

As he waits for me to continue, he strokes my hair and leans his head against mine in the way he knows will calm me. I silently marvel at how well he knows what I need, but I realize it's because he took the time and effort to ask and pay attention when we first started spending time together. Nobody has ever done that for me before.

I tell him the entire story, and when I finish, he asks, "How do you feel about your mom lying to you about Jack?"

"I don't feel great, that's for sure."

"Do you think it was better for little-girl Wendy to believe Jack left you?"

"Maybe," I admit. "It's too soon for me to think rationally about what Mom did, though. Or about what Jack did, for that matter."

"Understandably."

We're both silent for a minute.

"Do you want to meet Andrea?" I ask.

"I think I will at some point, but I don't know if I'll be ready by this weekend."

"You don't have to be. Don't let her schedule determine this for you. You can meet her next month or next year or ten years from now if that's what feels right for you."

"That's exactly what I needed to hear." I rub the collar of his maroon Polo shirt between my fingers as I consider what I want to do. "I think maybe I need to talk to her on the phone first and get to know her a little before I meet her."

"That sounds like an excellent plan. And if she doesn't understand that, it means you're making the right decision to not let her into your life yet."

"Very true."

We're silent for a moment before he asks, "Do you want me to meet her while she's here? I can see what she's like and try to figure out if I think she might want something from you other than getting to know the sister she didn't know she had."

My chest feels like it's going to explode from the care this man is showing me. "You'd do that for me?"

He squeezes me. "Of course I would. But you don't have to decide right now."

"Thank you. I'll think about it."

I shift so I can look him directly in the face.

"Thank you for coming over."

"You're welcome. I'm happy you chose me as your person to call."

I purse my lips. "Wellllll …"

"Well, what?"

"I did talk to Leslie first. Sorry."

Randall shakes his head. "Don't be sorry about that. She's your closest friend. I don't want you to think I always need you to prioritize me over her. But did talking to her not help you?"

"It did. She's good at helping me talk things out. But she doesn't understand what it's like to have a father who doesn't love her, and she can't hold me like you can." I run my hands up and down his arms, thrilled by the fact I can do so now. "I'm addicted to these arms. Whenever I get upset or sad or lonely or stressed, I need them around me, making me feel safe."

One of his eyebrows quirks up. "You still only want me for my cuddles, huh?"

I bob my head back and forth and stifle my smile. "Maybe." I finally grin at him. "But you do often manage to know just what to say to help me feel better, too. How do you do that?"

He shrugs. "I have no idea. Are you feeling better now?"

"So much better." I'm glad I have him to help me through this.

"Good. By the way, I like your pjs."

I giggle. "I wondered when you'd comment on them."

My tank top and shorts combo is soft, comfy, bright pink, and covered with armadillos wearing purple cowboy hats.

"I've been dying to say something ever since I walked in here, but I didn't want to mention it when you were upset."

"I got them when I was in Texas last summer."

His lips twitch. "I mean, I thought I was into lacy lingerie, but this little outfit is incredibly sexy."

"That's exactly what I thought when I saw it hanging on the rack in the gas station."

He bursts out laughing. "You bought these pajamas at a gas station?"

"It was a big gas station. Everything's bigger in Texas, you know."

He tugs on the hem of my shirt. "I wouldn't know. I've never been."

"You've never been to Texas?"

"Nope."

"Then we'll have to go sometime." I hold my breath when I realize that's a significant offer for me to make.

"I'd love that."

"Yeah?" I breathe out.

"Yeah."

While we're smiling at each other, I yawn.

"You tired, my little armadillo cowgirl?"

I nod and cover my mouth when I yawn again. "It's getting late, and it's been a long day."

"It has been. I'll head out soon, but first, when you called me earlier, you mentioned we didn't discuss how often we'd see each other. Can we talk about that now?"

"We can." I think about it for a minute before suggesting, "How about three times a week—including weekends?"

"That sounds reasonable. What about talking on the phone?"

"Once a week? Like to *really* talk? But if we need a quick chat about something, I don't think we should limit that."

"I like that. And how about in two weeks, we debrief and discuss how it's working?"

"Yes, counselor." I giggle.

He tickles me and I fall off his lap when I squirm away from his hand. The next thing I know, I'm cradled in his arms, and he's carrying me toward my bedroom.

My eyes widen. "What are you doing?"

He stops. "Tucking you into bed. Is that okay?"

I swallow hard and nod. "Yes, but I need to take off my makeup and brush my teeth first."

"Okay." He carries me to the bathroom door and sets me on my feet. "Do what you need to do, and then I'll tuck you in."

"You don't have to tuck me in."

"I do. No arguing."

"Yes, sir."

I take care of my evening routine, and when I exit the bathroom, Randall is inspecting the family photo hanging on the wall outside my room. He holds out his hand to me, and I take it. Then he pulls me so my back rests against his front, facing the picture.

He says, "These are the brothers I've heard you talk about?"

I nod. "Daniel and Ryan. They're nineteen and seventeen. And that's my mom, obviously, and my dad."

"Is your dad's name O'Halloran, or is that Jack's last name?"

"It's my dad's name. He adopted me when I was ten."

Randall's arms wrap around my shoulders from behind. "Jack gave up parental rights?"

"Yes."

"I'm sorry. That must've been hard."

"It's okay. It still hurts sometimes to think about it, but my dad is the best dad anyone could ever ask for. And I did technically ask him to be my dad. He and Mom dated for several years before she agreed to marry him. Dad and I finally wore her down. He wanted the three of us to be a family, and I wanted nothing more than for him to be my dad."

"He sounds like an amazing guy." Randall's voice is wistful, and my heart goes out to him.

"He is." I spin in his arms so I can look up at him. "I'm sorry things are so hard with your dad."

"Me, too, but that's a topic for another night." He presses a kiss to my temple. "Let's get you to bed."

He follows me into my room, and when I slip under the covers, he pulls them up to my chin, kisses my forehead, and then sits on the edge of the bed next to me.

"You gonna tell me why you have a framed photo of Patrick Swayze on your dresser?" he asks, lips twitching.

My face heats as my eyes shoot to the photo in question. "Uh, you weren't supposed to see that."

"Oh, but I did, and unless you want me spreading this information around, you need to tell me the story behind it." He grins.

I force myself not to smile back. "Fine. If you look closely, you'll see it's signed."

Randall looks over at the picture again, squints his eyes, and nods his head. "I do see that. It's even made out to you. But that explains nothing."

"I'm a fan, okay? And my brothers thought it would be hilarious to write him a love letter on my behalf. A month later, they got that signed photo in the mail. They gave it to me for Christmas, and they made me promise I'd display it for at least a year. I thought it was funny, so I agreed. Whenever they visit, they check to make sure it's still there."

"So do I need to worry about Mr. Swayze swooping in and whisking you out of my arms and off to Hollywood?"

"I wouldn't say that's out of the realm of possibility. My brothers also sent him my photo." I smirk at him.

He places his hand over his heart and gives me a pained look.

"Then I'm doomed. There's no way he'll be able to resist coming for you."

I giggle. "Well, it's been eight months since they wrote to him, and I haven't heard from him yet, so you might still be in luck."

"The only rational explanation for that is he lost your contact info."

I pull his head down to me and kiss his cheek. "You're sweet, you know that?"

Randall shrugs. "I do my best." Then he gives me a look that sends a rush of heat through me, and he smooths a strand of hair off my face. "You going to be okay?"

I nod, even though I don't want him to leave me.

"Want me to stay until you fall asleep?"

I nod again. "Yes, but there's a tiny problem with this whole scenario of you tucking me in."

"What's that?"

"You can't bolt my door from the outside without a key. I'll have to do it from inside." I would give him a key, but I don't currently have an extra one.

"Then I'll stay right here until you fall asleep, and then I'll go sleep on the couch."

"No. You're too tall to sleep on my couch. You'll be in pain tomorrow."

"I'll be fine. We spoon on that couch all the time."

The mention of spooning makes me want his body curled around mine. I close my eyes for a second and hope I'm not crossing a line when I say, "Can you handle sleeping here with me? Just for tonight? Everybody fully clothed?"

He studies my face for a few moments. "Yes, I can do that."

"You sure?"

"Yup."

"I think Daniel left some sweatpants and a shirt the last time he was here. He's a little smaller than you, but they should still work."

I tell him where to find the clothes and a new toothbrush. While he's changing, I second and third guess my request for him to stay the night. When he comes back into my room looking like every woman's dream in the tight gray sweatpants and white T-shirt, I know for sure this is a bad idea, and I say so.

"This was a terrible plan. I shouldn't have asked you to do this —not after everything we talked about today." I toss the covers off me. "Change back into your clothes and I'll let you out."

I try to get out of bed, but Randall lightly presses on my shoulders to keep me in place. "No, we're mature adults who can handle sleeping in the same bed without tearing each other's clothes off. I want to be here for you. Please let me do that."

nine

. . .

Randall

I hope I sound more confident than I feel, but I'm not about to walk out Wendy's door after she asked me to stay. In all honesty, I need to do this for me as much as for her. I need us both to know I can exercise the kind of control this situation demands.

After locking the door and turning out the lights, I climb under the covers next to her. We're on our sides facing each other, and I can barely make out her features in the darkened room.

"You good?" I ask.

"Mmhm." She giggles.

I smile at the sound. "What's funny?"

"You smell minty fresh."

"That's because I *am* minty fresh. So are you. It's too bad I can't kiss you."

"Nobody to blame but yourself."

"If there were ever a situation to change my mind, it might be this one," I admit.

"But you're not going to?"

"I'm determined not to cave on the first night."

"Good. I'm glad, even though I really want to kiss you."

I say, "Well, if you're dying to put your lips on someone, I'll bring Patrick's picture over here for you to kiss."

Wendy's giggle makes me smile.

"Oh, please do," she says.

"Nope. I've changed my mind. I'm not sharing your bed with anyone else."

"You'd better not."

Her eyes close, and after a minute of silence, I wonder if she already fell asleep.

"Thank you for staying." Her hand finds one of mine under the covers, and she laces our fingers together, sending a warm feeling racing through my body. "I didn't want to be alone."

"I know you didn't. That's why I'm here."

"Randall?" She suddenly sounds unsure, which sends a pang to my gut.

"Yes? What is it?"

"Will you spoon me?"

"I'm dying to spoon you." And it may well kill me, but if she wants me to spoon her, I'm going to. "Turn over."

She flips so she's facing away from me, and I wrap my arm around her middle and pull her into me. Then I readjust the pillows until we're both comfortable.

"You good?"

"Mmhm. This is perfect." She rests her hand on top of mine on her stomach. "Night, Ponyboy."

"Night, Glinda." I kiss the back of her head.

She sighs, and within minutes her breathing and pulse even out into the calm rhythm of sleep.

Mine won't be calm anytime soon.

Music jolts me awake, and I'm confused for a few moments until I register I'm in Wendy's bed and she's sprawled mostly on top of me.

"Make it stop," she mumbles into my chest.

I flail my arm out but can't reach her nightstand, so I wrap an arm around her and slide us both over in the bed. Then I slap at the alarm until I connect with a button that stops George Harrison from declaring over and over that he has his mind set on someone.

"Morning," I tell her as I trail my fingertips up and down her back.

"You're still here." She lifts her head up enough to look at me through slitted eyes.

"Of course I'm still here."

Her head drops back down onto me. "I don't like mornings."

"Good to know."

"Mmmm."

She seems to be falling back asleep.

"Wendy?"

"Hmm?"

"As much as I love having your body on top of mine, I need to visit the little boys' room."

"Don't have any little boys, so there's no room here for them."

"I'm talking about the bathroom, you loon. I was trying to be discreet."

"Oh." She shifts off me and rubs her eyes. "Sorry. I need my caffeine."

I slip out from under the covers. "What's your morning caffeine of choice?"

"Dr. Pepper."

"I'll bring you one after I take care of business."

"No, I need to get up. I'll get it."

When I come out of the bathroom after changing back into my clothes, Wendy is standing in the kitchen with glassy eyes, hair an absolute wreck, cheek creased from sleeping on my shirt-clad chest, armadillo pjs all askew, and looking more beautiful than I've ever seen her. My knees buckle when I realize I don't get to wake up to this view every morning, *but I want to.*

"Why are you staring at me like that?" she asks me.

"Because you're the most stunning woman I've ever seen." I cross the room, wrap my arms around her from behind, and kiss the top of her head.

She laughs. "I look a total mess, and you know it. I'd be embarrassed to have you see me like this if I weren't so happy you're here." She grips my forearms. "You really are here, right? This isn't a dream?"

I press my lips to her head again. "Not a dream."

"And I didn't screw this all up by asking you to stay the night?"

I turn her around so I can look down into her face. "Why would that screw anything up?"

"Because you told me you need your space in this relationship, yet the very first night I wouldn't let you go home."

"I didn't want to go home. You asked me to help you deal with some shocking news, and I did that. I'm glad I could."

She lifts her hands to my neck and pulls on it. "Get your face down here so I can kiss it."

I raise an eyebrow at her.

"On the cheek," she clarifies. "It's not fair that you can always reach my head, but I can't reach yours."

I lower my cheek to her lips, and she gives me a kiss that somehow seems more intimate than a kiss on the mouth would. Then she turns my head and kisses me on the other cheek. Finally, she boops me on the nose, giggles, and steps backward out of my embrace, taking a little piece of my heart with her.

"You need to go home to change into some work clothes," she orders, "and I need to get ready."

The last thing I want to do is leave her, but she's right. The clothes I wore here last night don't fit Carter-Jenkins' dress code.

"Okay," I concede, "but I'll swing back by and pick you up for work."

"No, you won't."

"I will."

"No." Wendy shakes her head.

"Let me do this, please. Just today, if you don't want me to drive you every day."

"But people will see us come in together."

My eyebrows shoot up. "Do you not want our co-workers to know we're dating?" I don't like that idea at all.

She sighs and avoids my eyes, and I'm glad I haven't eaten

anything yet, because I'm suddenly feeling nauseous. Is she ashamed of me?

"Wendy?"

"I don't want people to not take me seriously at work."

My stomach starts roiling. "And you think dating *me* will make people not take you seriously?"

"No! No, it's not because it's you. It's …"

"It's what?" I say it a little more harshly than I intended, but I don't apologize.

She finally looks at me again. "It's hard for me to be taken seriously in the professional world. I'm a woman, and I'm short, and I'm curvy, and most men want to either pat me on the head or make inappropriate advances toward me, not view me as the kick-butt PR rep I really am."

My nausea turns to fury in a heartbeat, and my hands ball up. "Who's making inappropriate advances toward you?"

"That's the thing you're going to focus on here?"

"Tell me who it was, so I can have a nice little chat with them."

She takes another step away from me. "Randall, I don't need you to defend me at work. I don't want you to. That's exactly what I'm talking about. I need to be seen as a woman who can stand up for herself and whose work speaks for itself—not as someone who needs her boyfriend to fight for her."

I take a few deep breaths, because I know I need to calm down before I say something else wrong without realizing it.

"People automatically respect you," she continues, "because you're a Hamilton, because you stood up to your powerful dad, because you're kind and smart and funny, and, frankly, because you're a good-looking man."

Oddly, even though she complimented me in almost every way possible, I also feel like she punched me in the gut. "That's not true."

"It's *all* true, as well as the fact that handsome white men don't need to do one stinking thing to earn anyone's respect. You don't have any idea what it's like to be a woman in this industry—especially a woman who looks like me. I don't think you've forgotten the dress debacle from yesterday. You weren't the only man who was distracted by it."

We stare at each other for several long seconds.

I lean back against her kitchen counter and fold my arms over my chest. "I don't know what you want me to say."

"I don't know either. But it's not up to me to tell you what to say anyway. You want to start being the real you—not who I want you to be—so you're going to need to figure that out for yourself. I don't want you to tell me what I want to hear. I don't want you to agree to keep our relationship under wraps at work simply because that's what I want. Tell me what you truly think."

"I think—no, I *know* I don't want to hide our relationship. I want the entire world to know we're together, to know that for some unfathomable reason, a woman as incredible as you actually chose *me.*"

She starts to speak, but I raise a hand to stop her.

"As for the rest of what you said, I didn't realize that's what work is like for you—for women. But that helps me understand why you don't love the idea of everyone at work knowing about us. Let's talk about this again later when we're not so worked up about it. We won't tell anyone about us today. We'll treat each other like we normally do in public. Okay?"

Wendy nods and opens the door for me.

ten

...

Wendy

Much to my dismay, I can't talk to Leslie about Randall at work this morning because she's at a TV interview with her primary client, Diego Sanchez. He's the Chicago Cubs' newest acquisition, who also happens to be one of the best pitchers in all of baseball. Not that I'd know that if he wasn't her client. I know almost nothing about sports, but I do know a lot about Diego, and I like him. Last month, Leslie, Ash, Randall, and I came up with a plan for him to start a foundation to help immigrants with legal issues, and a few weeks ago he hired Ash to launch and lead the Diego Sanchez Foundation.

Though I try to focus on work, I can't stop thinking about my conversation with Randall before he left my apartment. I don't think he was upset when he left, but I can't be sure. On a normal day, I see him multiple times in the break room, at meetings, or even passing in the hallway. But when I haven't caught sight of him by early afternoon, I start to get antsy.

Considering the location of his office in relation to mine, there's rarely a good reason for me to walk by it, but I decide I'm going to make a pass by there anyway. I can't handle not knowing if he's avoiding me.

I carry a notebook and pen so I'll look like I'm heading to a meeting, in case anyone wonders why I'm roaming the halls. As I approach Randall's office, I can see his door is open and the light is on. Before I get there, I stop, because I realize I'm giving in to my insecurities by doing this. I need to trust that he truly wants to be with me, regardless of our disagreement this morning. I'm turning around to head back to my office when George Carter, the firm's owner, exits Randall's office and nearly bumps into me.

"All right, Wendy?"

"Yes, sir. I realized I forgot something," I say to explain my turnabout.

"I do it all the time," he says as he continues down the hallway.

I hurry back the way I came, but before I round the corner several doors down from Randall's office, someone clears their throat obnoxiously loudly behind me. I'm tempted to ignore it, but since I know who it is, I stop but don't immediately turn around, so he'll wonder if I'm going to do so.

When I finally spin toward him, Randall is leaned against the wall outside his office with one leg crossed over the other and his hands in his pockets as if he's on the set of a Ralph Lauren photoshoot. He's wearing the navy-blue suit that makes his eyes look like they were God's inspiration for the sky on a perfect spring day. I order my body not to launch itself down the hall at him.

"Can I help you with something, Mr. Hamilton?" I ask.

"I was going to ask you the same thing, Ms. O'Halloran."

"Hmm."

"Hmm," he mimics. Then he shrugs, smirks, says, "Okay, then," and disappears back into his office.

I roll my eyes at the empty hallway and consider whether to follow him in. Of course I can't resist, but I take my time getting there.

When I step into the open doorway, Randall is sitting in his chair with his feet propped on the desk and crossed at the ankles, and his hands are clasped behind his head. He's still wearing the smirk from before.

"Think of something you need help with?" he inquires. "A contract? A lawsuit? A plate of fried chicken bigger than your head? A lost orphan girl from Kansas?"

I take two steps into his office and raise an eyebrow at him. "This is you being normal?"

"Tell me one thing I said or did that is out of character for me," he demands.

When I can't think of anything, he spreads his arms wide. "Ladies and gentlemen of the jury, I rest my case." He bows his head.

I force myself not to smile. "You're ridiculous."

"*You're* ridiculous."

"You're *more* ridiculous."

"Who's ridiculous?" George's voice booms from behind me.

My eyes go wide as Randall jerks his feet to the floor and rearranges some papers on his desk.

I slowly turn to face George while Randall says, "No one, sir. We were … uh …"

George chuckles. "At ease, Hamilton. The both of you are ridiculous if you think I haven't noticed there's something going on here." His eyes bounce between the two of us.

My hand goes to my throat, "George …"

He holds a hand up to stop me. "You don't have to explain anything to me. In fact, I neither need nor want any details. And I don't care what the two of you get up to as long as it doesn't interfere with your work." He points his finger at Randall. "And stop calling me 'sir.'"

Randall nods. "Got it, ssss … George."

George nods back at him and says, "Carry on, then. Wouldn't want to get in the way of you figuring out which of the two of you is the most ridiculous. Though if you want the opinion of this member of the jury, it's definitely Randall."

George steps out and closes the door behind him, and I drop into one of the black leather chairs in front of Randall's desk.

"Looks like things are good with him, then." Randall cocks his head at me. "Why'd you come down here?"

There's no reason to skirt the truth, so I admit, "To see you."

He nods. "But if you came to see me, why were you heading the other direction?"

I pick at a fingernail instead of looking at him. "I came over here because I was afraid you were avoiding me after our conversation earlier. I hadn't seen you all morning." I pause. "Well, not since you left my place. And then I felt silly and immature for coming over, so I turned around."

"Wendy, look at me," Randall says.

I peek up at him through my lashes.

"Fully look at me."

I drop my hands, sit up straight, and look him in the eye.

eleven

. . .

Randall

"You can come see me for any reason you want at any time," I say to Wendy, "and I won't ever make you feel bad about it. Got it?"

She nods.

I continue, "I'm in this one hundred percent. I'm committed to you and only you. I'm committed to *us* and what I'm hoping we'll become. Got that?"

She nods again.

I ask, "Why do you think I might not be all in?"

She looks back down at her hands again but then quickly refocuses on me when she realizes what she's doing. "You said you stayed with Colleen for a long time after you didn't really care about her, and I know this is very new with us and that's not what's happening here, but I'm afraid it will and you won't tell me, and I'm not used to having a man be committed to me, and I'm sorry I'm putting you in the same boat as the guys in my past, but it's hard not to because I don't know what it's like to be in a normal relationship with someone who really cares about me." She sucks in a deep breath after her long, run-on sentence, but she doesn't break eye contact.

My chest hurts, and it's all I can do to stay in my seat. "I want to hold you so badly right now."

After a few seconds of silence, she says, "Then do it."

At first, I laugh because I think she's joking, but I grip the arms of my chair when she doesn't join in, and I realize she's dead serious.

"Come here," I say.

Wendy stands and slowly walks around my desk, and I swivel my chair to the side so I'm facing her.

When she steps between my knees, her gaze still laser-focused on mine, I say, "You don't have to do this. Anybody could walk in."

"I don't care."

"I think you do care, because you're trembling. I think you're doing this because you think it's what I want and maybe what you think you should do as my girlfriend. I want you in my arms so much, but I don't want this for you. I don't want someone to walk in here and find you on my lap and think less of you because of it."

A variety of emotions flicker across her face and through her eyes, but I don't help her communicate them. I'm not going to physically stop her from doing this, but I'm also not going to encourage it. It needs to be her decision.

"I hate it when you're right," she finally says, with a mock glare.

I chuckle. "I know you do. But even though I'm right, I can't tell you what it's taking for me to keep my hands off you right now." My gaze flickers down the length of her body and back up. "I don't have the words to explain how much I love those form-fitting business suits." I wish shoulder pads would go out of style, but somehow she makes even those atrocities look amazing.

She smooths a hand down her hip. "I get them tailored to fit me just right."

My pulse kicks up, and I force myself to focus my eyes on hers instead of drifting lower again. "If you don't want me to inspect the tailor's work for myself right here, right now, you'd better head back to the other side of this desk so I can tell you why you didn't see me this morning."

"We'll keep that inspection on the back burner for now, but we'll be revisiting this conversation at a future date." Wendy grins at me before flouncing back around the desk and making herself comfortable in the chair.

I say, "I was meeting with George and the outside team of lawyers about my father's lawsuit against Carter-Jenkins."

Her hand goes to her chest. "Oh. Can you tell me about it?"

"Not the details, but it's not going well. Dad's playing hardball."

"How are you feeling about all of it?"

"Terrible, because it's all my fault, and it's costing George a huge amount of money."

When Dad found out Ash and I were involved in the creation of Diego Sanchez's new foundation, he went ballistic. He's not a fan of immigration, and he was incensed that my brother and I wasted his law firm's billable hours on the foundation. We ended up quitting our jobs over it, and George Carter broke his contract with Murphy, Hamilton, and Walker for legal counsel, which had been Ash's role in the firm. Then George hired me as his in-house legal counsel. Needless to say, Dad wasn't happy, and he sued Carter-Jenkins for breach of contract.

"George knew exactly what he was getting into," Wendy says. "And you didn't ask him to break the contract. He did that all on his own."

"If he hadn't broken it, he couldn't have hired me, and while I didn't ask him to do that, Ash did."

"True, but again, that was George's choice. He would have broken that contract regardless. He despises your dad. He only ever agreed to work with your dad's firm in the first place because he knew it was Ash who would be working with us."

"Is it terrible that I wish we could launch a PR campaign against my dad, telling the world what he's doing—what he did to me and Ash?"

Not only is there a lawsuit, but Dad also forbade us from talking to our mom or sisters. We're obviously not going along with that, but we're being discreet, to protect them from his wrath. Dad also kicked Ash out of his home in our parents' pool house, and he won't let us set foot on his property. Not that I care much about the property itself, but it's where my mom and sisters live, which makes it harder to spend time with them since they're up in Evanston and Ash and I live near downtown Chicago. Plus, my brother and I were unable to attend Tonya's high school graduation party, which nearly killed both of us. I spent a good part of that day on Wendy's couch.

"That's an understandable wish," Wendy says, "but you know it's not George's style. And it's not yours, either," she adds.

I hang my head. "I know, but Dad's going to get away with being a jack... terrible human once again."

"You can say that word in front of me. I won't be offended. But back to your dad—one of these days, he'll get what's coming to him. I can feel it."

I plant my elbows on my desk and steeple my fingers together. "I don't know. Sometimes it seems like the worst people never get punished for anything, especially when they're rich."

"Let's hope that's not what happens here."

"The bad side of Dad ever going down, though, is it'll hurt my sisters and mom."

"Yeah, that's something to consider. Have you or Ash talked to your mom lately?" she asks.

"No. When this all happened, she said she wasn't going to let what was going on with Dad change anything between her and us, but it has."

"There was no way it couldn't. Maybe she needs time to figure out how to navigate it. And she has to prioritize your sisters' needs over yours, since they're still teenagers living at home, but you and Ash are adults. This situation is difficult for the girls, too."

"You're probably right."

Wendy grins at me. "I know I'm right."

I rest my chin on my hands and smile back at her. "I'm glad you came to see me, even if we didn't cuddle."

"I love hearing you say the word 'cuddle' almost as much as I love actually cuddling with you," she says. "Not many men would use that word."

"It's quickly becoming one of my favorite words to say."

twelve

· · ·

Wendy

"**I**'m not ready to meet Andrea this weekend," I tell my mom on the phone after work, "but Randall's going to meet her for me."

"Randall?" Mom squeaks out. "Randall Hamilton?"

I can't help but grin. "Yes. We're dating."

"You're *what*? Why didn't you tell me?"

Mom has known about my crush on Randall for a while now, but I didn't tell her what we'd been up to the past month or so.

"It only became official yesterday," I explain, "and I was so thrown off by what you told me last night that I didn't have the energy to tell you about him."

"Oh, honey, I can't tell you how sorry I am for hiding the truth about your father and not telling you about him or about your sister in person."

"I know you're sorry, and I understand why you didn't tell me the truth. But I wish you had at least told me about you kicking him out. When I was little, I didn't need to know all the reasons why."

Mom sighs. "Wendy, we were so young and so dumb—both me and your father. Neither of us had the first clue how to be a spouse or a parent."

"I doubt anyone does until they do it, but I can't fathom trying to figure all of that out as a teenager. Imagine Daniel or Ryan attempting to be a husband or a dad. Yeesh."

"Don't I know it? I adore your brothers, but they're still boys and are, in many ways, completely clueless. But enough about them. Tell me about Randall."

My lips automatically turn up into a smile. "It's early days, and we're taking things slow. He's had some bad relationship experiences in his past, as have I, and we both want to try to do it right this time."

"That's a great idea. But him meeting your half-sister doesn't seem to be taking things slow. That's a big move."

"Yes, but we've been friends for a while, and he knows me well. It's not like we met each other yesterday. He cares about me, and he wants to make sure she's not going to try to take advantage of me."

"I like this man a lot already."

"So do I." I know she can hear the smile in my voice.

"I'm so happy for you, honey. You deserve a man who'll treat you like a queen—like your dad treats me."

"Thanks, Mom. Now, when and where is Randall supposed to meet Andrea?"

"She's staying at the Lakeview Hotel downtown. She'll be in town for a wedding, and the only free time she has is Saturday morning. She said she'll be at the hotel restaurant eating breakfast between eight and nine."

I jot down the details on the notepad by my phone. "Okay, how will he know what she looks like?"

Mom clears her throat. "It seems he won't have any trouble picking her out."

"And why is that?"

"Because she looks exactly like you."

"Are you kidding me?" I'm not sure how I feel about this information.

"No, Jack said the two of you could easily be mistaken for twins. In fact, when she sent him a photo of herself, he thought it was you playing an elaborate joke on him."

"So there's no doubt she really is his daughter and not some con artist?"

"That's what it sounds like. The man has some strong genes."

"You two seem more like sisters than aunt and niece. I love that," I say to Leslie's aunt Starla and cousin Beckett over dinner on Friday night. The two came to visit from Missouri for the weekend, and Leslie invited me out for a girls' night with them.

"We're only ten years apart in age," Beckett explains, "and I lived with Aunt Star for several years before I got married. In fact, if it weren't for her, I might not be married, or I might have ended up with someone other than my husband, which would have been a tragedy." She laughs, and I smile at how much she sounds like Leslie.

"So apparently Starla gives fantastic relationship advice," I say, "if she helped both you and Leslie end up with the loves of your lives."

"I didn't always get it right with either of them," Starla says. "And please call me Aunt Star. I don't want you to feel left out with these two." She points to her two nieces. "After all, you're dating my niece's boyfriend's brother, so we're practically family."

"For a while there, Wendy was threatening to become my sister-in-law in a totally different way," Leslie teases.

Aunt Star's eyebrows raise. "Shannon?"

I can't help but blush when I remember the way I fawned over Leslie's twin brother when I first got wind of his existence and saw his picture. The man is exceedingly handsome, not to mention charming.

"Oh, yes," Leslie says. "She even called him 'Sexy Shannon.'"

"Hey," I retort, "you hated when I called him that."

"I did," she admits. "It was weird then, but it's funny now."

"So what happened?" Beckett asks. "How'd you end up with Ash's brother instead?"

"Long story short," Leslie says, "Randall's girlfriend broke up with him, and Wendy forgot any other man existed and pounced on him immediately."

I gasp. "I did not!"

"Did you—or did you not—find yourself curled up with him on his couch all of four days after his breakup? You totally pounced."

I swat my friend's arm. "It wasn't like that, and you know it!"

"How would I know, since you waited a month to tell me about it? And during that time you met my brother and seemed smitten with him."

"Every woman on the planet is smitten with Shannon," Aunt Star interjects.

"*I'm* smitten with Shannon," Beckett states with a grin, "and he's my cousin. And I'm married."

Leslie rolls her eyes at both of them and says to me, "I thought it was strange you lost interest in him after meeting him and getting along so well. I figured it was the distance issue, but now I know the truth."

"What I really want to know," Beckett says, "is how this all started with Wendy and Randall."

I groan and drop my head into my hands.

"Get used to it," Leslie says. "Anytime someone wants to know how you and Randall got together, you're going to have to tell this embarrassing story."

"Kind of like how you have to tell an embarrassing story about how you and Ash met?" I retort.

Aunt Star laughs. "I like you, Wendy."

"We're not talking about me right now," Leslie says primly and takes a gulp of her wine.

"Maybe we should," I reply.

"Nope," Beckett says. "Aunt Star and I know everything about Les's love life. Now we want to know all about yours, Wendy. I demand you tell us everything."

I give them more details than they probably anticipated, but I've discovered I adore talking about Randall.

"That may be the most romantic story I've ever heard," Beckett gushes when I've finished. "I love this man, and I haven't even met him."

I smile at her and then look at Aunt Star, who hasn't said a word since I began my story. "What do you think?"

"You want to know the truth?"

My stomach flips. "Yes." Leslie trusts her aunt's judgment, and I think I possibly should, too, although I also have a feeling I'm not going to like what she has to say.

"I think he meant everything he said, and his intentions are good. I say that not because I know him but because it sounds like he cared for you as a friend before he realized he wanted more. But don't ignore his history. I'm not saying he can't change. He probably can to some extent, and it's best that he wants the change for himself and not only because he thinks it's what you want or need.

"But the kind of changes he wants to make can't happen overnight, nor can the ones you want to make." She points at me. "You're both going to slip back into your old habits at times, and you'll almost certainly hurt each other in the process. You need to be prepared for that. You need to prepare your heart for that, because it sounds like you've already given it to him."

I stare at her as her words sink in.

"Sorry to burst your bubble," she says, "but I'm not known for holding back."

"Nor am I. I appreciate the candor, although it makes me feel a little sick." I take a steadying breath. "Because you're right. And you sound like you speak from experience."

"Decades of it. I've made so many mistakes with so many men I can't count them. But when you find the right man, it's worth it to work through the mistakes you both make—together."

"And you've found your right man?" I ask, although the giant diamond on her left ring finger has already answered the question for me.

She smiles as she touches her ring. "I have, but it took me almost forty years, and I nearly ruined it several times."

"She's not lying." Beckett chuckles.

Aunt Star gives her a mock glare. "Like you're one to talk."

Beckett shrugs. "What can I say?" She explains to me, "My husband and I didn't have an easy road, either. But we got through it, and the hard times helped form the unbreakable bond we have today."

"Okay," Leslie says, "enough of the Debbie Downer talk. We get it. Relationships are hard."

thirteen

. . .

Randall

"I saw your friend Melissa today. I don't think she likes me," Bobby Jacobs says to Ash and me over drinks and dinner at McConnell's Pub.

Bobby is Diego Sanchez's sports agent, and I'm not his biggest fan. But Ash seems to like him, so instead of sitting home alone while Wendy and Leslie are out on their girls' night, I agreed to come along to the pub.

I take a sip of my Guinness and let my brother respond to Bobby's declaration about our childhood friend Melissa, who recently moved back home to Chicago.

"Why?" Ash asks. "What did you do to her?"

Bobby sets his pint glass down harder than necessary and says, "Nothing. That's what I did. Why do you assume I did something?"

"Because you can be a total jerk, man, and I don't think you usually realize it."

I'm impressed by my brother's boldness and honesty. Bobby is known for his ruthlessness as an agent, and as a result, most people steer clear from him both professionally and personally.

"I've barely spoken to the woman," Bobby says. "What could she have against me?"

"Maybe that's your problem," Ash replies. "Try speaking to

her. Try being nice. Try smiling at her. In fact, I don't think I've ever seen you smile—not a real smile, at least."

"I can't smile and be nice in the Cubs' front office. I have a reputation to maintain."

Melissa works in Customer Relations for the baseball club, and Bobby has a few clients who play for the team, so he's in their office on a regular basis.

"Then I don't know what to tell you," Ash says. "If you want her to like you—and I'm rather interested in why you do—you need to actually talk to her and maybe try to get to know her a little. Ask her questions. Give her a compliment. This is basic stuff that even *I* know."

"Why do you care if Melissa likes you?" I ask Bobby.

"Why does any man care if a woman likes him?" he retorts.

I narrow my eyes at him. "I hope in your case it's because you want to get to know her, not only because you want to get in her pants. Melissa's our friend. Don't mess around with her."

"Oh, I see how it is," Bobby says with a smirk. "If you're going after her, I'll steer clear."

I hold my hands up. "No. I'm dating someone else."

His eyebrows lift. "Since when are you dating someone?"

"Since two days ago."

"Do I know her?"

"It's Wendy."

Bobby's jaw drops. "Wendy from Carter-Jenkins?"

"The very one."

"Good for you. I like her. But why aren't you with her right now?"

Ash tells him where our girlfriends are as a fresh beer appears in front of me.

"Thanks, Tammy," I say to our waitress. "How do you always know exactly what I need, exactly when I need it?"

"I'm finely attuned to your needs at all times, Randall Hamilton. And my tip better reflect that," she teases with a wink.

"Eh, we'll have to see if you keep up the excellent work," I tease right back. She knows I'll tip at least thirty percent, like I always do. "Where were you when we got here?" I ask. "Some guy we don't know took our order."

"Kitchen emergency. You don't want to know." She cocks her head at Bobby. "Who's your friend?" Tammy gives him the once-over, but she doesn't seem interested, even though Bobby's an attractive man. Maybe she thinks he's too old. I'm not sure how old he is, but I'd guess late thirties, and Tammy can't be much older than twenty.

"Tammy, this is Bobby Jacobs," I say. "Bobby, Tammy."

"Nice to meet you, Tammy." Bobby shakes her hand. "Have you worked here long?"

"A couple years. I go to school during the day and serve these two ugly blockheads at night and on the weekends."

"Hey!" I protest. "You know I'm the most handsome man you've ever seen."

"Whatever you want to tell yourself." She winks again and heads off to check on another table.

"Look at you being nice to a woman," Ash says to Bobby. "I knew you could do it."

Bobby ignores him and points at me. "You have a girlfriend now, young man. Stop flirting with the waitress."

"I wasn't flirting! We're friends."

"That was definitely flirting." He nudges my brother. "Ash, back me up."

"Yep," the traitor confirms, "you were flirting. I didn't notice, because you always flirt with her, but Bobby's right. You need to stop now that you're with Wendy."

I flick my wrist. "Tammy knows I'm not serious."

"Does she?" Bobby asks. "Because it seems like she's into you."

"It's nothing," I say. "She's like that with everybody."

"Whatever you want to tell yourself," Bobby says, echoing Tammy's words with more than a little sarcasm. "She didn't give me a second glance, and I'm pretty sure I'm better looking than you are."

"You're definitely not." He maybe is. "And you're old enough to be her father." I take an extra-long sip of my beer.

Ash gives me a sharp look. "You're drinking faster than normal, and there's been something off about you all night. What's going on?"

I take another big gulp and wipe my mouth with the back of my hand before responding. "Dad called."

"What? When?"

"Right after I got home from work. Before you got home."

"Why didn't you tell me?"

"I didn't want to ruin your night."

Ash takes a deep breath, holding in whatever he was going to say. Finally, he asks, "What did he say?"

I stare into my beer. "Basically that I'm a loser and he never expected me to amount to anything, and he reminded me that he has forbidden us to see or talk to our sisters and Mom."

My brother curses.

"I thought you were trying to clean up your language," I say.

"I don't think I can when it comes to Dad. There aren't other words to fully express how I feel about him. He's not supposed to be in contact with us, anyway. Why didn't you hang up the phone?"

"I don't know." I twirl my glass around. I do know. As much as I hate to admit it, I crave the man's attention and can't let go of the tiny bit of hope that someday he'll approve of me.

"I hope you don't believe what he said about you," Bobby says, to my surprise.

I don't answer him or look him in the eye.

Bobby continues, "He seems a lot like my old man, may he not rest in peace. Don't let him get to you. You're not a loser. Listen to the people who care about you, not him."

"I gotta hit the little boys' room," I tell Ash and Bobby a couple hours and several beers later.

"You need me to help you find it?" my brother asks.

"Haha. You're hilarious, Sober Sheila."

"You know how much I love it when you make fun of me for not drinking," he says.

"I actually like that you don't drink, because it means you'll always be able to pay my tab and carry me home."

"Whatever. Take care of your business, and then we'll head out."

"You don't get to tell me when I'm going home," I protest.

He rolls his eyes. "Go. And try to find a better attitude before you get back."

"So bossy," I mutter as I make my way to the back of the bar on slightly unsteady feet.

When I come out of the bathroom, I run into a woman in the dark, narrow hallway. I grip her waist to steady us both, and when I focus on her face, I realize it's Tammy.

"Tammy! Oh, my favorite Tammy who brings me delicious drinks. You okay?"

Her gaze flickers from my eyes to my mouth and back to my eyes. "I'm good. You?"

"Fine and dandy," I say. "Fine and dandy."

"You're still holding onto me," Tammy says, with another glance at my mouth. I wonder if I have something stuck in my teeth.

"Making sure you don't fall," I say, although I'm the one who's more likely to hit the floor, as my head is suddenly spinning. I knew shouldn't drink that last beer she brought me, but when Dad's words echoed through my mind for the hundredth time, I guzzled it down.

"Don't want you to fall." I tighten my grip on her as the room whirls around me. "That wouldn't do at all."

"Why wouldn't it do?" she asks softly as she steps closer to me.

"Well, we wouldn't want anything to happen to your pretty face now, would we?"

Before I can comprehend what's happening, her body presses up against me, and her mouth is on mine. I automatically kiss her back, but I have a niggling feeling there's a reason I shouldn't. When her tongue swipes along the seam of my lips, Wendy's face suddenly pops into my mind, and I freeze. I twist my head to the side and set Tammy away from me.

"I can't." I gasp for breath. "I'm sorry. I can't do this. I have a girlfriend."

Tammy's hand goes to her mouth. "Oh, no," she says. "I didn't know. *I didn't know!* I'm so sorry, Randall. I'm not that kind of woman. I promise. Ohhh." Her other hand rests on her belly. "I'm going to be sick."

She bolts into the women's bathroom, and a few seconds later I hear retching noises. The sound triggers my own gag reflex, and I rush back into the men's room to empty my guts into the toilet.

After I clean up, I steel myself to head back out, praying I won't see her. I walk back to our table as quickly and steadily as possible.

"You fall in?" my brother jokes as I approach.

"I gotta get out of here," I tell him. "Pay the tab, and double the usual amount of tip. No, quadruple it."

I don't say goodbye to Bobby as I lurch toward the door. Ash calls after me to wait for him, but I can't. I stumble out onto the sidewalk and suck in gulps of the humid night air. I need to get away from this place, but I can't make my legs take me toward home, so I lean my back against the outside wall of the pub and slide down it until I'm sitting on the filthy ground with my head in my hands.

"Randy," my brother's voice says from above me, "what's going on? Are you really this drunk?"

"No." I'm trying my best not to cry, especially not here in public. "Well, I'm drunk, but … but …"

He squats down next to me, and when I look at him, I spot Bobby hovering behind him. I don't want him to know what I've done, but I don't see any way around it.

"But what?" Ash prompts.

"She kissed me." I squeeze my eyes shut. "And I kissed her back." I drop my head into my hands again.

"You kissed who? Wendy?"

"No." I suck in a few breaths. "Tammy."

A curse falls from his lips, and then he says, "Please tell me you're joking."

"I'm going to lose her." I feel like I'm going to be sick again. "I'm going to lose the best woman I've ever known, but I don't deserve her anyway. Not if I can do something like this."

"You're not wrong," Ash says. "Now get up off the ground so we can go home and figure out if there's any possible way to salvage this situation."

He grasps my hand to pull me up, and when I make no move to get up, Bobby grabs my other hand, and they haul me to my feet.

Then my loving brother adds, "But don't get your hopes up."

fourteen

. . .

Wendy

"Is there someplace around here we can do karaoke?" Beckett asks when we're finally leaving dinner after too much food and an abundance of laughter. "I've been dying to try it, but of course none of the bars in Cherry Hill have a karaoke machine."

"Carrie who?" Aunt Star asks.

"Karaoke," Leslie says. "It's where you sing popular songs along with the instrumental music, while the rest of the bar listens."

"That sounds interesting," Aunt Star says, "but I think I'll just watch you girls."

"Nope," Leslie declares. "We're all doing it. No excuses."

Aunt Star replies, "I doubt I'd remember any of the words if I had a lot of people looking at me."

"The lyrics are on a little screen," I explain. "Come on, it'll be fun! There's a place a few blocks away."

As I lead the way down the sidewalk, Leslie loops her arm around mine and says, "You're thinking about him, aren't you?"

I smile. "Of course I am. And you, obviously, are thinking about his brother. What do you think they're doing right now?"

She looks at her watch. "It's after ten, so they're probably home from dinner with Bobby and watching *SportsCenter* in their underwear."

My eyebrows jolt up. "They sit around watching TV in their

underwear?" I shouldn't picture that in my mind, but there's no way not to, and I honestly don't want to stop.

"I've never seen it," she says, "because it would be weird if Randall walked around in his skivvies in front of me, and Ash is still pretty shy about his body. But I know my brother does it, so I'm guessing those guys do, too, when there's no ladies around. Or at least Randall probably does. He's not shy about anything."

"Hmm." I shake my head to clear it of thoughts of my boyfriend in very little clothing. "We should talk about something else, or I'm going to turn around and head to their place to verify your prediction."

Leslie giggles, and I can't help but join in.

When we enter the bar, two women are singing "Walk Like an Egyptian" and doing the hand motions. They've obviously been drinking most of the night, because they're laughing and stumbling around.

"Do we have to dance?" Aunt Star asks over the music. "I don't want to dance."

"No, you don't have to dance. Are we all going to do a song together?" I ask.

"Yes," Leslie says, "I'm not going up there by myself."

"Any requests for songs?"

"Whatever you want," she replies. "Pick something that'll be fun. There's a table opening up over there in the corner where it hopefully won't be as loud, so we'll go snag it."

I make my way to the bar to flip through the binder of song options, choose one, and sign us up. A few names are on the list ahead of us, which means we'll need to settle in for a while. We'll also need a little liquid courage because karaoke is more intimidating than you think it'll be once you get up there. With that in mind, I stop by the bar to get us a round of vodka shots before heading back to the table with the four shot glasses held precariously between my fingers.

"Why don't I help you with those?" a familiar deep voice says, and I nearly drop the glasses.

I stop but don't turn to him, for fear I truly will drop the shots. "Joel?"

"In the flesh." He deftly slips the two of the shot glasses out of my hands and says, "Where to?"

I finally look up into my former co-worker's handsome face. "Um, follow me. Thanks."

"No problem."

I lead him to the table, and we dole out the glasses.

"I'm Joel," he says to the others, shaking hands all around. "I used to work with Wendy."

The other women introduce themselves while giving me questioning glances, as I seem to have lost my ability to talk. I'm dying to cover my face with my hands, as I know I'm beet red, but I realize that would bring more attention to it.

Leslie looks back and forth between Joel and me a few times and asks, "Did you work together for a while?"

"Yes, the whole time she was at Greene PR, so …?" He looks at me. "Five years or so?"

I nod.

"I've tried calling you a few times since you left," he says to me, not needing to add that I never called him back.

"Life's been a little crazy," I say, giving him the lamest excuse in the book.

His hand settles on my shoulder and squeezes lightly, and then he leaves it there. I can't make myself shrug it off, which was always my problem with him.

"Here's hoping it gets less busy," he says in a low voice near my ear.

"That's doubtful, because her boyfriend can't seem to stay away from her," Leslie says pointedly, though the fact that Randall's not with me now doesn't back up her words.

Joel's hand slides off my shoulder, and he sticks it in his pocket. "Well, it was nice to meet you ladies." He turns to me. "Great to see you, Wendy."

"You, too."

Once he's out of earshot, Beckett points at me. "There's a story there, and we need to hear it."

"I might have kissed him once." My face turns red again. "Or twice."

"Or more than twice?" Aunt Star asks.

"Perhaps."

"You gotta give us more than that," Beckett says, "but let's do these shots first. Maybe that'll loosen your lips." She grins at me.

We down the shots, and after some coughs and sputtering, the others look at me expectantly.

I don't want to admit this, but after everything else I've told them tonight, I figure I might as well come clean. "After pretty much every evening work event we attended together, we'd …"

"Go out for drinks?" Beckett guesses.

"Make out?" Leslie suggests.

"Head home together." Aunt Star doesn't make it a question. She knows.

I clear my throat and avoid looking any of them in the eye. "All of the above."

They're all silent for a moment.

"Is he one of the guys you were talking about earlier who wanted to sleep with you but wouldn't commit?" Beckett asks gently.

I nod. "He never wanted anything more than a physical relationship, yet for some reason I could never tell him no. I kept thinking at some point he'd want more than that, but he never did."

"How did it feel to see him again?" Leslie asks.

"I felt …," I search for the right words, "… embarrassed and … confused."

"Why confused?" Aunt Star asks.

I look at Leslie. "You can't tell Ash what I'm about to say."

"I won't. I promise. If this is something you need to talk to Randall about, he needs to hear it from you, not his brother."

I take a deep breath. "Confused because when I first heard his voice, before I was embarrassed, I was excited. And then when he put his hand on my shoulder, I couldn't make myself move away." I twirl my empty shot glass and focus on it instead of the other women. "I don't want to be with him anymore. I really don't. I only want to be with Randall. But if that's the case, why didn't Joel repulse me? Why did I let him carry our drinks and put his hand on me?"

"He caught you off guard," Leslie says. "Don't read anything into that. The important things are you don't want to be with him, and you didn't do anything inappropriate. If you tell Randall any of what just happened, he's not going to be mad. He may well be pissed off at the way the guy treated you in the past, but he won't be angry with you. You didn't do anything wrong."

"Up next," a voice announces over the speakers, "Wendy and friends with 'You Give Love a Bad Name.' Come on up, ladies!"

The other women burst into laughter as we stand.

"You couldn't have picked a more appropriate song," Beckett says.

fifteen

. . .

Randall

"We told you to stop flirting with Tammy," my brother says, "multiple times."

Bobby helped Ash get me home, and then he headed back to his hotel. I don't blame him. I don't want to be around for this conversation, either.

"I don't need an 'I told you so,' jerkface."

"Jerkface?"

"I'm trying to clean up my language."

"Let's hope you're more successful with that than you are with relationships."

"Stop. If you're trying to make me feel worse, it's not going to work, because there's no possible way I could feel worse than I do right now." I put my hand over my mouth. "I think I'm going to be sick again."

Ash sighs, disappears into the kitchen, brings me a Tupperware bowl in case I need to hurl, and plops down beside me on the couch. "I'm not asking this to be a jerk. I only want to try to understand. What were you thinking?"

"I wasn't thinking. I shouldn't have drunk that much, but I was trying to forget what Dad said to me."

Then I tell him what happened with Tammy.

"So you didn't initiate the kiss?" he asks.

"No! Why would I do that?"

"Okay, settle down. Did you put a stop to it immediately?"

I cover my face with my hands. "No."

He huffs out a breath. "Why not?"

"I don't know, okay? I didn't set out to kiss her, but her lips were right there on mine, and it's like my mouth went on autopilot." I groan. "I'm never drinking alcohol again."

"So you were kissing her, and then what?"

"I finally remembered Wendy, so I pulled away from Tammy and told her I have a girlfriend."

"How did she respond to that?"

"She was horrified. Said she's not that kind of woman. Then she ran into the bathroom and threw up. So did I."

"Not to add to your misery, but I think you've ruined McConnell's for us."

I hang my head. "Don't remind me. I have to apologize to Tammy, though. This wasn't her fault. I led her on without realizing it."

"Did you tell her who you're dating?" Ash asks.

"No." I peek over at him. "Why?"

"Because she knows Wendy. She and Leslie go to the pub all the time, too."

I flop back against the couch, my head tilted up toward the ceiling. "How did I think this couldn't get any worse? What am I going to tell Wendy?"

"The truth—every last detail of it. You can't keep this from her."

"Is the fact that I wouldn't kiss Wendy yet going to make this even worse?"

"You really want me to answer that?"

"No."

"Do you want to keep talking about this?"

"No."

"Then go to bed and sleep it off. But don't put off telling Wendy. She needs to know, and you need to get this off your chest."

He stands and pulls me to my feet. "Can you make it to your room okay?"

"Yep." I start to head that way. "Thanks."

"For what?"

"I don't know. I guess for being here."

I make a pit stop in my bathroom and then crawl into bed. As I'm about to drift off to sleep, I remember I'm supposed to meet Wendy's sister in the morning, and I sit straight up, which makes me queasy again. I sit on the edge of the bed and put my head between my knees for a minute until the feeling passes, and then I set my alarm. I can't mess anything else up with Wendy.

I wake to the sound of clanging—like something metal hitting the floor—and my head feels like it's going to split apart.

"Sorry," Ash calls out.

I groan and roll over. Through my slitted eyes, I catch sight of my alarm clock. I close my eyes, but then they pop back open, and I focus on the clock again.

I curse loudly, and Ash hollers, "I said I'm sorry."

When I sit up, my head spins, but I manage to stumble to the door and out into the hallway.

"Good morning, beautiful," my brother says when I enter the living room.

"I gotta go," I say, lurching toward the apartment door.

"The bathroom's the other way."

"No," I say, "I'm supposed to be meeting Wendy's sister *right now.*" The reality of the situation finally fully hits me, and I rush to the bathroom and dry heave over the toilet.

"Seriously, what is wrong with you?" Ash stands in the doorway with his arms crossed over his chest. "I have to say, this level of screw-up is excessive, even for you."

"I'm going to ignore your attitude," I gasp out between heaves, "because I need your help."

"You could have helped yourself by setting your alarm *and* by not getting drunk last night."

"I did set my alarm. I promise. I must have set it wrong." I straighten up, hoping the nausea is over for the moment. "You gotta drive me to the hotel. It's the only way I might make it." I push past him and rush back into my room to change my clothes, since I'm still wearing the ones I wore last night, and I need to look presentable for Andrea. "There's no way I'll find anywhere to park down there."

I surprise myself by how fast I can change my clothes while my head feels like it's going to explode. All the while, Ash watches me from the doorway.

"Let's go," I say, when I'm standing in front of him and he's not moving.

"You gotta brush your teeth first, man. And put on some cologne. You reek."

"Then get out of my way."

He moves, I quickly brush my teeth and douse myself in Obsession for Men, and we rush out the door.

"Tell me why I'm helping you," Ash says as we pull out of his parking spot.

"Because you love me, even if I'm the dumbest man to ever live. Drive faster!"

"No. I'm not breaking the law simply because my brother is dumb."

"Ash—"

"I'll get us there as fast as I can, all right? Calm down." He reaches over and flips open the glove box. "And grab a piece of gum out of there. You still smell like something died in your mouth."

It's exactly nine o'clock when we pull up in front of the hotel. I jump out without asking Ash if he's planning to wait for me, but if he doesn't, I'll have no right to be upset. I rush into the lobby and look around for the restaurant.

"Can I help you, sir?" a bellhop asks me.

"Yes, I need to find the restaurant."

"Which one?"

"You mean there's more than one?"

"There's one over there," he points, "and one over there." He points in the opposite direction.

I groan so loudly he backs away.

"Sorry," I say as I rush toward one of the restaurants. "I'm late for a meeting."

When I reach the hostess stand, I raise a hand in greeting but race right past, frantically looking around for a redheaded woman who looks like Wendy.

"Are you looking for someone?" the hostess asks from behind me.

"Yes, a woman with red hair." I spin toward her and hold my hand five feet from the floor. "About yea tall."

"I haven't seen anyone this morning who looks like that. Sorry."

I quickly make my way back across the lobby to the other restaurant, where I repeat the process with another hostess.

"Someone matching that description was here, but she left a couple minutes ago."

I look at the ceiling and take a deep breath to calm myself as my heart descends to my feet. "Did you happen to see which direction she headed?"

"No. Sorry."

I once again rush back into the lobby, hoping to catch a glimpse of Andrea heading out the door or to the elevators. I don't spot her, but I do spy my brother walking toward me.

"Is she still here?" he asks.

"I just missed her. What are you doing here?"

"I had the valet park the car. You're paying for it, by the way."

"Whatever. I don't care."

"Do you know what room she's staying in?"

"No. And I don't know her last name, so I can't ask the front desk to call her room. There's no way they'll do that if all I have is a first name."

"You could try O'Halloran. That's maybe not her name, but you could give it a shot."

"No, that's Wendy's stepdad's last name." He's not technically her stepdad, since he adopted her, but I don't have time to go into the entire explanation with my brother.

"Oh. Try anyway. You've got nothing to lose."

The man at the front desk is no help. Without a last name, he refuses to attempt to find an Andrea amongst the hotel's guests. There's no doubt he believes I met her at a bar last night and am trying to track her down.

I trudge toward where my brother is waiting for me in one of the lobby chairs.

"I'm going to have to leave the state. The *country*. There's no coming back from this with Wendy, is there?" I drop into the chair next to his.

"Wendy's a good woman, but I don't know how understanding she'll be about this double whammy."

"She shouldn't be understanding at all." I shut my eyes and try to ward off yet another bout of nausea.

"Open your eyes back up. We need to watch for this woman, in case she went back up to her room for a few minutes before heading out for the day. She might come back through the lobby."

I open my eyes as hope fills me. "You're right."

"What does she look like?"

"Wendy."

"I guess that makes sense."

"They look enough alike to be twins, apparently."

We wait for two hours before I'm willing to give up, but when Ash says he needs to leave to meet up with Leslie and her family, I realize waiting any longer isn't going to help. I need to go home, psych myself up, and then tell Wendy what I've done.

sixteen

. . .

Wendy

I've been pacing the floor in my apartment all morning, my cordless phone in hand, wondering how things went with Randall and Andrea. He should have been home by nine-thirty, but it's now almost noon, and he hasn't called, even though I've left two messages on his answering machine. I'm growing almost frantic with worry.

When the phone rings, I answer it immediately. "Hello?"

"Hi. It's me." Randall's voice is void of any emotion, which scares me.

"What's wrong? What's going on? Was Andrea terrible? Is that why you haven't called yet?"

"No, she's not the problem." he says. "Can we talk? Can I come over?"

"Of course you can come over, but you're scaring me. What's going on?"

"I'll tell you when I get there."

The fact that he doesn't tell me to not worry, like one would expect in this situation, ratchets my anxiety up several notches.

"Okay," I say. "See you soon."

While I wait, I can't obsess over all the scenarios of what he might tell me, because I don't know where to start. The only thing I'm halfway sure about from the brief conversation is the problem wasn't with my sister. So if not that, then what?

It feels like déjà vu when I buzz him up, crack the door, and take a seat in the easy chair to wait for him. But this time when he enters, he avoids my eyes and doesn't insist I sit with him on the couch.

"I don't know how to say this," he begins, still not looking at me, "but I've completely screwed everything up."

I can't imagine what he might think he's done to mess everything up in the past eighteen hours since he dropped me home after work yesterday, but something is obviously wrong.

He takes a shuddering breath. "I'm going to tell you what I did in broad terms, and then you can ask me anything, yell at me, kick me out, whatever."

If I don't have a stroke before he gets this off his chest, it'll be a miracle.

"I got drunk and kissed Tammy at the pub, and then I woke up late and missed breakfast with your sister."

My heart stops. It completely stops. I fully intend to see St. Peter any second. When I don't, I can't decide which of the three things Randall suggested I want to do first. I have no desire to look at him, much less have him continue to sit on my couch across from me, but I also want details. I want all the details, but I seem to have lost my voice along with my heart.

"Will you say something?" he asks.

I stare at him and finally choke out, "What do you expect me to say?"

"That you hate me and never want to see me again."

I consider saying it, but I don't.

"I need you to give me a few minutes." I stand and walk to my bedroom as calmly as I can and close the door behind me. Then I sit on the edge of my bed and do my best not to hyperventilate.

Do I hate him? No. Do I ever want to see him again? Not anytime soon, honestly. If he had a halfway decent explanation for anything he did, he would have tried to explain. But he didn't. While I do want to hear exactly what happened both last night and this morning, I'm not prepared to hear it yet. Considering my insecurities, I'm afraid I'll either forgive him too quickly or completely overreact. I'd rather imagine the worst for now, and then hopefully when he tells me the details, I'll be less disappointed in the truth.

Even though I'm ready to tell him to leave, I wait a few more minutes to do so, simply because I want to leave him in suspense a little longer. I know it's petty and childish, but all my mature-adult energy is currently channeled toward holding myself together.

Randall is sitting with his head in his hands when I walk back out of my room.

"I want you to go," I say numbly. "I'm not ready to hear your explanations."

He nods, stands, and heads to the door without looking in my direction. In fact, he hasn't looked at me since he got here. He also hasn't apologized, though I'm not going to point that out to him.

When he reaches the door, he finally turns and looks at me with anguish-filled eyes. "I'm sorry, Wendy. And I'll be sorry until the day I die for hurting you, for disappointing you, for *betraying* you. I didn't mean for any of it to happen, and I'll understand if you never forgive me." And then he's gone.

I slowly sit down on the kitchen floor and hug my knees. For some reason, I can't cry. I can't wrap my mind around what happened, yet it's whirling with wild thoughts and visions of Randall kissing another woman.

There's no point in getting up. There's no one I can call. Leslie is out with Ash and her family all day. Ryan has a baseball tournament this weekend, so Mom and Dad aren't home. I don't have anyone else in my life I could call even if I knew what to say to them.

The phone rings some time later, but I don't move. It can't be anyone I want to talk to, and my body is so stiff from sitting on the hard floor, I'm not sure I can move anyway.

"Wendy," a voice comes out of my answering machine, "this is Melissa. I don't know what's going on, but Randall called and asked me to check on you. He said something happened, and he knows Leslie isn't available for you to talk to, and he doesn't want you to be alone. If you're there, please answer."

Tears finally start to fall, but I don't make an attempt to wipe them. I don't want to think about how it makes me feel that Randall asked his friend to check in on me because he's worried about me.

"Okay," Melissa says when she realizes I'm not going to pick up the phone, "if you need to talk or to be with someone and not talk, I'm here. Call me, please. I'm worried, although I don't know what I'm supposed to be worried about. At least call me so I know you're okay. I'll be home the rest of the day."

I know I should call her back, but I don't want to get up off the floor, because there's nowhere else to go that won't make me hurt more. I can't go to the couch where I've spent so much time in Randall's arms. I can't go to my bed, where my sheets still hold his scent. I can't even curl up in the easy chair, because it's where I was sitting when he told me he kissed someone else—when he wouldn't even kiss *me*. Randall Hamilton has ruined my entire home for me.

With that realization, I push myself off the floor and make my way to the phone to call Melissa back.

"It's Wendy," I say when she answers. "Can I come over?"

"Of course. Let me come get you."

I don't try to argue, because I'm in no mental state to potentially deal with a chatty cab driver or figure out the bus route to her place near Wrigley Field. "I'll be waiting downstairs so you won't have to try to park. Thanks, Melissa."

"Glad to be of help. See you soon."

seventeen

. . .

Randall

I have nowhere to go and no one to talk to. When I got home from Wendy's, Ash was gone, and he'll be out with Leslie the rest of the day. All my other friends disappeared when Colleen dumped me for Kevin, and they all chose to stay friends with the cheaters instead of me. I can't call my mom, not because Dad forbade me to talk to her, but because I can't admit to her what I've done. I won't be able to handle the sound of disappointment in her voice. I briefly consider calling Bobby Jacobs, because he already knows the worst of what I've done, but I figure he doesn't want to deal with my shambles of a life.

It's not that I deserve to have someone help me deal with my misery. I'm fully aware I brought this all upon myself, but I feel like if I have to spend one more minute in this apartment by myself, I'll lose my mind. I have to go somewhere, anywhere, even if I'm alone. But I can't escape yet—not until I hear back from Melissa. I need to know that Wendy has someone looking out for her. The two women don't know each other all that well, but they've spent enough time together I'm hoping Wendy will open up to Melissa.

I flip through the TV channels while I wait. There's nothing I want to watch, but I'm hoping something will distract me from my own thoughts for at least a few minutes. Instead, my channel surfing is backfiring on me. I've already caught glimpses of two kissing scenes in movies as well as love song music videos on both VH1 and MTV. I finally land on an old western movie, and I pray it won't inexplicably contain a love scene.

It doesn't, but when a woman starts yelling at John Wayne on the screen, I can't help but think of Wendy, and it feels like a vice is crushing my chest. Yelling—or at least telling me her thoughts and feelings—is exactly what I expected her to do. Instead, what I did was so bad I managed to silence a woman who usually speaks her mind with no provocation whatsoever.

When the phone rings, I grab it before it can ring a second time.

"It's me," Melissa says. "I'm going to pick her up and bring her to my place."

I let out a long breath. "Good. Thank you."

"You're not going to tell me what this is about?"

"No, I'll let her tell you what she feels comfortable with. But so you know, it's all my fault."

"I figured it was."

I huff out a laugh. "Fair enough."

"Am I going to have to pick sides?"

"Yes, and you'll choose her."

"Oh, Randall." Melissa sighs. "What have you done?"

"You'll find out soon enough."

"I'll take care of her."

"I appreciate it, and I owe you."

"You don't owe me anything. We're friends, and this is what friends do, even when the other person is a numbskull. Plus, Wendy's also my friend. I care about her, too."

"You're right. Thanks again."

When we hang up, I decide I'm going to try to get in touch with Bobby. I have nothing to lose, because he already knows I'm a walking disaster.

He lives in Los Angeles, but when he's in town, he stays at the Drake Hotel, where Diego Sanchez has also set up house in a massive suite. I call the hotel, and they won't connect me to his room since I don't know the room number, but the nice lady on the phone says she'll get him a message to call me.

I decide to give Bobby a half hour to call me back, and then I'll head out to do something to attempt to get my mind off Wendy. I hope she'll give me a chance to explain, but I'll understand if she doesn't, and I know if she does and eventually forgives me, she probably won't want to be with me anymore.

While I wait, I keep watching the western, trying and failing to get invested enough that I forget everything else. Instead I check the time every two minutes and then go take another aspirin since my hangover headache is still hanging on.

I'm about to head out the door when the phone rings.

It's not Bobby.

"Randall Hamilton, what did you do to Wendy, and where in the world is she?" Leslie demands. There's a lot of noise in the background, so I have no idea where she's calling from.

I answer the most important part of her question first. "She's with Melissa."

"Good. I'm glad she doesn't have to get through whatever you did to her on her own. Now, what did you do?"

"Ash didn't tell you?"

"He wasn't going to tell me anything, but it was obvious the second I saw him that something was wrong. I finally wore him down enough to admit you did something to hurt my best friend, but he won't tell me what. Says that's your responsibility. So spill before my time runs out on this pay phone. I don't intend to waste another quarter on you."

"I got drunk and kissed Tammy at the pub, and then I set my alarm wrong and missed breakfast with Wendy's sister."

"Are you kidding me?" she says. "You wouldn't kiss your girl-friend, but then you went and kissed a waitress you barely know?"

"I was drunk," I say feebly, as if that's a viable excuse.

"You're twenty-six years old. It's time for you to stop getting drunk and start taking some responsibility for your life. I hope you didn't screw things up between her and her sister, too, by not showing up in time."

"The sister didn't know if anyone was going to show up or not," I reply.

"And you really think Wendy wouldn't have gotten word to her if nobody was planning to meet her? She would have at least sent a message through her parents to let Andrea know she wasn't ready to meet her yet. Instead that poor woman sat there waiting and wondering if anyone was going to come. Imagine her disappointment when nobody did."

Now I feel worse, which I didn't think was possible. "I'm sorry, okay? And I told Wendy I was sorry, but she didn't want to hear my explanations."

"Not that your explanations are worth hearing."

I close my eyes. "Can you cut me some slack here?"

"No, I can't. You don't deserve it. Now, give me Melissa's number so I can call and see how Wendy is."

I give her the number, and she hangs up without saying goodbye. The phone immediately rings again. This time it's Bobby.

"What are you doing for the next few hours?" I ask him.

"Nothing. I have dinner plans, but I'm free until then."

"Want to play racquetball?" Hopefully the physical activity will help take my mind off my life.

"Sure. When and where?"

I give him the address of my gym and tell him to meet me there in thirty minutes.

"What are we really doing here?" Bobby asks while we're taking a water break in between games.

"I needed to get my mind off Wendy."

"I figured. You tell her what you did?"

"Yeah, but you only know half of what I did."

He gives me an assessing look. "What else did you do?"

I tell him about missing breakfast with her sister and then about my brief interaction with Wendy.

Bobby lets out a long whistle. "You're going to be lucky if she ever looks at you again, much less wants to date you."

"That's real helpful."

He shrugs. "What do you want me to say?"

I hang my head. "I don't know. I guess I keep hoping some-body will give me at least a tiny kernel of hope that I didn't completely blow this whole thing up with her when it had barely started."

"Well, you did blow it up, but you two were friends before this, right?"

I nod. "Which makes it worse."

He's quiet for a minute before saying, "I'm not sure that's true. It might make her more likely to try to work this out."

I tilt my head to look at him. "What makes you say that?"

"I think she'll eventually realize this is out of character for you. She'll understand it was a mistake. Add in the fact that her friend is dating your brother and how awkward it'll be for everyone if you two don't make up, then maybe there's a chance."

"You think?"

"I said *maybe*. But you're going to have to work for it. Since Wendy won't talk to you yet, the first thing you can do to try to fix this is to find out the sister's last name so you can leave her a message at her hotel."

eighteen

. . .

Wendy

"**B**efore I tell you what he did," I say to Melissa once I'm curled up on her couch, "I want to thank you again for doing this for me. I know it might be weird for you, because you haven't made a secret of the fact that you're interested in Randall."

Melissa grew up with Ash and Randall, and she recently reconnected with them when she moved back to Chicago after going to college and working in New York City for several years. She has also become good friends with Leslie, and I've spent some time with her as well.

"I'm not interested in him anymore," Melissa says. "When I was at dinner with him, Ash, and Leslie last week, I could tell he wasn't into me, and I decided I should move on. And now that I know you two are together, that seals the deal for me. You're my friend, and I don't try to steal men from my friends." She grimaces. "Not that I have a habit of stealing men from anyone, mind you."

I nod. "I'm sorry I didn't tell you there was something between me and him. I should have, because that's what a good friend would have done, but we didn't tell anyone until a few days ago. In fact, he and I didn't even acknowledge what was happening between us until then."

"You're forgiven," she says. "Now, tell me what he did to you so I'll know exactly why I'll be yelling at him later."

I laugh at her statement but then quickly sober up when I remember what I'm about to tell her. "I might as well start at the very beginning," I say, "so you'll understand the full impact of what he did."

When I'm finished, she asks, "Can I hug you? Or will that make you wish things were okay and *he* was the one with his arms around you?"

"Please hug me," I say. "I can't let him ruin hugging for me, too."

Melissa takes a seat next to me and wraps her arms around me. I sink against her and rest my head on her shoulder as we sit in silence for a minute.

"What am I supposed to do now?" I finally ask her.

"What do you want to do? Do you want to know the details? Do you want to try to work things out?"

"I want to know the details for sure. At the moment, I don't want to try to work things out. I want to yell at him and then forget I ever met him."

"You sure about that?"

I sigh. "No. Well, I'm sure about knowing the details. Not about the other."

"Do you love him?" she asks gently.

I take a deep breath. "I ... I think I might. I think this wouldn't hurt so bad if I didn't."

She squeezes me tighter. "I don't know Randall as well as you do, but I've spent enough time with him lately to know there's no way he meant to do any of what he did. He would never set out to hurt you like that."

"I know he wouldn't," I admit. "This is ultimately a forgivable offense. We've not been dating long, and deep down, I know there's more to the story he's not telling me, though I'm not sure why he didn't explain it without me asking him to. But it happened, and what's to say this won't be a pattern with him? I can't live my life wondering when he'll kiss some other random woman again."

"No, you can't. But you can ask him if it's a pattern—if he's done anything like this before. I think he'll tell you the truth."

Brrrring!

Melissa lets go of me so she can answer the phone. After greeting the other person, she hands the phone to me. "It's Leslie."

"How'd you know I was here?" I say into the phone.

"The person whose name I'll never say to you again told me," Leslie explains.

I allow myself to smile at her loyalty. "It's going to be hard for you to never say his name, since you're going to marry his brother."

"I don't care. I'm going to do it." She doesn't comment on the "marrying his brother" part, and I wonder if Ash is listening on her end.

"You can say his name," I say. "And where are you?"

"At a pay phone outside the restaurant where we were eating lunch. I made Ash tell me why he was acting weird. Then I tried calling you but didn't get an answer, so I called no-name man to yell at him, and now here I am. How are you doing with all this?"

"At first, I was numb. Then Melissa came and got me, and we've been talking about it, and I'm feeling better. Not great, not ready to talk to him, and not ready to forgive him until I know more, but better."

"Do you need me to come be with you? Because I will."

Tears fill my eyes. "No. I appreciate it, but you need to spend the day with Ash and your family, like you planned. Melissa has me covered."

I smile at my new friend through my tears, and she nods and grabs my hand.

"You sure?" Leslie asks.

"Positive. Don't think about me any more today. And tell Aunt Star she was right."

"She won't be happy to hear that."

"I know."

"Bye, friend. Love you."

"You, too."

Melissa hangs the phone up and asks, "Did you eat lunch?"

When I tell her I haven't eaten all day, she heads out to grab us some sandwiches from a deli up the street. While she's gone, I flip through the TV channels trying to find something to distract me. It doesn't work.

After we've eaten and talked about many things other than Randall, Melissa asks if I want to get out of the house or stay in the rest of the day. I opt for staying in, and I suggest having a movie marathon. She runs out to the nearest Blockbuster with strict instructions from me to not bring back any romance movies, and she returns with *National Lampoon's Vacation, Adventures in Babysitting, Ghostbusters, The Sting,* and *The Muppet Movie.*

She also carries a bag with other items in it I can't see, and when I ask her about it, she says, "I have an idea. You might think it's silly, but it might be exactly what you need. Give me a second to get it set up."

I raise an eyebrow. "Get what set up?"

"You'll see."

She grabs a roll of tape out of a drawer and heads off to her bathroom with the bag, and I hear paper ripping. I have no idea what she's up to. A few minutes later, the water runs, she lets loose with a few unmentionable words, and then she comes back into the living room wearing a soaked shirt and holding two water guns.

"Come on," she says. "Let's do this."

I hesitantly stand. "Do what? Are we having a water gun fight? I'm so confused."

"Come with me." She nods toward the bathroom.

I follow her into the small space and burst out laughing. She has taped pages from a *GQ* magazine onto the walls of her shower. Every single man in the photos is dark haired and wears a suit. The one at my eye level looks freakishly like Randall.

Before she can say a word, I grab a water gun from her and start emptying it onto the picture. I start with the head, move down to the heart, and finish a couple inches lower.

Melissa cackles. "You have excellent aim."

"Join me," I say. "You know you want to."

We spend the next ten minutes reloading our guns and unleashing on the suited men until the pages tear and fall down into the bathtub. Then I turn on Melissa and start spraying her. She shrieks but retaliates, and we both end up gasping on the floor in a puddle of water.

"Oh, I needed that." I grin at her. "I like you, Melissa."

Partway through *Vacation*, the phone rings, and Melissa goes into her bedroom to answer it so I can keep watching. After the movie's over, while we're waiting for the videotape to rewind and are grabbing snacks for movie number two, she asks me about my sister.

"I don't know much about her," I say. "Her name is Andrea, she lives in Little Rock, and she's in town for a wedding." I sigh. "I need to get in touch with my father to see if he can let her know I still want to meet her at some point, but I don't have the energy to deal with him right now."

"Does he live in Little Rock, too?" Melissa asks.

"No, he lives in Green Bay. Or at least I think so. I haven't heard from him in a while, so he might be somewhere else by now."

"Do you think your sister has his last name?"

That's an odd question for her to ask, but I say, "No, he didn't know about her until recently, so her mom wouldn't have given her his name. Mom said her last name is Doyle. Isn't it weird that not only does she look like me, with the red hair and green eyes and all, but her last name—that didn't come from our father—is also Irish?"

"It's quite a coincidence," she says. "Does your father also have red hair?"

"Bright red and curly. What's funny is his last name is MacDonald—like Ronald."

nineteen

. . .

Randall

"I want you to know," Melissa says in a hushed voice over the phone, "I'm doing this for Wendy and her sister. *Not* for you."

"I get it," I say. "But I appreciate the help. Hopefully I can make this one thing right."

"You're going to need more than hope. Anyway, Andrea's last name is Doyle. And if it's helpful in any way, her father's last name is MacDonald. I don't know his first name, though."

"Thank you. Truly."

"Yeah. Gotta go before she gets suspicious."

"Bye."

I sit right down to write a letter to Wendy's sister.

> *Dear Andrea,*
>
> *I'm a friend of Wendy O'Halloran, and I was supposed to meet you for breakfast this morning. Please accept my apologies for missing it, as I set my alarm wrong and didn't arrive until just after 9:00. I can only imagine how disappointed you felt when nobody showed up.*
>
> *Wendy thinks she'll want to meet you, but she's not*

ready yet. She's still adjusting to the idea of having a sister. I offered to meet you today instead, so I could find out a little about you for Wendy, and so I could tell you a little about her. In a nutshell, she's an amazing woman, and you're incredibly lucky to have her as a sister.

She said this morning was the only time you were free this weekend, but if there's a chance I could still meet you for even five minutes tonight or tomorrow before you leave town, I would love to do so. If you're interested, please call me at 312-555-5309. You can call anytime, no matter how late or how early.

Again, I'm sorry I left you waiting this morning.
Sincerely,
Randall Hamilton

I stick the letter in an envelope and then head back to the hotel and drop it off at the front desk, extracting a promise from the clerk that she'll hand deliver it to Andrea's room. Then I go straight home so I'll be there if she calls.

The only problem with this plan is I'm home alone again, but now I have a glimmer of hope that I can make at least one thing right with Wendy.

"Are you Wendy's boyfriend?" is the first thing Andrea asks me as we sit in the hotel lobby very early the next morning.

"I was. I'm not sure now." Apparently I have no problem being honest with strangers before the crack of dawn.

She gives me an assessing look. "Because you missed breakfast with me yesterday?"

"That and something else I did Friday night." There I go with the honesty again.

Andrea laughs. "You don't hold back, do you?"

"I kind of feel like I'm talking to Wendy. It's wild how much you two look and sound alike."

"So it's true, then? I thought Jack was exaggerating when he told me that."

"Not at all. Since we don't have much time before you need to leave for the airport, let's get down to business. Can you tell me how you found out about Wendy?"

"It's a long story, and if Wendy wants to hear the entire thing, I'll tell her. But for now I'll tell you that for my whole life, my mom told me my father died before I was born, and I had no reason not to believe her. So imagine my surprise when my mom sat me down a few months ago and told me the truth. She had an affair with a married man and thought it would be easier to tell everyone—not only me—that the man who got her pregnant was dead. But in reality, he was alive, and Mom knew he had at least one other child: Wendy. I'm an only child, so it was shocking to find out I'm actually not. Then I tracked Jack down, talked to him, and here I am.

"I understand Wendy being leery of meeting me. This is all so new and strange, and I wasn't sure about meeting her, either. But when Jack told me she lives in Chicago, and I was headed here for a wedding, I figured I should take a chance and see if she'd meet me."

"I'm glad you did," I say.

"There's something else I told Jack not to tell Wendy yet, because I wanted to tell her myself, but I feel okay telling it to you." She presses her lips together before saying, "I have a daughter."

My eyebrows shoot up. "Wendy has a niece?"

Andrea nods. "She's six. Her dad and I were never married, and he's not in the picture anymore, so Mom helps me out with Emily. That's where she is this weekend—with my mom."

A smile spreads across my face. "I think Wendy will be very

excited to learn about Emily."

"Really?" Andrea seems relieved by this news.

"Yes. She loves kids."

"I haven't told Emily yet that she has an aunt. I don't want to get her hopes up in case things don't work out with Wendy."

"I understand that." I look at my watch. "We only have a few minutes left, and I have a lot of questions, but the most important one is this. Forgive me for my bluntness, but what do you want from Wendy?"

"I do forgive the bluntness," Andrea says. "You're trying to protect her, like I'm protecting my daughter. And the answer is I want a sister—someone I can count on and who can count on me, someone I know I can always call when I need a friend, someone I can be myself with, and vice versa. I know it would take a while for Wendy and me to get to that point, but ultimately that's what I want. I don't have any family other than Emily and Mom, and I want more of a family for my daughter. I want her to have aunts and uncles and cousins she can love and who will love her."

Andrea is so earnest, I know she's telling the truth.

"You couldn't have given a better answer," I say.

"It might sound contrived, but it's true."

"I believe you. And now I'm even angrier at myself for missing breakfast yesterday, because if I hadn't, maybe you'd be sitting here talking to Wendy now instead of me. I'm sorry I screwed that up for both of you."

"Don't be so hard on yourself," she says. "I believe this all happened the way it was supposed to, though we might never know the reasons why."

twenty

. . .

Wendy

I fell asleep during our fourth movie, and when I wake up on Melissa's couch Sunday morning, there's a pillow under my head and a blanket covering me. I'm thankful once again for Melissa's friendship and how she went above and beyond yesterday to help me through the day. But today I need to put on my big girl pants and deal with Randall, whatever that might mean. A pit forms in my stomach from thinking about it.

When I head to the bathroom, I pass Melissa's open bedroom door, and she's sitting cross-legged on her bed reading a book.

"Morning," I say from the doorway.

She looks up and smiles. "Good morning. You feeling better today?"

"A little."

She nods. "Good. You're welcome to stay here today, too, if you want. I have a few errands to run, but my home is your home."

"I should probably get back to my place. I need to talk to Randall, and I'd rather do that in my own space."

"I get that. Let me know when you're ready for me to take you."

"You don't have to drive me. I'll get a cab."

"I'm driving you. End of discussion."

"Okay. Thanks. I'll be ready soon. I want to get this over with."

"I know you don't want to talk to me," Randall's voice comes out of my answering machine, "but I have something to tell you that will make you happy. So please call and let me tell you about it. We don't have to talk about the rest of it if you don't want to." I think the message has ended and am walking away from the machine when his voice speaks to me again. "I'm so sorry, Wendy. So sorry." His voice breaks on the last word, and it sends a pang to my heart, which irritates me.

Now I don't want to call him, because I'm afraid he's trying to manipulate me into talking to him by claiming to have good news. What could he possibly have to tell me that would make me happy? In my heart, I know he's not the manipulative type, but I also thought he wasn't the type to kiss another woman a day after declaring he was fully committed to me and only me.

While I shower and get dressed, I talk myself back into calling him. We need to work this out to some extent because we work together and because of Leslie and Ash. As much as I don't feel like acting like an adult in this situation, deep down I'm thankful the circumstances are forcing me to.

I take my cordless phone to the kitchen table to make the call. I still don't feel comfortable on any of my other furniture, and I'm going to need to get over that soon, but I'm not ready quite yet.

My pulse races as I wait for Randall to pick up.

"Hello?" He says from the other end of the line.

"Hey. It's Wendy."

He gives me a tentative, "Hi."

I don't respond. I'm going to let him take the lead on whatever he wants to tell me.

"I met your sister this morning," he says, and my heart stops.

When it starts back up, I say, "You did?"

"I did, and I like her, Wendy. I like her a lot, and I know you will, too."

"You don't think she wants anything from me?"

"What she wants is a sister." He pauses. "And an aunt for her daughter."

My hand goes to my chest. "I have a niece?"

"You do. Her name is Emily, and she's six."

Tears prick behind my eyes at this unexpected but welcome news.

"Andrea's married?" I ask.

"No. Her mom is helping her raise Emily."

"What else did you learn about her?"

"Not much, except she doesn't have any other siblings. We didn't have a lot of time to talk, but she told me a little about how she found out about you." He explains what she told him.

"So her mom lied to her about our father, too."

"Yes, unfortunately you two have that in common." He sighs. "I'm so sorry I messed this up. If I hadn't, you maybe could have met her this morning."

Now I sigh. "That's water under the bridge now, though."

"Yes, but I got her phone number, if you want to call her." He gives it to me, and I write it on a piece of scrap paper.

"Well, I'd better let you go," he says.

I'm tempted to say goodbye, but instead I say, "Wait."

"Yes?" I detect a hint of hopefulness in his voice.

"Will you tell me what happened? I think I'm ready to hear it now." I also wonder if I'm wrong about that.

"Do you want me to tell you over the phone or in person?"

I think about it for a minute. The conversation would probably be best in person, but I don't think I can be in his presence right now.

"On the phone."

"Okay." He sounds resigned. "Feel free to interrupt me any time you want to ask questions or scream at me."

His statement reminds me he doesn't know me as well as I think he does, which is a reminder I don't know everything about him, either.

"I'm not going to scream at you," I say, although I very well may want to. "That's not something I do."

"Sorry," he says. "I shouldn't have assumed that of you. Let me amend that to saying you can speak your mind at any time."

"That I plan to do."

"Good. I want to know your thoughts, no matter how much they might hurt me."

Nausea settles deep into my belly at his words. "I have no intention of hurting you, Randall."

"I know you don't." He sighs. "I can't quite seem to say the right thing here."

"Just tell me what happened."

"I went to McConnell's with Ash and Bobby. Tammy was our waitress, and I flirted with her, like I always do. Bobby told me I needed to stop, since I'm with you now, and I don't know if flirting is simply ingrained in me or if I'd already had too much to drink, but I didn't stop."

My heart aches from what he's telling me. But at the same time, I realize he didn't have to tell me he didn't stop flirting. He could easily lie to me, but he didn't.

He continues, "I want you to know I'm not in the habit of getting drunk. The only other time I've been drunk in the past year is the night Colleen broke up with me. Anyway, I went to use the restroom, and when I came out, I ran into Tammy. I grabbed onto her simply to steady both of us, but looking back, I can see how she took it as something more after all the flirting. Then I told her I didn't want her to fall and hurt her pretty face, and she kissed me."

What he said doesn't sound unforgivable. I don't like that he got drunk or flirted with Tammy, but I think I can eventually move past all that. However, when it comes to the kiss, there's one more thing I need to know.

"Did you kiss her back?"

twenty-one

. . .

Wendy's question will echo in my mind for weeks to come. I wish I could tell her I didn't kiss Tammy back, and I'm tempted to preface my answer with an excuse, but I won't lie to her or try to sugarcoat it.

"Yes. I kissed her back."

The silence on the other end of the line nearly ends me. I want her to yell, to scream, to tell me exactly how terrible of a boyfriend I am, but she does none of that.

"Why?"

Her voice isn't soft or timid, which is promising. She's not going to roll over and take it. She's going to fight back, whatever that means for her.

"I was drunk. I know that's an awful reason, but it's the one I have. I wasn't thinking straight, and my mouth automatically kissed her back. But then I came to my senses, and I pulled away from her and told her I couldn't kiss her because I have a girlfriend."

"How did she respond to that?"

That wasn't the response I expected, but I answer. "She was horrified, said she's not that type of woman, and then she threw up."

"On you?"

I wonder if she's hoping I'll say yes.

"No. In the bathroom. I could hear her. And then I threw up. Also in the bathroom, if you're wondering. The men's bathroom, that is. We didn't puke side by side or anything."

"Don't try to lighten the mood," she says.

"Sorry." I sigh.

"Why did you get drunk? Is there a reason you drank that much?"

I don't want to tell her what my dad said to me, but I realize it's important for her to know all the facts, so I do. I tell her every word he said in his quest to tear me down.

"Randall," she says softly, "that's not true about you. I hope you know that."

"I mostly do, but it's hard to hear something like that from a parent."

"I know. But please don't believe it. I wish you had called me as soon as you talked to him. We could have worked through it and probably avoided all the rest of what happened."

I swallow the lump in my throat. "I'm sorry I didn't."

We're both quiet for a long time.

"Tell me what you're thinking," I finally say to her when I can't take the silence any longer.

"I'm thinking I'm really sad. I'm sad about what your dad said to you. I'm sad that because of what he said, you let yourself drink so much that you kissed someone other than me. I blame the alcohol on the actual kiss, but I blame you for putting yourself in that position. I'm also sad that Tammy got to know what it's like to kiss you when I haven't gotten that chance yet. And I'm sad for her. She didn't deserve for you to put her in that situation. You hurt her, too, you know. And in addition to the sadness, I'm disappointed."

I didn't think I could feel worse, but I do. I would have preferred yelling to this calm resignation and disappointment. However, I didn't miss the "yet" she said in relation to us kissing, and I hold onto that tiny little word, although I have no intention of pointing it out to her.

"I have a feeling I'm more disappointed in me," I say.

"That's doubtful. Now, tell me how you missed breakfast with Andrea."

I explain about setting my alarm wrong.

Wendy asks, "So how did you end up meeting her? Did you wait in the lobby again for her later?"

"No, I asked Melissa to find out Andrea's last name from you so I could get her a message at the hotel. For the record, Melissa didn't want to help me, but since it was ultimately going to help you, she did it."

"Oh."

I don't know how the last-name conversation went down between Melissa and her, but I can guarantee she's now replaying it in her mind.

To my surprise, she says, "Thank you for doing that."

"You're welcome. I'm sorry I messed it up to begin with."

"I'm not going to blame that one on you," she says. "Anybody could have made the alarm mistake. I've done it myself a few times, stone cold sober. I forgive you for that."

I close my eyes and let out a long breath. "You do?"

"I'm not a monster." She now sounds exasperated, which is a step up from disappointment. "I can understand when people make an honest mistake."

"Sorry."

"Stop apologizing," she snaps. "I know you're sorry for all of it. I know you didn't intend for any of this to happen, but it did, and what happened Friday night *is* your fault. There's no amount of apologies on your part or understanding on my part that can change that."

Feisty Wendy has finally returned, much to my relief.

"So where do we go from here?" I ask.

"We go back to being friends."

Her voice is filled with enough confidence I don't doubt her decision, and my heart drops to my knees. I shouldn't be surprised, but I guess I was holding on to too much hope after all. At least she still wants to be friends, though. That might give me a chance to eventually win her over again.

"Okay," I say, because there's no good alternative to agreeing.

"And by friends, I mean the way we were before the cuddling. There will be no more of that."

"I assumed as much." Although my arms feel achingly empty at the thought of not holding her again.

"And no more cute nicknames or banter or any of the rest of it."

My heart has now exited through my toes and no longer exists within my body. There's a gaping hole where it used to reside, and it's completely my fault.

twenty-two

. . .

Wendy

I wish Randall would at least try to argue with me about where we go from here. I suddenly realize I want him to fight for us, but I don't think he's going to, and that makes my chest hurt. I don't want this to be over. He has valid reasons for why he did what he did, even though I hate some of those reasons and it'll be a while before I can get the image of him kissing Tammy out of my mind.

Because of that, I'm not going to let us go right back to where we were. I need some time to make sure neither of us is going to revert to our old habits, and I need to make sure I can truly forgive him for kissing another woman. But I also need him to forgive himself and to want us to work this out.

He asks, "Is there a possibility we could be more than friends again someday, or have I blown that chance?"

The tightness in my chest loosens a bit. "I have a question that might help me answer that."

"I'll answer anything you want to ask."

"Is this a pattern with you? Do you routinely make big mistakes like this with women? Because if you do, my response to you is no, we'll never be more than friends. I can't live my life wondering when you're going to break my heart again. But if you can honestly say this was a fluke and you don't make a habit of messing up your relationships like this, we can maybe someday get back to where we were. Maybe."

"Well, I do mess relationships up," he says, "like I've told you, but not like this. I've never cheated—not even a kiss. I've never done anything like this before. And I'm going to try to prevent anything similar from ever happening again by not drinking alcohol anymore."

"That's a good start. And if you want to try to get back to where we were, you have to be yourself in the process. Make the decisions and do the things and say the words that are true to who you are and who you want to become. Don't do any of it simply because you think it's what I want or because you think it'll win me back. I'm not saying you should never sacrifice or compromise or do things that will make me happy even if they don't particularly make you happy, because those are important aspects of a relationship. But don't become someone you're not or fall back into letting other people's wants and needs control you, Randall. Please."

He's silent for several seconds before saying, "I'll be myself. I promise. And if you want me to be me, then you need to compromise on the banter. I can't be myself with you without it."

My heart rate increases enough to confirm I want the banter. "Okay."

"I also need you to do something for me."

"What's that?"

"Don't shut down on me again. I always want to know how you're feeling, even if you're mad at me or aren't sure what you're feeling. I need you to let me in."

"I'll try," I say. "In most parts of my life, when it comes to the fight-or-flight reflex, I'm a fighter all the way. I tell people how I feel and try to work through conflict. But thanks to my romantic history, I often choose flight with men. The reason I don't fight is I assume things won't go the way I want them to, because they rarely do. Yesterday I should have asked you to explain, but instead I shut you out. I'm sorry I did that." I pause. "I might need you to help me to not shut you out again in the future."

"I will. And I should have given you the whole story yesterday. I didn't because I didn't want you to think I was making excuses for my behavior. But now I can see how that hurt you more than telling you everything from the start."

"Aren't we a messed-up pair?" I ask.

"Maybe so," he replies, "but I have no doubt it'll be worth trying to work through all our mess."

I add, "Together."

"Yeah?"

The hope in his tone makes my heart leap the tiniest bit, but I need to be careful we don't move too fast. "As friends first."

"Friends with bantering," he counters.

I allow myself to smile. "Friends with bantering."

"You're really going to try again with no-name man?" Leslie asks.

"I am. But slowly—starting out as friends again."

I've finally forced myself to sit in my easy chair, and Leslie is on the couch across from me, but I made her sit on the opposite end from where Randall used to.

"You sure that's the best idea?"

"I thought you'd be all for this," I say. "It'll make things easier for you and Ash if Randall and I aren't avoiding each other."

"This isn't about me and Ash. It's about you and your heart. I don't want him to break it again."

"Neither do I, but what he did isn't who he is. He made a terrible mistake, and I don't think he'll do it again."

"But he kissed somebody else, when he wouldn't kiss you."

"Am I upset that he kissed her?" I nod. "Absolutely. The thought of it still makes me want to vomit. But that has nothing to do with the fact that he didn't want to kiss me yet. He had valid reasons for that—reasons that prove how much he cares for me. I know he's not perfect, and maybe I won't ever be able to get past him kissing her, but I won't know unless I give him another chance."

"I guess that makes sense, but don't let him walk all over you."

"I won't. I *haven't.* In the past, I would have either pretended to forgive him from the beginning and acted like everything was fine, or I would have completely walked away because I didn't want to deal with it. But like Aunt Star said the other day, when you're with the right man, it's worth the effort to work through your mistakes together."

"And he's the right man?"

"If I didn't think he might be, I wouldn't be willing to try to work this out."

"Okay, then I'll support your decision. But I'm still mad at him."

I shrug. "Me, too. Now, I need to play the best friend card and ask you to do something weird."

"Anything."

"Will you change my sheets for me? They still smell like him, so I can't go near my bed until they're gone."

"Of course, and I'll take them home with me to wash so you don't have to touch them."

"I love you, Leslie Beckett."

"Ditto."

As soon as Leslie leaves, my mom calls to find out what Randall learned about Andrea. In order to tell that story, I need to tell her everything that happened with him.

"Honey," she says when I've finished, "I know you're hurting from what Randall did, but I'm proud of you for talking to him and deciding to try to work through it."

"Thanks. You really think I'm making the right decision?"

"I do. Do I think it'll work out in the end? I don't know. But I'm glad you're not giving up on him. You seem to truly care for him, and vice versa. Now, tell me about your sister."

twenty-three

. . .

Randall

"She's really giving you another chance?" Ash asks.

I'm lying on my back on the couch again, like I was the night I told Ash about the cuddling. "Kind of," I say to the ceiling. "We're starting as friends, although I'm not exactly sure what that means. We didn't talk about how often we might see each other or talk to each other. But I'm certain it means I can't touch her."

"Can you handle that?"

"I'll have to. I need to earn her trust back."

"I think you can, if she's willing to give you the chance."

I turn my head to look at him. "Really?"

He nods. "It might take some time, but she's a smart and perceptive woman. If you commit to making this relationship work and becoming the man you want to be, she'll see it."

I look back at the ceiling. "She's so much better than me."

"She's not."

My head whips back toward him, and he holds a hand up before I can respond.

"I'm not saying she's down at your level, whatever you think that might be. I'm saying you're up at her level. You're a good man, regardless of your occasional harebrained decisions, and you deserve a woman like Wendy."

A lump forms in my throat at his words, but I manage to choke out, "Thanks."

Brrrring!

As my brother answers the phone, my heart pounds. I know it's probably not Wendy, but the fact that it could be her is something I couldn't have imagined twenty-four hours ago.

"Hey, kiddo," he says, so I know he's talking to one of our sisters, and I try not to be disappointed.

"Yeah, we're both here. … Do you want me to come get you? … Okay, when you get here, pull up to the curb and have Sonya run in and tell Jeff you're here. He'll call up and one of us will come down to park the car. … Nope. Don't argue with me. That's the way this is going to happen. … Yeah. See you soon."

He hangs up the phone and unnecessarily says, "That was Tonya."

"I never would have guessed."

Ash rolls his eyes at me. "Dad left town for a couple days, and the girls want to come down and have dinner with us and watch a movie. I guess I should have asked if that was okay with you, but I assumed you'd say yes."

There's only one other person in the world I'd rather spend my evening with than my sisters. "Of course I'd say yes."

"We want to go to that Irish pub you guys always talk about," Sonya says.

I suck in a breath as Ash sends a sharp look in my direction.

"We've been there a lot lately," he says to them. "I'm tired of pub grub. How about Italian instead?"

Thankfully the girls are happy with his suggestion. If we got into a debate about it, they'd undoubtedly try to ferret out the real reason we're avoiding McConnell's. And while I need to go back by there and talk to Tammy, I don't want to do it with an audience, nor do my sisters need to know why I want to talk to her.

"What movie did you bring?" I ask with a feeling of dread. They usually force us to watch a romantic comedy, which I secretly enjoy, but I can't deal with anything relating to romance tonight.

"*The Untouchables,*" Tonya says.

My eyebrows jump. "No way."

"Have you seen the men in that movie?" Sonya puts her hand over her heart. "Yum."

I pretend to gag, though it's not much of a leap from what I'm really feeling at the thought of my teenage sisters being attracted to grown men.

"You're really going to complain about our choice?" Tonya asks.

"Did you hear me complain? Nope, you did not. But keep your drooling to a minimum while we watch, please. I don't want my dinner to come back up."

"Speaking of dinner, let's go," Ash says.

"When are you proposing to Leslie?" Tonya asks Ash over dinner. Neither of our sisters is known for beating around the bush.

"None of your business," he responds.

"It is *so* our business," Sonya retorts.

"How do you figure that?" he asks.

"Because we need to start planning our wardrobes, finding our dates, and all the other things that go along with a wedding," Tonya says.

"There will be no dates," I say to them.

Tonya rolls her eyes. "Stop with the protective big brother nonsense. Our dating lives are none of your business."

Ash gives her a pointed look.

"Okay," she says, "I realize the hypocritical nature of my statement, but we love Leslie."

"We do," Sonya chimes in. "And we want her to be our sister as soon as possible."

"We do. So get on with it," Tonya orders. "But just so you

know, I'd prefer the wedding to be during one of my college breaks, not on some random weekend during the school year."

Ash chuckles. "I'll make sure to plan my wedding around your schedule."

"You'd better." She grins at him.

"What are you most looking forward to about college?" I ask Tonya, to take the spotlight off Ash and Leslie's hypothetical wedding. My brother is starting to sweat, though he's attempting to play it cool.

"Not being at home," she says without missing a beat.

My face falls.

"Stop looking like your dog died," she says to me. "We've told both of you over and over again none of this insanity with Dad is your fault. He's an awful person, you did what you needed to do, and we support it. But that doesn't mean things are easy at home."

"Mom misses you two so much," Sonya says. "She even cries sometimes."

Her words are a knife to the heart. I've only seen Mom cry once in my life, and it kills me that what I did—what Ash and I did—put her in this position.

"Stop it," Tonya says to me again, although I didn't say a word. "You didn't do that to her. Dad did."

"How long is he out of town?" I ask.

"Until Tuesday."

I look at my brother and he nods. He's thinking the same thing I am.

"When you get home tonight," I say to the girls, "tell Mom to call us. We want to see her tomorrow if she's free."

"She can't call you," Sonya says. "Dad checks the phone bill. He'll see that someone called your number and will lose his mind."

"How did you call us, then?"

"From the pay phone at 7-Eleven."

"Then tell her to go to 7-Eleven."

"She doesn't go to 7-Eleven. Or use pay phones."

"Something tells me she might in this situation. Just tell her."

"We will," Tonya says. "We promise."

"Hey, you don't get to promise for me!" Sonya tells her.

"But do you promise?"

Sonya pouts but says, "Yes."

The rest of us laugh at her, and she glares at us.

Then Sonya turns to me. "It's been over a month since you and Colleen broke up. When are you going to find a new woman?"

I narrow my eyes at her. "What makes you think I'm ready for a new woman so soon?"

"Because you always have a girlfriend," Tonya answers. "I can't remember a time when you didn't have one."

Her comment shouldn't sting, but it does. "Maybe I'm trying something different." I avoid Ash's eyes, because I'm sure he's giving me a look I don't want to see.

"Why's Ash giving you that look, then?" Sonya asks.

I sigh. If I want to have a good relationship with my almost-grown-up sisters, I should be honest with them. "There is a new woman, but we're taking things slow," I explain. "We're friends right now, but there's potential for more." While I want to be honest, they don't need to know all the details.

"Do we know her?" Tonya asks.

"Is it Melissa?" Sonya guesses.

"No, it's Wendy." The girls met her several weeks ago when Leslie and Wendy took them out for a girls' night.

"Ooooo," Tonya says. "She's fun."

"She is," Sonya agrees. "We like her."

Tonya points a finger at me. "Don't screw it up."

I school my features and then roll my eyes to try to keep them from guessing I already have. "Thanks for the vote of support."

"That's what little sisters are for."

twenty-four

. . .

Wendy

"You and Randall, huh?" My co-worker Brian smirks at me from my office doorway on Monday morning.

My heart stops. I forgot Brian saw Randall and me holding hands in the parking garage after work on Friday, and I don't know how to respond.

"Cat got your tongue?" He steps into my office, takes a seat on the couch, and makes himself comfortable. Brian asked me out soon after I started working at Carter-Jenkins, and I turned him down, but he didn't make things weird and has always treated me with respect. Usually I enjoy chatting with him, but his presence is making me nervous since I don't know what to tell him.

"I like Randall," he says. "He's a good guy."

"He is," I finally say. "We … uh, we've been spending some time together."

"I'm surprised you're not being more open about this. You're not worried about what people will think about you dating a co-worker, are you?"

"No," I say, maybe too quickly. "We're taking things slow. Not much to tell at this point."

"Hmmm."

Brian obviously doesn't believe me, but there's nothing I can do about it. There's a zero percent chance I'll tell him the whole truth.

"Did you need something else?" I ask him pointedly.

"No." He stands. "But I can take a hint." As he walks out, he adds, "There's nothing to be ashamed of."

"I'm not ashamed," I call after him, but he's gone.

I give him thirty seconds to return to his office, and then I'm out the door like a shot, headed to Leslie's office. I don't bother knocking, and I swing the door shut behind me.

Leslie sits back in her chair and studies me as I take my usual seat in the plush purple chair by her desk.

"You need something?" she finally asks.

"Brian thinks I'm dating Randall."

She nods slowly. "Okay. What did you tell him?"

"We're spending time together and taking things slow."

She shrugs. "You didn't lie. There's nothing wrong with telling people that."

"I don't think he believed me."

"Why do you care if he believes you, especially when you told him the truth?"

"He also suggested I'm ashamed."

"Ashamed of what?"

"He didn't specify, but I'm afraid he thinks I'm ashamed of dating Randall."

"Are you?" she asks. "I mean, you aren't technically dating anymore, but are you ashamed of him?"

"No!"

"Not after what he did this weekend?"

"No," I say in a much softer tone of voice.

"What if everyone here knew what he did?"

"Still no."

"Then don't worry about what Brian thinks."

"But he'll talk, and then everybody will think we're dating. I don't want to have to explain that we're not dating anymore or the reason why, but that won't matter, because people will figure out we're not dating if we're not going to lunch together or flirting with each other or whatever."

"You need to talk to Randall about this and see how he wants to handle it. You're not the only person involved in this situation. Work through it *together,* like you said you wanted to do."

She's right. Now I truly am ashamed—ashamed that I'm acting like a teenager and also that it didn't occur to me that I should have gone to Randall with this instead of to her.

"It's okay that you came to me," she says, reading my mind. "I've done the same with you when it comes to issues with Ash. We're good sounding boards for each other. But now you need to talk to him."

"Now now?"

"You might not want to hash it all out here at work, but at least tell him you need to talk about it in the very near future."

I stand and straighten my skirt. "Okay. Thanks for being my sounding board."

"My pleasure," she says. "Now go." She shoos me with her hand but also smiles so I know she's not irritated with my interruption to her day. "I've got phone calls to make."

I head straight to Randall's office when I leave. When I knock, he glances up and his face runs through various emotions before settling on a welcoming smile.

"Come in," he says. "Take a seat."

I enter and close the door behind me, resulting in raised eyebrows on his part.

"This conversation is of a personal nature." I settle on the edge of a chair and try not to dwell on how good he looks with his jacket and tie off, a few shirt buttons undone, and his sleeves rolled up to his elbows. "None of our co-workers need to hear it. In fact, that's what we need to talk about: our co-workers thinking we're dating. I don't want us to discuss how to handle that right now, because I want you to think about it, and I need to as well, but we need to talk about it later today, if possible."

"At lunch?"

I shake my head. "I've got a lunch meeting already. We'll have to do it after work."

"In person or on the phone?"

"In person." I don't want to have another intense conversation with him over the phone. I want to see his expressions and body language while we're talking.

"In public or in private?" he asks.

"Public." We can't be alone in private for a while, current situation notwithstanding.

"Do you have a suggestion for where?"

I think for a moment, and then I have what could be either a brilliant or a terrible idea. "McConnell's."

His face pales. "No."

"Have you apologized to Tammy yet?"

"I haven't had time. Ash and I were with our sisters last night."

My heart melts a little. "You were?"

"Yeah, Dad's out of town. And we're having dinner with Mom tonight, so I'll have to meet you after that. *Not* at McConnell's."

I steel myself. "I'm going to insist on McConnell's."

Randall folds his arms over his chest. "Why?"

"Because I think it'll help us work through this to go back to the scene of the crime. And it should help Tammy if we're both there. It'll help prove to her that neither of us blame her for what happened. She deserves that. And if she can't deal with the awkwardness, or if we can't, then we'll leave and never go back there. But I'm hoping we can help her move past it, even if it's weird for us. I want us to do this hard thing together."

He nods, his expression unreadable. "Okay. I can do that."

"Good." I stand. "Call me when you get home from dinner with your mom, and I'll meet you outside the pub."

"Will do. Thanks."

"For what?"

"Making me be an adult in this situation."

I laugh. "You're not the only one who needs help in that area."

As I exit Randall's office, Brian is heading down the hall toward me. He says nothing, but he shoots me a giant grin accompanied by a knowing look. I give him a sunny smile in return and silently curse the universe for his timing.

twenty-five

. . .

Randall

M om gives me a tighter and longer hug than she's ever given me in my recollection, and I squeeze her right back. I've never doubted my mother's love for me, but like my brother, she rarely shows affection, and she's been described as "scary" by more than one person, including myself.

When we take a seat at our table in a restaurant in a suburb none of us frequent, she says, "I don't want to talk about your father tonight. Tell me what's been going on in your lives."

Ash tells her what's happening with his new job and with Leslie, and I listen without giving any commentary.

"You're being awfully quiet," Mom says to me when they've exhausted the recent developments in Ash's life.

I shrug. "I guess I'm tired. Long weekend."

"Care to expand on that?"

On the way here, Ash suggested I tell Mom about Wendy. He seemed to think she'd be supportive of me instead of judgmental about what I've done, but I'm not so sure.

Before I can decide what to tell her, she says, "If it makes a difference, the girls told me you're dating Wendy."

Of course they did.

"Is there something going on that you didn't tell them?" she asks.

I nod, and then I tell her the highlights of our brief relationship —both the good and the bad.

When I finish, she says, "I know I said we weren't going to talk about your father, but I have to say this. Considering the example he set for you, I'm impressed by the way you're both working on having mature, healthy relationships with women, even when you make mistakes." She looks at me. "I'm so proud of you for owning up to your mistake and doing what you can to fix things with Wendy. Your father doesn't admit it when he cheats on me, and he has never apologized for it or tried to make things right with me."

"Mom." Ash's voice and face are both tinged with horror. I'm sure my face looks much the same.

"Don't tell me you don't know about his long line of mistresses," Mom says. "I've known it for years—decades, even. Here lately it's been that new young secretary at the office. She's with him on his so-called business trip right now."

Although I've always suspected Dad wasn't faithful to Mom, I didn't know for sure, and the confirmation from my mother makes me feel sick. I reach for her hand and take it in my own. "Mom, I'm so sorry."

"Why do you stay with him, then?" Ash demands. "Why put us through living with him and dealing with him? Why do the girls have to keep living under his roof?"

I give my brother a harsh look and am about to lay into him about his attitude, but Mom answers before I can.

"Leaving the father of your children and the provider of everything you and those children depend on isn't as simple as you would think. Imagine what divorce proceedings would be like with him—and the aftermath. You think living with him was terrible. That's nothing compared to what it will be like when Sonya leaves home and I finally leave *him.*"

I'm stunned Mom is telling us all this. "You're really going to leave him?"

"Yes, as soon as I know Sonya's college education is paid for, I'm filing for divorce."

"Do it now," Ash says. "I'll pay for her college if she doesn't get scholarships."

"I can't ask you to do that. You've done enough for the girls already."

"You're not asking," he says. "I'm telling. I'll cover both girls financially while they're still in school, and I'll take care of you, if he manages to leave you with nothing, though we'll fight him tooth and nail to make sure you get what you deserve. Get out now."

"I echo everything he said," I say, though I'm certain I won't be able to afford to help financially support her and my sisters if I leave my current job for something I like better, like I've dreamed of doing. But I'll stay at Carter-Jenkins forever if it means Mom can divorce Dad and we can get Sonya away from him a year earlier. "We'll take care of all of you, Mom."

Tears fill Mom's eyes, and all she can say is, "You boys …," as she dabs her eyes with her napkin. Then she takes a deep breath and says, "I can't let you do this. I can't. I won't."

"You can and you will," Ash declares.

Mom says to Ash, "You can't make the kind of promise you made to me without talking to Leslie about it. I know you're not engaged yet, but something tells me you will be soon. Your father has rarely talked to me about financial decisions, but I want both of you boys to always consider your wives when you make any kind of big decision like this."

"Leslie will be okay with it," Ash says.

"You can't make that assumption, even though I'm pretty sure you're right. Talk to her, and we'll go from there."

My brother closes his eyes. "You're right." When he looks at Mom again, he says, "I guess I'm still learning, huh?"

"You'll be learning about how to live with a woman until the day you die, son."

He gives her a wry smile. "That's not very reassuring, but I get it. I'll talk to her. But for now, let's discuss what happens next if she says yes. Before you tell Dad what you're up to, we'll need to get a few things in order."

Ash proceeds to talk to Mom about their finances and property, hiring a private investigator to provide proof of Dad's infidelity, and all sorts of other things she needs to do to prepare for the legal battle Dad will wage against her.

I sit back and listen as my little brother lays out the plan, and I marvel not only at his vast legal knowledge and ability to strategize on the fly but also Mom's sudden willingness to leave Dad and to let us in on the private side of her life, which she has never done.

The more Ash talks, the more energized Mom becomes. My mother is an intelligent and resourceful woman and, like Ash and Dad, she can get things done that most other people can only dream of doing. She can organize anything and can get people to help her or agree with her while making them think it was their idea in the first place. She has always been a force to be reckoned with, except when it comes to Dad. Now that I think about it, in a way she reminds me of Wendy—strong and confident in every area except her love life.

When the two of them stop to take a breath, I ask Mom, "Do you still love him?"

Ash gives me a sharp look, but I ignore him and focus on Mom while she considers what to say.

"No," she finally says. "To be fully honest, I never truly loved him in the way a wife should love her husband. I mostly loved the lifestyle and the family and the things I thought he could give me. You boys know my parents didn't earn their money until after I was married. I didn't like being a poor nobody. Your dad could solve that problem for me, so I let him."

"Do you regret that?"

"No, because I wouldn't have you kids if I hadn't married him. I wouldn't trade you and your sisters for any alternate version of my life. But I do wish I had mustered up the courage to leave him long ago. For your sake, I'm so sorry I didn't."

twenty-six

. . .

Wendy

"Hi, Andrea?" I say to my half-sister's answering machine. "This is Wendy O'Halloran. I'm sorry I missed you. Feel free to call me back anytime." Then I leave my number.

I hang up the phone and take some deep breaths to calm my racing heart. When I got home from work today, I decided I'd bite the bullet and give her a call. Since I'm now pretty certain she doesn't want anything from me beyond a personal connection, I'm comfortable talking to her. However, that doesn't mean I'm not nervous about it.

Now I'm not sure what to do with myself. I don't want to run any errands, since she might call back, and I also need to be home for Randall's call later. But I can't just sit here doing nothing, so I stick a TV dinner in the microwave, and when I'm finished eating my lackluster meal, I pick up my new copy of *Caribbean Blues* by Mary Higgins Clark and try to lose myself in the mystery.

It works, because when the phone rings, my body jerks in surprise. I glance at the clock, and based on the time, I know it's probably not Randall yet, so it might be Andrea.

"Hello?" I say into the phone.

"Wendy?" a voice eerily like my own says.

"Yes, is this Andrea?"

"It is. Thanks for calling me. I enjoyed meeting your … friend yesterday."

Since she hesitated on the word "friend," I wonder what Randall told her about our relationship.

"Yeah," I say. "I'm glad you and Randall were able to work that out after he missed breakfast on Saturday. I'm sorry for that, by the way."

"Don't worry about it. He explained what happened and he apologized."

We're both silent for a moment, obviously not knowing what to say to each other.

She finally asks, "How do we want to do this? Do you want to ask me questions? Do you want me to ask you questions?"

"How about we take turns?"

"That sounds good. You want to go first?"

"Sure. Can you tell me about Emily, or is that too personal to start out with?"

"No, that's great. I'm glad you want to know about her. She's six and just finished kindergarten. She loves to read and play with her friends, and she does gymnastics. The girl is a ball of energy, and gymnastics helps channel that energy so I don't lose my mind." She chuckles.

"Does she have red hair?" I ask.

"Strawberry blonde."

I smile as I try to picture the little girl in my mind.

Andrea says, "Jack told me you have two brothers, but he didn't tell me anything about them. Are you close to them?"

"Their names are Daniel and Ryan," I explain. "Daniel is nineteen and just finished his freshman year at Marquette University in Milwaukee, and Ryan will be a senior in high school this coming year. I love them to death, but we're not especially close, since I left home for college when they were very young. Do you have other siblings?"

"No, it's only been me and mom until Emily came along. Mom doesn't have siblings, and when her parents died when I was a baby, she left Wisconsin for Little Rock because a friend hooked her up with a job here. While she built a good life and we have friends, it's not the same as having family."

"I understand that," I say. "Do you mind telling me how you found out about me?"

"I don't mind at all. My whole life, my mom told me my father died while she was pregnant with me. In fact, she told everyone that. But I now know I was the result of my mom's affair with your married father. As I said before, when Mom's parents died when I was a baby, she left Milwaukee for Little Rock. It was partly for the job, but mostly because she wanted to get away from the memories of her parents and what happened with my— our—father. She broke things off with him when she found out she was pregnant, and she never told him, since he had a family. She didn't want to cause any trouble. Mom says she didn't know he was married when she first met him, but she did find out about you and your mom before she knew she was pregnant.

"Then about a month ago, she sat me down and told me the truth. She knew about you, but she didn't know whether Jack was still married to your mom or had other kids or not. She left it up to me to decide if I wanted to find out."

When she takes a breath, I say, "Do you know why she decided to tell you after all these years?"

"She knew how much I was struggling with not having family and realized that when she's gone, I'll have nobody but Emily. This was her way of trying to provide a family for us."

"Is she …" I'm not sure how to put this delicately. "Is there a reason she thinks she might not be around much longer?"

"I wondered that, too, when she told me, but she swears she's not sick or anything."

"Good. So how did Jack respond after you tracked him down?"

"I can't say he was delighted to hear from me, but he was willing to talk to me and tell me a little about himself and about you. From our conversations, I gathered the two of you aren't close."

"No," I say. "We're not. He left when I was two. Actually, let me amend that. That's what my mom always told me. In reality, she found out about his affair and kicked him out. I've only seen him a handful of times, and my stepfather adopted me when I was ten. He's who I consider to be my dad, not Jack."

"So your mom lied to you, too?" Andrea asks.

"Yes, and I only learned the truth when she called to tell me about you."

"*She* told you about me? Not Jack?"

"I haven't spoken to Jack in ten years."

"Oh." She sounds disappointed.

"You didn't miss out on anything by not knowing him. Take it from me."

"I don't know if that makes me feel better or not," she says.

"Are you mad at your mom for not telling you until now?"

"I am. We're not estranged or anything—we love and depend on each other too much for that—but things are strained between us."

"I'm sorry."

"How about you and your mom?" Andrea asks.

"I was mad initially, but not so much now. But our situation is a little different than yours."

"Yeah."

Andrea sounds sad, and I hate that for her. She didn't ask for any of this to happen.

"I'm glad you're in my life now," I say.

"You're not just saying that to make me feel better, are you?"

"I'm not. And I want to know a lot more about you and Emily, but we'll have to do that another time, because I have plans here in a few minutes. Do you want to set a time for another call? I'm sure you're busy, so it might be easier to plan it instead of making random calls."

"I'd love to."

twenty-seven

. . .

Randall

"**Y**ou ready for this?" Wendy asks when she marches up to the front of McConnell's, where I've been waiting for several minutes.

"As I'll ever be."

She nods and slips her hand into mine. When I glance down at her with a surprised look, she says, "United front. For Tammy."

"For Tammy," I echo, gripping her hand tightly, ignoring the hammering of my heart from the contact.

We walk into the pub together, and I can't decide whether I'm happy or not when the only empty table is in Tammy's usual section. Wendy pulls me in that direction, and we settle into the seats at the high-top table.

I can't help but scan the room for any sign of Tammy, and when I spot her, she's heading our way but hasn't noticed who we are yet. The second she spots me, her steps falter, but she doesn't turn around like I expect she will. Instead, she takes a visible breath and continues toward us, her gaze focused firmly on the table.

When she reaches us, she pulls out her order pad and says in a tense tone, "What can I get you folks tonight?" without looking up or acknowledging she knows us.

Wendy shoots me a pointed look and tilts her head toward Tammy.

"Tammy," I say, "I need to apologize for the other night."

Her eyes finally meet mine, and then she glances over at Wendy. Her eyes go wide, and her hand covers her mouth. "Oh, no. No, no, no."

"Listen to me," I say in a low voice so nobody at the surrounding tables can hear. "What happened wasn't your fault. It was all on me. I was drunk and not thinking straight. I shouldn't have flirted with you or done anything to lead you on, but I did, and I'm so sorry."

Wendy adds, "You have nothing to feel bad about, and there are no hard feelings on my part. Randall made the bad decisions, not you."

"But it *was* my fault," Tammy says, and then she looks at me. "I didn't know you had a girlfriend, but I knew you were drunk, and I did it anyway." She turns her anguished gaze to Wendy. "I'm so sorry. I'll never forgive myself for it."

"I hope you do," Wendy says. "Because I forgive you. Like he said," she points at me, "his fault."

Tammy shakes her head. "My fault. I made the move. And I could get fired for what I did."

The look on her face reveals she's terrified that might happen.

"Nobody here will find out about it," I assure her, as my heart goes out to her. "I promise. Your job is safe."

"Tammy," Wendy says, and Tammy looks at her. "I know as well as anyone how charming this man can be and how he can make a woman feel like she's the only person on the planet, without even realizing he's doing it. Yes, you played a part in what happened, but he was the one who was responsible for turning off the charm with you and making it clear he was dating someone, and he didn't. Let him take the responsibility for that, and please forgive yourself for your part."

Tammy looks back and forth between the two of us and gives a tentative nod. "Okay. I'll try."

"Now," Wendy says, "we didn't come here to make you feel awkward, but we've fully managed to do so, and we're going to go now. I'm going to act like I'm not feeling well, so nobody will wonder why we're leaving already."

"Okay," Tammy says again before taking a step back, giving each of us one last apologetic look, and walking away.

Wendy slides off her chair and says to me, "Don't look at her. Don't draw any attention to her. Get off that chair, put your arm around me as if you're comforting your sick girlfriend, and let's go."

She places her hand on her belly and makes a face as if she's trying not to be sick, and I wrap an arm around her shoulders and lead her out. Once we're outside on the sidewalk, she slips out of my grasp, leaving me with a distinct feeling of loss.

"That went about as well as it could have," she says.

"I guess. I hope she forgives herself."

"Me, too. I don't think we can come back here. It'll make her feel awkward every time."

"I'm—"

Wendy's hands fist at her sides. "If you say you're sorry one more time …"

I hold my hands up. "I hear you. Where do you want to go to discuss the work situation?"

"Let's go to that diner over by Leslie's apartment. I need one of their sundaes."

"Diner it is."

We're silent as we walk the few blocks to the diner, though it's not an uncomfortable silence. She doesn't attempt to take my hand again, much to my disappointment, but she stays closer to my side than a friend would.

Once we're seated and the waitress takes our order, Wendy says, "Brian thinks we're dating, and I didn't tell him we're not."

My heart beats a little faster. "Why not?"

"He took me by surprise, and I wasn't sure what to say. I guess I was embarrassed, because I didn't want to admit that we dated for all of two days and now we're not together anymore." She points a finger at me. "Do not apologize for creating that situation."

I act like I wasn't going to do that exact thing. "So what did you tell him?"

"That we're spending time together and taking things slow."

"Well, that's the truth."

"Yes, but if people at work think we're dating, but we don't act like we are, they're going to know."

"And you care if they know?" A few days ago she didn't want our co-workers to know anything.

"I don't think I would care if there wasn't a chance we might date again, but I don't want to seem wishy-washy."

Her declaration that we might date again makes me want to get up and pull a Fred Astaire in the middle of the diner, but I restrain myself. "You're not being wishy-washy."

"I know that, and you know that, but since I don't have any intention of telling anyone at work what you did, it'll look like we can't get it together and figure out what we want."

"I don't think anyone will think that. All relationships have their ups and downs."

"True, but our co-workers don't need to be privy to how ours went down almost immediately."

"So what are you saying? What do you want to do about this?"

"When we're at work," she says confidently, "we pretend we're dating."

My heart leaps into my throat, and my eyebrows join my hair-line. "What?"

"I thought you'd be happy about that."

Am I? I think about it for a few seconds and determine I'm not. "I don't want to pretend with you. If I flirt with you or hold your hand in the hallway or kiss you in the break room, I want it to be because we both want it, not because we're putting on a show."

"You put on a show at McConnell's when you held my hand and put your arm around me."

"Those were your decisions, and they were to help Tammy, which I understand. But I didn't have time to think about it or get a say in it. Did I enjoy touching you? You'd better believe it. But I don't want to touch you for other people's benefit. From here on out, I'm only touching you if you want it for *you*."

twenty-eight

. . .

Wendy

I held Randall's hand for me today, too, not only for Tammy's sake, but I don't think I can tell him that. While it felt so right for my hand to be in his, it also felt so wrong to sit there while he apologized to another woman for kissing her. I'm glad I was with him when he did it, because I wanted to make sure Tammy understood she wasn't fully to blame. But that doesn't mean I enjoyed envisioning the two of them kissing in that very room.

"Tell me what you're thinking," Randall says.

"You really want to know?"

"I do. Don't hold back."

"I'm thinking about you kissing Tammy."

His face falls. "I wouldn't have minded you holding that back."

I shake my head. "You can't pick and choose what you want to hear me say."

"I know. But I'm afraid that kiss is going to haunt us forever."

"Hopefully not forever," I say, "but probably for a while." And I can't imagine the memory won't taint my first kiss with him, if we ever get to that point.

The waitress brings our ice cream, and we don't speak for a while. I try to focus on enjoying the treat instead of thinking about the man sitting across from me, but it doesn't work.

"We still haven't solved the problem of what to do at work," he says.

As I take a few more bites of my hot fudge sundae, I think about what I want, not only for how we interact at work, but also for where I want our relationship to go. Sitting at a standstill isn't going to get us anywhere. If I want to see if I can forgive him and move past what he did, I have to take steps to get there.

I sit up straight and look him in the eye. "I want to hold your hand. For me—nobody else."

Excitement flashes in his eyes, but he keeps his expression neutral. "Friends don't hold hands."

Why is he fighting me on this? "Friends with bantering do," I counter.

"I don't recall any bantering happening today."

I huff out a frustrated breath. "Are you trying to make me change my mind?"

"No, I'm making sure this is what you want. Don't do this because it's what I want."

I place one hand out palm-up on the table while keeping my gaze directed on his. He looks between my hand and my eyes a few times before wrapping his hand around mine. I feel a flutter in my belly when his skin touches mine, which gives me hope we can move forward.

Again, we don't speak for several minutes, but we steal glances at each other while we continue to hold hands and eat our ice cream. Since he's using his right hand to hold mine, he's forced to use his left hand to eat, which is becoming quite amusing. The man is apparently as far from ambidextrous as a person can be.

"You need me to feed that to you?" I tease.

He shoots me a stern look. "I'm pretty sure feeding each other is not included in the friends-with-bantering-and-hand-holding contract."

I shrug. "You could always let go of my hand."

"I'm not letting go of your hand until I drop you off at your apartment."

His declaration makes my heart pound, but I try to keep him from seeing how his words affect me.

I press my lips together and then say, "What if you need to go to the little boys' room?"

"You don't have any little boys," he says. "So there's no room for them."

"Look at us bantering." I squeeze his hand and try not to think about where we were the last time we had that conversation.

"It's about time."

I roll my eyes. "It's only been three days."

"What can I say?" He shrugs. "I'm a banter-holic."

"You're ridiculous, is what you are."

"I know. George confirmed that for us the other day."

I give him a soft smile. "I missed you, Ponyboy."

He shoves his now-empty dish to the side and reaches across the table to take my other hand in his. "I missed you, too, Glinda." He searches my eyes. "Can we do this? Are we really going to try to make this work again? You want that?"

I nod as tears prick behind my eyes. "I want to try." I look down at our joined hands and then back up at him. "I know you didn't intend to kiss Tammy and you would never knowingly hurt me like that. However, that doesn't mean I'm certain I can move past it or fully trust you to not do something like it again. But I'm not willing to give up on us. I want to try to move forward with you from here, but it might take me some time."

He lets go of one of my hands and wipes away the lone tear that trailed down my cheek. "I'll give you all the time you need. If at any point I do or say something that's moving too fast for you, let me know, and I'll back off. Okay?"

"Okay." I hope I don't need to—or want to.

Then I take a deep breath and psych myself up to bring up something I've been trying to avoid thinking about, but I can't do that any longer. "There's also something I need to tell you."

His thumb sweeps over the back of my hand. "You can tell me anything."

"There's this guy I used to spend some time with at my old job."

Randall's jaw clenches. "What about this guy?"

"I saw him Friday night."

"What? I thought you were with Leslie and her aunt!"

"I was." I squeeze his hand. "Keep your voice down. I ran into him at the bar we were at."

"What did he do to you?" he demands. "Did he hurt you?"

"No. Well, not physically, and not Friday night."

"What are you trying to tell me?"

"He's one of the guys I used to kind of date but who didn't want more than a physical relationship. And when I saw him again, I didn't hate it. And when he touched me, I didn't hate that, either."

Randall's nostrils flare. "He touched you?"

"He put his hand on my shoulder. And then Leslie told him I had a boyfriend, and he stopped touching me and went away."

"Okay." He shakes his head. "I still don't get why you're telling me this."

"Because I should have told him I have a boyfriend. I should have told him not to touch me. But I didn't." I look down at our entwined hands. "I'd been drinking. If Leslie and her family hadn't been there, I might have ended up doing what you did."

"Oh, babe," he says, the term of endearment slicing through my heart. "No, you wouldn't have."

I glance back up at him. "You don't know that."

"Did you want him to touch you?"

"No."

"Did you want to kiss him?"

"No! But did you want to kiss Tammy?"

"No."

"See?"

Randall shakes his head. "It's not the same. You didn't follow through. I did."

"I still feel bad."

"You shouldn't. You did nothing wrong. Please don't stress about this or compare it to what I did." He squeezes my hand. "Promise me you won't."

"I can't promise, but I'll try."

"Try your hardest." He looks at his watch. "Do you need to get home? It's getting late."

"Soon," I say, "but I want to hear about dinner with your mom before we go."

His grip tightens on my hand, and I watch the rest of his body visibly tense.

"What?" I ask. "What happened?"

"She's leaving my dad."

My jaw drops. "No way."

He nods. "I'm pretty sure we convinced her to do it."

"We'll unpack that statement in a minute, but tell me why you're stressed."

"Because it's going to get ugly. Dad's going to try to destroy her."

"He won't succeed." I shake my head.

"Why do you say that?"

"Well, I've only met your mom briefly one time, but from what I experienced that night and from what you and Ash and Leslie have said about her, I know she's strong enough to make it through anything your dad throws at her. And to be fair, I think he's been trying to destroy her for a long time, but she hasn't let him."

He nods and some of the tension leaves his body. "You might be right."

I caress his knuckles with my thumb. "I'm sure I'm right. Now tell me about you and Ash convincing her to do it."

He tells me about their conversation and his and Ash's vow to support their mom and sisters in every way necessary. By the time he's finished, tears are streaming down my face. He pulls a napkin out of the dispenser and attempts to dry my cheeks, but he's so bad at it with his left hand, I end up laughing and pushing his hand away.

"I didn't mean to make you cry."

"These are happy tears," I explain as I finish cleaning my face up. "I've always known you and Ash are good men, but this is another level of good. I'm in awe of you both and am so proud of you." I'm so proud my heart hurts.

Randall blushes. "Thanks. I wasn't sure I should tell you everything, because I didn't want to sound like I was bragging. To be honest, I'm nervous about the financial side, if they do end up needing that kind of help. I'll give them everything I have if it comes to that, but I'm more of a spender than a saver. Ash probably has ten times the amount of savings I do."

"You know Ash won't care if he gives them more than you can."

"He won't care, but I will."

"I know." I take his other hand again. "But you don't know if that will happen. It might all seem overwhelming now, but there's no point in stressing about it. Focus that mental energy on supporting your mom and sisters practically and emotionally. That's what they need the most right now."

twenty-nine

. . .

Randall

I only see Wendy in meetings and in passing in the hallway at work on Tuesday and Wednesday, and when I haven't seen her at all by Thursday afternoon, I head off in search of her, because I can't stay away from her any longer. I find her in her office, talking on the phone. She smiles at me and holds up a finger, and I lean against the doorjamb to wait.

I take the opportunity to let my gaze wander over her soft red waves, her pale throat, and her silky green button-up shirt. The desk hides her bottom half, and I hope she's wearing the narrow black skirt with the slit up the side that drives me to distraction. In reality, the skirt isn't all that revealing, but that slit ... I shake my head to stop that train of thought before it pulls out of the station.

Wendy hangs up the phone, removes all expression from her face, and says, "May I assist you with something, Mr. Hamilton?"

I tap my finger on my chin and in a serious voice say, "I believe you may, Ms. O'Halloran. I've come in search of some light banter with a side of hand holding."

She fights a smile. "Then you've come to the right place." She sweeps her hand toward the chair across from her. "Take a seat, and we'll begin."

I obey her command and then say, "Shall we start with the light bantering?"

"We shall. You may commence."

I chuckle. "You sure we haven't already commenced?"

Her lips twitch. "Perhaps."

"Why are we talking like we're in a Jane Austen novel?"

She clasps her hands in front of her and says earnestly, "Please tell me you're a Jane fan."

"I've only read *Pride and Prejudice*," I say, "because inexplicably it was required reading at my all-boys prep school. But it was a slog to get through. I liked the story all right, but ol' Jane could have used a lot fewer words to tell it." As I speak, Wendy's face gets redder and redder, and I'm tempted to keep going to see exactly how much I can rile her up about this, but I decide I don't want her to give me a dressing-down in the office, so I refrain.

Wendy opens and closes her mouth a few times before she can grasp the words she wants to say. "Okay, that … I mean … "

Maybe she can't grasp the words.

Finally, she says, "That's not bantering, that's sacrilege."

"It's sacrilege for a man to not like overly wordy early nineteenth century romance?"

She growls at me, and the sound is so cute coming from her, I laugh.

Wendy narrows her eyes. "Are you laughing at me, Mr. Hamilton?"

"Indeed, I am."

"Then you can forget about the side of hand holding."

She lifts her head imperiously and attempts to look down her nose at me, which is a failure, since although we're sitting, her head is still several inches lower than mine. She tips it back so far I can see up her nostrils. I chuckle again, knowing it'll irritate her even more.

"Wendy," a man's voice filters through the doorway, "do you … oh, sorry."

Wendy's face flushes as she quickly drops her chin, and I turn and watch Brian's eyes flit between me and her.

"I'll come back later," he says and starts to turn away.

"No, come on in," Wendy says. "Randall's leaving."

I face her and raise an eyebrow, and she gives a slight shake of the head. She's not dismissing me because of anything I said. I'm guessing she wants to ensure Brian doesn't think our relationship means we'll be slacking off on the job.

I push out of the chair. "See you tonight, Wen."

Her head cocks to the side, but she nods at me. We don't have plans tonight, but I want Brian to think we do. I hope she understood my motive, but I can't exactly explain it.

I pass Leslie's office on my way back to my own, and I don't look in because I'm sure she's still upset with me, but she calls out to me, so I stop. She uses her head to motion me in, and I enter and take a seat.

In a low voice, she says, "Ash told me about your mom."

I nod. He told me Leslie said she'd support him in doing whatever he thought was best for everyone.

"I told him this, and I'll tell you, too. If there's anything I can do to help, please let me know."

"I appreciate that, but I don't think you understand how bad this might get. You don't want to get involved."

"You're wrong. I do want to get involved. I love Ash, and I love your family—your dad excluded, obviously—and I'll do whatever I can to help make this easier on all of you."

"Thank you."

I pick up a baseball from her desk and toss it from one hand to the other. She stands, reaches across the desk, and snatches the ball out of the air. "That's a signed Willie McGee ball Diego got for me. Don't touch it."

"Sorry. But I'm surprised you asked a Cubs player to get you a ball with a Cardinals player's autograph on it."

"Diego's a good guy. You know that. And I didn't ask him to get it, but he knows Willie is my favorite, and he got it for me out of the kindness of his heart."

"I'm also surprised you're talking to me," I say.

She purses her lips. "If Wendy can forgive you, so can I, but I'm still mad about what you did."

"As you should be." I'm glad Wendy has a friend like Leslie in her corner. "Hey, Wendy told me about some guy she ran into Friday night."

Leslie's eyebrows raise. "She did?"

"Yeah. She seems to think that if you ladies hadn't been there with her, she might have done the same thing I did. I completely disagreed. Am I right on that?"

"You're correct. She didn't act like she was into him at all. She didn't flirt with him or really even talk to him. He talked to the rest of us. In fact, she was distressed that she didn't hate him on sight."

I nod. "Can you talk to her about it? Make sure she knows it's nothing like what I did?"

She nods. "I will. Now, back to your family, if you need me to get the girls away from the house while your dad is still around by taking them out to eat or to a movie or whatever, I'm more than willing. I'm sure Wendy would be, too. Did you tell her what's going on?"

"Yes. She also said she'll help support all of us however she can." Although I don't want Wendy involved in my family's mess, either. I want her as far away from my dad's reach as possible.

"Of course she did." Leslie purses her lips as she thinks about something, and I give her time to process it. She finally says, "Ash said your dad will be out of town again next weekend, right?"

"Yeah. Not this coming weekend, but the next."

"Why don't Wendy and I take your sisters somewhere for the weekend, so you and Ash and your mom can strategize and do whatever else you need to do to prepare for what's coming, without having to worry about the girls?"

Ash certainly found himself a winner in the woman across the desk from me. "Would you really do that?"

"Yes. Granted, I'm not sure Wendy is free then, but if she is, I have no doubt she'll be on board."

"Okay, let me talk to Ash about it, and you check with Wendy. And, of course, we'll need to somehow figure out if the girls have plans already."

"I'll run down to the pay phone in the main lobby and call the house to see if I can catch one of them. None of your parents' household staff would recognize my voice, so I shouldn't get caught if one of them answers the phone."

"Has anyone ever told you how brilliant you are?" I ask her.

"Not often enough," she says with a smirk.

"Ash and I will pay for everything," I say.

"You will not. Girls' weekends are to be fully funded by girls … well, women. Your sisters won't be paying for anything."

I shake my head. "No, you're doing this for our family. We'll pay for it."

"Don't make me yell," she threatens. "Because I will. And you won't like what our co-workers will hear me say about you, because most of it will be vicious lies."

I hold my hands up in surrender. "You drive a hard bargain, Leslie Beckett."

She shrugs. "How do you think I keep a loose cannon like Diego Sanchez in line?"

thirty

. . .

Wendy

"I know exactly where we can go," I say to Leslie when she stops by my office on her way out of work to talk to me about the girls' weekend. "My aunt and uncle have a vacation home on Lake Geneva. There's a small private beach, a dock with a boat and a couple of WaveRunners, and the house is amazing. The girls will love it."

"That sounds perfect," Leslie says, "but your aunt and uncle might be using it themselves next weekend."

"Doubtful. They only go a few times a year. I don't understand it, because if I owned that house, I'd be there every weekend. In fact, I think I spend more time there than they do. And if they're planning to be there, the house is plenty big for all of us, and they'd get a kick out of hosting us. I'll give Aunt Bonnie a call when I get home and get it all set up." I tap my fingers on my desk. "What if we invite Melissa to go with us, too?"

"Ooo, yes, let's. I want to get to know her better, and she's already met the Hamilton sisters, and they like her. But we need to make sure not to say anything to her about the divorce. Ash said they don't want anyone else to know yet, including Tonya and Sonya."

"Got it. I'll call Melissa when I get home tonight, too." I flip open my day planner and check my work schedule. "I can take off at noon next Friday. If you can, too, that'll give us plenty of time to pick up the girls and head out of the city before traffic gets crazy."

"I can leave at noon. And I'll make sure the girls can, too, but I'm guessing so, because they said they don't have any plans. They said they'll get their mom to drive them to another part of town to meet us, so hopefully nobody they know will see us with them."

"Do you feel like we're living in a soap opera, with all the drama and clandestine meetings surrounding the super-rich, powerful family of the men we're dating?"

"Okay, first of all, you implied you and Randall are dating, which will need to be discussed. And second, yes, I do feel like I'm living in an alternate universe at times. The Hamilton world is so far removed from my own that it's often mind boggling. But I wouldn't trade Ash for anything, no matter how crazy things get with his family. Now, let's talk about whether you and Randall are dating. Are you?"

"No." I briefly close my eyes. "I don't know. We're saying we're friends, but when I was with him Monday night, it didn't feel much different from before. I'll admit I've kind of been avoiding him at work since then, though."

"That's understandable, but you can't do that forever."

"I know. I'm just not sure how to act around him with an audience—especially with *this* audience."

"I get that, but you're going to have to figure it out."

"I will. Keep reminding me of that, please."

"Will do. Also, have you thought about when you're going to call Andrea?" she asks.

"Oh! I forgot to tell you I talked to her the other night." I tell her about the conversation.

"I'm glad you two hit it off. Do you think you'll try to meet her soon?"

"I haven't had much time to think about it, but yeah, probably in the next month or two."

"If you want to go to Little Rock, I can go with you," she says. "We can stay at Shannon's place. He has an extra bedroom."

"That would be great. I'd like to go there instead of meeting her somewhere else, because I'd like to meet Emily, too, if Andrea decides she's ready for that."

Leslie smiles at me. "You have a niece."

I smile right back. "Awesome, right?"

"I'll talk to my brother this week and see if there are any weekends that wouldn't be good for him, and then when you're ready, we'll start making plans."

"Perfect."

"What's perfect?" Randall asks from the doorway. "Me?"

"Hardly." Leslie rolls her eyes.

"Okay," he concedes as he leans against the doorframe, "I can see how neither of you would think I'm perfect at the moment. But I want to try to fix that. How about the four of us go out Saturday night and have some fun? I'll be on my best behavior. I promise."

Butterflies take up residence in my belly, and I move my gaze from his eyes to Leslie's. She quirks an eyebrow at me and gives a slight nod, giving me the green light for her and Ash while letting me make the decision. I return my focus to Randall, who wears an earnest and hopeful expression.

"Like a double date?" I ask him.

"You can call it whatever you want," he says. "Whatever makes you feel comfortable."

"I won't feel comfortable if you're on your best behavior," I say. "That would be extremely weird. And boring. Especially if the point is to have fun."

He throws his head back in a laugh. "You're right. Is that a yes, then? As long as I'm my usual, ridiculous self?"

I nod my head slowly. "It's a yes."

Randall gives me a smile that whips the butterflies into a frenzy. "Great. I'll pick you up at seven."

"Where are we going?" I ask.

"That's a surprise." He winks at me. "I'll give Ash the details for him and Leslie. See you ladies then. Well, I'll probably see you before then, too."

When he's gone, Leslie says, "I think this will be good."

"You do? You don't still hate him?"

"I never hated him. I just wanted to throttle him."

"And you don't anymore?"

"Only sometimes." She grins at me.

"Same."

Leslie laughs. "Understandable. And something tells me that will never change, even after you're able to move past what he did. Anyway, I think it'll be great for the two of you to be together in a laid-back situation with friends. You can just have fun without the pressure and the potential for heavy conversations."

I nod. "I see what you're saying. A lot of our time together has been pretty heavy. We need to relax and have fun."

"You do. The two of you are both very fun people. You need to make room for that in your relationship." She smiles. "And hopefully being with all of us will help Ash loosen up a little."

I return her smile. "You mean he's not an inherently fun guy? Who would have guessed?"

"I'm working on him," she says, "but you and Randall can definitely help."

"Here's the deal," Randall says as we all stand outside Filene's Basement Saturday night. "We're going in as teams: Leslie and I are one team, and Wendy and Ash are the other." He gives us each a twenty-dollar bill. "We each must buy something for our date to wear for the rest of the evening for twenty bucks or less. The reason for the teams is to ensure we each buy something silly. Well, actually, it's to ensure Ash buys something ridiculous for Leslie, because otherwise he'd buy something nice. The rest of us won't have an issue with making our date look goofy."

Everyone but Ash laughs at that. He simply gives his brother a deadpan look.

Randall continues, "We have twenty minutes to carry out this mission. Aaaaand, go!"

He grabs Leslie's hand and takes off running. She looks back at Ash with a smile and a giggle as they disappear into the department store.

"Come on, big guy," I say to Ash, who hasn't moved. "Let's get cracking."

Ash sighs as he fiddles with his watch. I assume he's setting a timer of some sort.

"I don't know why I agreed to this," he says.

"Because you love Leslie, that's why. And you need some fun in your life." I grasp his elbow and tow him toward the store. "We're shopping for Leslie first. Something tells me that will take longer than finding something for Randall."

Ash drags his feet but doesn't completely resist. "What if I see someone I know when I'm wearing whatever Leslie picks out for me?"

"They'll think you've loosened up in your old age." I open the door and push him through. "Now, stop being a stick in the mud and start thinking about how much Leslie is going to enjoy all of this."

That puts a smile on his face. "She will, won't she?"

"For sure. So what are we thinking for Leslie? A crazy hat? A huge, gaudy, bejeweled pin for her shirt? A holiday-themed tie?"

Ash thinks for a few seconds. "Let's start with the hats and go from there."

thirty-one

· · ·

Randall

"**W**ho knew you could look sexy in a men's sweater vest?" I ask Wendy as I finger the bottom of the obnoxiously bright, multi-colored vest she pulled over her blue sundress on our way to dinner.

We're waiting to be seated at the casual restaurant I chose for the evening. I knew the rest of us could handle wearing something crazy to a formal restaurant, but since I didn't want my brother to have a stroke, I chose a place that was more low-key.

She says, "Not as sexy as you look in that tiara."

Wendy giggles as I take her hand and pull her closer to me. I'm thankful she doesn't tense up or pull away from me.

She glances toward Ash and Leslie and then up at me. "Did you have fun picking out Ash's scarf with Leslie?" she asks, referring to the silky, pastel-striped scarf tied jauntily around my brother's neck.

"I did. She really wanted to get him some ladies' shoes, but they didn't have any big enough for his enormous feet."

"Even if there'd been some big enough, I doubt we could've convinced him to wear them. I'm surprised he's wearing the scarf."

"He's only doing it for Leslie. He wouldn't do something like that for anyone else. Well, he'd probably do it for our sisters, but that's it. How was shopping with him?"

"It took him a few minutes to get into it," she says, "but I got him there. My strategy was to find the most over-the-top options I knew he'd never go for, so then he wouldn't feel as bad about picking out something not quite as ridiculous. I think he chose well."

Leslie is sporting a pair of gigantic Christmas-tree earrings Ash and Wendy found in the clearance section. The trees even light up.

"You're pretty smart, you know that?" I say to her.

Wendy shrugs. "I have two little brothers. I know how to get men to do things they don't think they want to do."

"Oh, yeah? Have you used your tricks on me?"

"Wouldn't you like to know?" She grins at me.

I tighten my hold on her hand. "I'd like to know all your tricks."

"Well," she taps a finger to her lips, "there was this one time—"

The hostess calls my name, so I don't get to hear whatever story Wendy was about to tell. As we walk through the restaurant, I glance back at my brother to see how he's dealing with the stares and whispers as we pass the other diners. His face is red, but he's hanging in there.

"Ash is hating this, isn't he?" Wendy asks.

"Yep," I say gleefully. "I'm so happy our table is on the opposite side of the room from the door."

Her nose wrinkles. "Your brother's discomfort makes you happy?"

I laugh. "Of course it does, but only if I'm the one purposefully causing the discomfort. Otherwise, the person who makes him uncomfortable better watch out."

She smiles up at me as we reach the table. "Even if it's Leslie? Or your sisters?"

"Okay, it's fine if it's someone who loves and cares about him. But nobody else gets to mess with him."

"You're a good brother," she says to me as we take our seats.

"He has his moments," Ash says to Wendy, "but this isn't one of them."

The women both laugh.

"It is," I say to my brother. "Look how happy your gorgeous girlfriend is that you're wearing that ridiculous scarf. You've made her day. No, let me amend that. *I've* made her day by coming up with my little game."

Ash looks at Leslie and can't help but smile at her, but then he glares at me. "You don't get to call her gorgeous."

"Why not? It's true."

"It is," he practically growls, "but you're not supposed to notice her looks. And it's not smart to say things like that in front of your …" His sentence trails off as he looks at Wendy.

"Friend?" Wendy supplies.

"Uh, yeah. Your friend … who's a girl … I mean woman … that you hold hands with."

The table is silent for a second before Leslie says, "Who's up for a fruity cocktail?"

Wendy raises her hand and waves it. "Me!"

I shoot Leslie a grateful look for changing the subject from the status of my relationship with Wendy. Leave it to Ash to mention the elephant in the room. As the women discuss their drink choices, my brother shoots me an apologetic look.

"Okay, on to the next game for the evening," I say.

Ash groans. "No more games."

Wendy claps her hands and bounces in her seat. "Yay for more games." She points at Ash. "What did I tell you about being a stick in the mud?"

My brother glances at Leslie and then back at Wendy. Then he says in a monotone voice, "Yay for more games."

We all laugh as I wonder what Wendy said to him.

"So what's this game, then?" Leslie asks.

"Whichever one of us can get the waitress to say the word 'hot' the most times during the meal gets to decide what we do after dinner."

Wendy rubs her hands together. "You're all going down."

"Oh, yeah?" I ask. "And what are we doing after dinner if you win?"

"Something that'll make *you* uncomfortable," she says with a smirk.

"I'm on Wendy's team again," Ash says.

I shake my head. "This isn't a team event."

"It is now," he replies.

Wendy and Ash win by a landslide. I knew they would, because even though Ash didn't want to play, he's the most competitive person I know. I was also hoping they'd win, because I'm dying to know what Wendy has planned for us next.

"It's like you two didn't even try," Ash says to me and Leslie.

I sneak a glance at his girlfriend, and her smile tells me she wanted to lose as well. I have a feeling she wants to see me in an uncomfortable situation.

"Maybe we didn't," I admit.

"You purposefully put yourself in a position to be uncomfortable?" Ash asks me. "Why?"

"Because it'll be fun."

"How are we related?" my brother asks.

"Beats me. Anyway, Wendy, what's your plan?"

"We're going to that place down the street that has late-night bowling."

"Oookay. And what about that will be awkward for me?"

"You have to bowl left-handed, and you can't say a word." She smirks at me.

We've already established I'm not great with my left hand, but I can deal with that. Not talking? That might be a problem.

"And what happens if I *do* say a word?" I ask.

"For every word you say, that's one less minute I'll spend at your apartment afterward."

My eyebrows shoot up. "You're coming to our apartment?"

She nods, and my breath catches in my throat.

"What are we going to do there?" I ask.

"That's for Leslie to decide."

My gaze shoots to Leslie and back to Wendy. "She'll be there?"

"Well, I'm not going there with you alone."

I wink at her. "You afraid of what you might do to me if we're alone?"

She rolls her eyes. "Yeah, I might smack you upside the head."

Ash chuckles, and I glare at him.

"Hey," he says, "you've laughed at my expense several times tonight. It's my turn now."

I've never laughed as much as I did during wordless bowling. I narrowly missed dropping the ball on my foot multiple times, much to Ash's delight. And seeing Wendy's gleeful face when I couldn't verbally celebrate a strike or express my disappointment at a gutter ball warmed my heart. I might have overdone my frustration a bit simply to see that look on her face. I think I also impressed her with my ability to keep my mouth shut the entire time. And she loved that I left the tiara on, even though the rest of them removed their new items.

After bowling, we went back to the apartment, where Leslie made us play "Spoons." The winner of each round got to wear the tiara, which Ash protested, but he played along. The more tired we got, the more aggressive and competitive we all became, and I put an end to it when Ash nearly took Wendy's hand off grabbing for the last spoon. Then Leslie asked Ash to walk her home, and I'm doing the same for Wendy.

"Did you have a good time tonight?" I ask, her hand gripped firmly in mine.

She looks up at me with a sweet smile. "I did. We haven't ever spent time together with the goal of having fun, and I loved it. We need to do more of that."

"Yeah, we do. And I love that you want to keep spending time with me. Thanks for giving me another chance."

"I don't want that one thing you did to define our entire relationship. You deserve the chance to prove that's not who you are, and spending time with you is helping me to move past it."

A sense of relief washes over me at her words. "I'm glad to hear that."

I walk her all the way to her door this time.

"You can kiss me once on my cheek," she says primly.

"Both cheeks?" I ask hopefully.

"I'm not sure we're at that level yet," she teases. "Just one cheek tonight."

"I'll take whatever I can get." I lean down and press my lips to her cheek, and then I leave them there, resting lightly against her soft skin.

"You done?" she asks after about ten seconds.

"Huh-uh," I voice without moving my lips.

She pokes me in the belly, which makes me jerk away from her.

"Hey, I wasn't done," I protest.

"Ridiculous man."

I grin at her, raise her hand to my lips, and kiss each of her knuckles before letting go of her.

"You going to keep standing there gazing at me with adoration?" she asks, when I don't leave.

"Yep, until you go inside."

"Not gonna happen."

"Why?"

My heart clenches when she says, "Because I want to watch you walk away."

thirty-two

. . .

Wendy

"Can I take you to lunch today?" Randall asks when he stops by my office Monday morning.

My stomach quivers as I glance at my open day planner. "Yeah, but I need to be back by one for a meeting."

"I can make that happen. Think about where you want to go."

He's gone before I can respond. That's probably for the best, because he's wearing the navy-blue suit again, and if he had stuck around much longer, I may have started drooling. It's going to be hard to get through lunch with him without making a fool of myself.

The next few hours are filled with a flurry of phone calls, and before I know it, Randall is leaned up against my doorjamb again, looking so delectable it ought to be a crime.

"Ready?" he says.

"Yep. Let me grab my purse."

"You don't—"

I cut him off. "I do need it. We're supposed to take turns paying, remember?"

I can tell he's tempted to roll his eyes, but he refrains.

"I want to pay," he says. "In fact, you agreed to let me take you to lunch, which implied I would be paying."

"Not gonna happen. Plus, there's more than one reason why

women carry purses, you know. They're not just for carrying money around."

I can tell he wants to make a comment, but he thinks better of it and instead holds out his hand to me. "We need to get cracking, if we're going to have you back here in an hour."

As we walk through the office, several co-workers see us, and they all glance at our joined hands, but nobody comments on it. Brian must have spread the word enough that nobody's surprised to see us together.

"Where are we going?" Randall asks as we wait for the elevator.

"Surprise me."

He takes me to a hole-in-the-wall Chinese restaurant a few blocks away.

"I didn't know this was here," I say.

"Best kept secret in downtown Chicago."

We pile our plates high at the buffet and sit at a tiny table for two in a corner of the cramped dining area. Our knees touch under the table, and neither of us moves away from the other.

"Have you been wearing your tiara?" I ask him.

"Of course. And I make Ash tell me how lovely I look in it."

I giggle. "I can't imagine him doing such a thing."

"Oh, he's a totally different guy when it's just the two of us."

"I don't believe that for a second."

He smiles. "Would you believe me if I said you look amazing today?"

I feel my face heat. "I guess so."

"You guess so? You need to *know* so."

I take a deep breath as warmth floods my chest. "Okay. I believe you."

"You also need to believe that if you don't start eating that food," he points to my plate with his chopsticks, "I'm going to eat it."

"Um, there's no need to eat my food when you can simply go back over to the buffet and get more of your own food."

"But where's the fun in that, when I can irritate you by eating yours?" he teases.

"You need to understand," I now point my chopsticks at him, "that if you ever take my food without my permission, you *will* regret it."

"And you need to understand that I will definitely test you on that one of these days."

"You won't mind losing a finger?"

"No offense, Munchkin, but I don't think you're capable of removing one of my fingers with a pair of chopsticks."

I shrug. "I could if I turned them into shivs."

"*Shivs?* Did you have a stint in prison I don't know about?"

"Yes." I struggle not to smile.

"Oh, this is gonna be good," he says as he tilts his chair onto its back legs. "What did you do?"

"I got caught skinny dipping in Lake Michigan and was arrested for public indecency. I spent a week in jail."

The look on his face is priceless as his front chair legs reconnect with the floor. I manage to hold a straight face for several more seconds before I crack and start giggling.

He says, "I still can't tell if you're serious or not."

"I'm not serious about being arrested," I admit.

He gives me a searching look. "But you were serious about the skinny dipping? And getting caught?"

"Maybe." I give him a smirk.

"You can't leave me hanging." He leans toward me. "Tell me if this happened."

"It's true."

His eyes grow huge. "Really?"

"Yes. I went skinny dipping in Lake Michigan … when I was four. My mom caught me all of ten seconds after I whipped off my bathing suit."

Randall briefly closes his eyes. "Why would you mess with me like that?"

"I wanted to see the look on your face."

He chuckles. "Was it worth it?"

"Definitely."

We grin at each other for a few seconds before I dig into my meal.

"I'm excited for the girls' weekend with your sisters," I say between bites of orange chicken.

"Thanks for making it happen. You have no idea how much it means to us that you're doing this."

"We're happy to do it. We want to help, and we want to get to know your sisters better. It's a win-win."

"Speaking of sisters, have you talked to Andrea again?"

"I've talked to her a few times." I tell him what I learned about her and Emily during the conversations.

"You think you'll want to meet her, then?"

"I do. Leslie's going with me to Little Rock as soon as I'm ready. We'll fly down for the weekend and stay with Shannon."

I detect a tensing of Randall's jaw when I mention Leslie's twin's name, and I wonder if he's jealous. Instead of responding, he shovels some food into his mouth.

"I'm hoping I'll get to meet Leslie's parents while I'm there, too. They don't live too far from the city."

He nods and takes another bite, and his leg shifts away from mine.

I ask, "Did you meet Shannon while he was here last month?" I already know the answer, and I don't know why I'm pushing him on this, but his silence is irritating me.

"Yeah, I took him to the airport. Nice guy." He fills his mouth once again.

"Say whatever you're thinking," I order him. "If you're jealous, admit it."

He puts his fork down, swallows, and says, "Fine. I'm jealous. I wish I could be the one going with you when you meet Andrea and Emily."

"So you're jealous of *Leslie?*"

"Yeah." He won't meet my eye.

I shoot him a piercing look, even though he can't see it. "Anyone else you might be jealous of?"

"Can you leave it alone?"

"No. I can't. We're not dating, Randall. You have no claim over me or where I go or who I go with or who I stay with. And honestly, even if we were dating, you still wouldn't have control over those things. I make my decisions. Got it?"

He finally looks at me. "Do I not get to voice my opinions or my feelings about your decisions? Because if not, I can't do this. I'm not just along for the ride. You said we're in this together, but if that's not truly the case, let me know now."

I take a deep breath before replying. "We *are* in this together. And your opinions and feelings matter to me. But I gave you the opportunity to share them about Shannon, and you didn't. So don't act like I don't value what you have to say."

Randall tosses down his chopsticks, leans back, and crosses his arms over his chest. "You didn't exactly give me the opportunity to voice my opinion. You accused me of being jealous of a man I know you've had interest in dating in the past, which makes me wonder if there's a reason I *should* be jealous. So forgive me if I'm not excited about you spending a weekend at his place."

thirty-three

· · ·

Randall

I know it's ridiculous for me to be jealous in this situation, especially considering what I've done. But Shannon truly is a nice guy. And he's smart and charming and, though I hate to admit it, better looking than me. I can't imagine there are many women who wouldn't want to be with him.

"I like Shannon," Wendy says, "and I enjoyed spending time with him while he was here last month. We talked on the phone a couple times after he went home, and he suggested we try a long-distance relationship."

I nod as my chest feels like a boulder has rolled onto it.

"But I said no. Do you want to know why I said no?"

I nod again.

"Use your words, Randall."

I breathe deeply through my nose. "Don't patronize me. And yes, I want to know why you said no."

"Because of you."

The boulder shifts so it's not pressing down on me as heavily. "Really?"

"Yes, really," she retorts. "Goodness knows I've had reason enough to question that decision, but I stand by it." She jabs a finger on the table in front of me. "And the fact that I'm here with you right now proves that."

I drop my head for a few moments before looking back up at

her. "I'm sorry. I should have told you exactly what I thought instead of shutting down when you mentioned Shannon. I hate using Colleen as an excuse, but when you said another man's name, it took me back to her telling me she was sleeping with my friend. I know I need to get over that, but obviously I'm not yet."

"Oh, Randall," she breathes out softly.

Wendy slides her hand across the table, and I take it in mine.

"I'm sorry," she says. "I wasn't thinking. For a minute, I forgot you have some hurdles, too. Can you forgive me for pushing you about Shannon?"

"Yes." I swipe my thumb across her knuckles. "Can you forgive me for letting my own issues keep me from being excited about you meeting your sister and niece?"

"Of course. And I want you to know I'm proud of you for telling me you want your opinion to matter to me, even when I was being a jerk to you. Thank you for being honest."

"I'm learning," I say, "even if I don't always go about it in the right way." I glance at my watch and let go of her hand. "Eat up. We need to get you back to the office soon."

I'm in bed reading a book late Thursday night when the phone rings. I reach over to get it, but it stops ringing, so I assume my brother answered. Considering the hour, it's almost certainly Leslie calling him.

A couple minutes later, he calls out from the other room, "It's for you!"

I stick a bookmark into my book and grab the phone from the bedside table.

"Hello?"

"I'm hanging up now," Ash says, and the line clicks.

"It's me," Wendy says.

I can't stop the smile that spreads across my face. "Hi. What were you and Ash talking about?"

"He thanked me once again for giving up my weekend for your sisters."

"Ah. Still planning to leave at noon tomorrow?" I readjust my pillows and slide down so I'm lying on my side.

"Yes. But Melissa has plans tomorrow night, so she's driving out to meet us Saturday. Ash said you have a meeting with a divorce lawyer tomorrow afternoon."

"We do. He's the best in the entire state, and he despises Dad, which should make him fight even harder than normal."

"That's good to hear."

When she says nothing else, I prompt, "Did you have a reason for calling?"

"No, I haven't talked to you in a couple days, so I thought I'd call. Did you do anything tonight?"

My smile grows bigger at the thought she might be missing me. "Hung out here at home with Ash. We played some games on the Nintendo and now I'm reading in bed."

"Whatcha reading?"

I roll over and pick up the book, as if she can see it. "James Michener's *Alaska.*"

"Wow. That's a huge book."

"Yep." I flip to the back of it. "More than eight hundred pages." I set it back down. "What did you do tonight?"

"Packed for the weekend and talked to Andrea again."

"Did you learn anything interesting about her?"

"We mostly talked about our jobs. She's a second-grade teacher, and in the summers she works part-time at the public library."

"So she's a reader, too."

"Yes, we had a good time talking about our favorite books and authors. We have quite a few in common."

"Like Jane Austen?" I guess.

Wendy chuckles. "Like Jane Austen and L.M. Montgomery and Mary Higgins Clark and … Danielle Steel."

"Why did you hesitate before saying Danielle Steel?"

"I might be a little ashamed to admit I read romance novels," she admits.

"Don't be ashamed of reading books you enjoy. There's nothing wrong with reading romance novels."

"Read a lot of them yourself, do you?"

"Tons." I smile. "I'm quite partial to the bodice rippers."

Wendy bursts into laughter. "How do you know that term?"

"Who knows where my vast amounts of knowledge come from? If you ever go to a trivia night, you need to take me along. I clean up in the 'random facts' category."

"I'll keep that in mind. And maybe you should consider being a cover model for those bodice rippers as your next job."

I chuckle. "You think I'd be good at that?"

"Well, I've never seen you without your shirt on, but I've felt those pecs and abs, and I'm pretty sure you could give Fabio a run for his money."

I'm not nearly as ripped as Fabio, but I can't help but grin at her words. "I'd need to grow my hair out."

"Nah," she says. "We need some variety in romance cover models. Not all of them should have long hair. I'm a fan of shorter hair myself."

"Oh, yeah? And what color are you the biggest fan of?"

"Hmm. I'm thinking dark brown is just right."

My grin grows even bigger. "And I'm thinking red hair is perfect for the heroine. Long, wavy red hair, that is. And a tiny, curvy body in a low-cut dress. Yep. That sounds just right."

Wendy clears her throat. "Uh-huh."

I've obviously embarrassed her, but I can't tell if that's good or bad.

"Speaking of jobs," she says, "when are you going to seriously start thinking about getting a different one?"

I sigh and roll onto my back to stare at the ceiling. "I can't do anything about that right now. Switching careers will likely cost money for education or training, and I'll almost certainly make less money than I do now. With everything up in the air with my mom and sisters, I can't afford to do anything different."

"I'm sorry."

"Thanks. Me, too."

"Are you second guessing your offer to help them financially if needed?"

"Never."

"That's what I thought you'd say."

My heart swells at her words.

She adds, "You don't hate it at Carter-Jenkins, do you?"

"No," I admit. "Not like I did at Dad's firm. It's a much better place to work in every way possible. So I don't mind working there, but it's not what I want to do forever."

"You forgot to mention you also get to work with me."

I smile. "That's the best part of working there and the thing I'll miss the most if I ever leave."

"You'll leave. It'll happen someday. I won't let you give up hope for finding a job you truly love."

"I'm going to hold you to that. Now," I say, "on to more important things. Are you wearing the sexy armadillo jammies again?"

"Jammies?" She giggles, and I goofily grin at the ceiling. "I am," she confirms. "What are *you* wearing?"

I should have anticipated she'd turn the question back on me, but I didn't, and now this conversation is about to get awkward.

"You think you can handle the truth?" I ask.

She sucks in an audible breath. "I don't know, but I don't want you to lie to me."

Here goes nothing. "I'm wearing a suit."

"A suit? I told you not to lie to me, Randall Hamilton!"

"My birthday suit," I amend.

thirty-four

. . .

Wendy

I've been a bundle of nerves all morning, because after talking and flirting with Randall on the phone last night, I decided there's something I need to do today, and it has to happen before I leave work at noon. At 11:45, I head to Randall's office. His face lights up when he spots me lingering in his doorway.

"Is it noon?" he asks.

"Not quite yet," I say as I close his door and lock it.

He raises an eyebrow at me. "Is this the moment I should be wishing I keep a weapon in my desk?"

I purse my lips and tilt my head to the side. "You might need to defend yourself."

"What's going on?"

I stand opposite him with the desk between us and clasp my hands together. "There's something I'd like us to do, but only if you're okay with it."

"And that would be …?"

"I think we should kiss. On the lips."

He breathes in deeply through his nose, and his grip tightens on the pen in his hand. "Now?"

I nod. "I know you wanted to wait, and I understand why, but I think we can handle it and not let it turn into more until we're ready for that. And don't take this the wrong way, but I want to get it over with. I want to see if we can kiss without the Tammy thing ruining it. I keep worrying that I'll never be able to kiss you without thinking about you kissing her, and I need to find out if that's true before we take this any further. So will you kiss me?"

His Adam's apple bobs as he swallows and nods. "I can do that."

I take a shaky breath. "Yeah?"

"Yeah. I've been dying for this moment to come. Come around here."

I round the desk, and he takes my hands and pulls me so I'm standing between his legs. Due to our height difference, his face is only a few inches lower than mine in this position.

"Are you sure this is what you want?" he asks.

"Yes." I place a hand on his jawline. "And you're not saying yes because it's what I want?"

He covers my hand with his own, sending a tremor through my body. "No," he says. "I'm ready for this step. I've been ready, but I wanted it to be your decision. You're positive you want to do this now, here at work?"

I nod. "We won't see each other all weekend, and I can't wonder about this any longer. Doing it here will ensure we don't do anything more. If we don't meet Leslie in the lobby in ten minutes, she'll come looking for us."

Since neither Leslie nor I own a car, Ash offered us his for the weekend. When we get off work at noon, Randall will drive the two of us home to change and get our bags, and then we'll head to their apartment to pick up the car.

"We'd better get on with it, then," Randall says, "because this won't be a quick peck on the lips."

"I would hope not."

I give him a trembling smile, my nerves on high alert. What if I'm right, and all I can think about is Tammy? What if all these feelings I have for him go away if that happens? What if I don't enjoy it? What if *he* doesn't enjoy it?

He tugs me down so I'm sitting on his lap. Then he wraps one hand around the nape of my neck and slides his fingers up into my hair, but instead of pressing his lips to mine, he trails light kisses along my jawline from my ear to my chin. Just when I think he's going to finally kiss my mouth, he repeats the process on the other side of my face. My heart is pounding, and I want to beg him to stop teasing me, but I don't.

He finally makes his way to my mouth, and I sigh. The moment our lips touch, I forget about everything but the sensations coursing through my body. I wrap my arms around his neck and press closer against him, and he deepens the kiss while using his other hand to anchor me to him. After much too short a time, his mouth pulls away, but he continues to hold me close as he presses his forehead against mine and we catch our breaths.

"Well?" His eyes are closed, and his voice is tinged with anxiety.

Instead of answering, I capture his lips with mine again. He growls into me, and he lets himself go in a way he didn't before. His hands roam over me, and mine grip the front of his shirt.

This time I'm the one who pulls away, because he doesn't seem to be thinking about stopping. I press a last quick kiss to the corner of his mouth and slightly lean away from him, my chest heaving and heart hammering.

He groans and throws his head back. "Are we really going to have to wait *days* to do that again?"

"Yeah, I didn't think that part through, did I?"

"I think I can forgive you for the lack of foresight." He lightly tickles my side, and I giggle as I swat his hand away.

Then he sets me back on my feet and straightens his shirt as I smooth my hair down and make sure all my clothing is in its proper place, while mentally ordering my heart to settle down.

"That's my favorite skirt," he says.

"Oh, yeah?"

"Yep. It's the slit that does it for me." He gaze dips down to the sliver of exposed thigh and his pupils dilate.

My heart rate picks up again. "Hmm. Good to know."

"Care to share anything that does it for you?"

"Your navy suit," I say without hesitation.

He grins and points to his eyes. "It makes these babies pop, doesn't it?"

I cross my arms over my chest and shake my head at him. "You're a mess, did you know that?"

"I've been told that a time or two." He puckers his lips at me. "Do I have lipstick on my mouth?"

I swipe a thumb over his lips. "You're good. How about me? Is my makeup okay?"

"You look stunning, as usual."

"Thank you," I say with a blush, "but that didn't answer my question."

"Other than your lipstick being gone, your makeup is perfect."

I lean against his desk and grin at him. "Did we really do that?"

"We did." He reaches to pull me back between his legs and settles his hands on my hips. "You sure you want to take my sisters on a girls' weekend instead of staying here with me? I can think of some fun things we can do." His hand slides to the slit in my skirt, but I redirect it up to my waist.

I'm dying to stay here with him, but I can't, and that's probably a good thing. I need time to process what happened before we do it again or take this further than my heart might be ready to.

"What I want isn't pertinent," I say, "because we both know I need to get your sisters out of town, and you need to focus on your mom."

"I'm pretty sure my focus will be on something other than my mom."

I trace my finger along his hairline, and he can't stop the shiver that rolls through his body.

"Some*thing?*" I ask.

"Maybe some*one.*" His grip tightens on my hips. "But I'm not naming any names. Don't want to make you jealous."

My stomach twists. "You're really going to joke about that?"

He winces and his gaze turns apologetic. "I'm sorry. I wasn't thinking."

I sigh. "I know. And I don't want you to second guess everything you say to me, so please don't worry about it. We're both bound to say stupid things sometimes."

He nods and glances at the clock. "We've got a minute before we need to meet Leslie. Want to kiss me one more time?"

I press my lips to his forehead. "Done." Then I twirl out of his grasp and head for the door. "See you in one minute!"

thirty-five

. . .

How am I supposed to get up and walk out of my office after what just happened?

I've never been more surprised than when Wendy asked to kiss me. I figured I'd have to wait months for her to feel like she was ready and, like her, I was afraid she wouldn't be able to lose herself in it due to thinking about the last woman I kissed. I'm glad we overcame that obstacle, but I don't know how I'm going to make it through the weekend without seeing her.

I'm still sitting at my desk, staring off into space while reliving the last ten minutes in my head, when Leslie appears in my doorway.

"Yoo-hoo, you forget about us?"

I shake myself out of my stupor. "No. Sorry." I study her face for a moment to try and decipher if Wendy already told her about the kissing, but her expression doesn't give anything away.

"Well then, hop to it," she orders. "We need to hit the road."

"Yes, ma'am."

I grab my keys and wallet out of my desk drawer and follow her out. Wendy is waiting for us in the lobby, and she avoids looking me in the eye, but her mouth holds a hint of a smile. The two women chatter as we make our way to my car. Normally I would join in, but today I simply listen.

When we reach my Porsche 944, Wendy maneuvers her tiny

self into the minuscule backseat, giving Leslie shotgun, since she's at least six inches taller. Before I pull out of the parking spot, I angle the rearview mirror so I can see Wendy while still having a view out the back window.

As soon as we're out on the street, Leslie says, "Now that I have both of you trapped, I expect one of you to tell me why you," she twists around and points to Wendy, "can't stop smiling, and you," she trains her finger on me, "have barely said a word since I found you looking all dreamy eyed in your office."

"I didn't look dreamy eyed!" I protest.

"You looked like one of those cartoon characters with hearts floating around their head." She flutters her fingers around her face for emphasis.

Wendy giggles, and Leslie turns on her again and says, "You know you're going to tell me as soon as we're alone, so why not tell me now?"

Wendy and I lock eyes in the mirror, I give her a tiny nod, and she says, "We kissed."

Leslie is silent, and when I glance at her out of the corner of my eye, her mouth is wide open.

"It's true," I say. "We made out in my office like a couple of hormonal teenagers. Your little friend back there knocked my socks off." I figure if we're going to talk about it, I might as well go for broke.

"You did *not* make out in your office."

I give a fake gasp. "I don't think you have any room to talk about kissing someone at work, Ms. Beckett."

Her cheeks turn pink. "That's not what I meant. I don't care where you kiss each other. I'm surprised, is all."

I shrug. "Well, to be clear on the location, it was in the vicinity of our mouths. And I was surprised, too. This one," I point my thumb behind us at Wendy, "waltzed into my office wearing that delicious little skirt, locked the door, climbed on top of me, and demanded I kiss her. Who was I to say no?"

"Randall!" Wendy glowers at me in the mirror.

"You were going to tell her the whole story anyway, and you know it."

"Maybe so, but you don't have to make it sound so tawdry."

"Tawdry? It wasn't tawdry. It was sexy, you coming in and asking me to kiss you, knowing we could get caught but not caring, you little exhibitionist."

"Ah, see?" Wendy says. "You're changing your story. First you said I demanded, then you said I asked. Which is what happened, for the record."

"You know I love it when you get feisty." I wiggle my eyebrows at her. "Makes me want to kiss you again, and we'd have an audience this time, which I've discovered gets you revved up."

"I'm going to ignore that ridiculous statement. Plus, it would be kind of hard for you to kiss me when I'm trapped back here in this shoebox of a backseat," she retorts.

"Are you complaining about my car?"

"Yes. It might be pretty, but it's not very practical."

"My car is not *pretty*. It's cool."

"It's dumb."

Leslie has been silent during this whole exchange, her focus ping-ponging between us, but now she says, "I find it quite entertaining that you two can go from kissing to snapping at each other in such a short amount of time."

"Wendy loves it that way," I state. "She enjoys the variety."

"Oh, I do?" she retorts. "Says who?"

"Me." I raise an eyebrow at her in the mirror. "Am I wrong?"

"No." She pouts, which is so adorable I almost crash into the car stopped at the light ahead of me because I'm gazing at her.

"Eyes on the road, not on the redhead, Hamilton," Leslie says.

She adjusts the mirror so I can't see Wendy, but I shift it right back to where it was.

"I need to keep an eye on her," I say, "to make sure she's not carving our initials into the backseat."

That earns me an eye roll from the woman in question. Then she mouths, "You're a mess."

I burst out laughing, and Leslie looks back and forth between us. "What did I miss?"

"Nothing to worry your little head about," I say. "Some things are sacred."

"Very few things," Wendy says with another roll of her eyes.

I pull up to the curb in a no-parking zone in front of Wendy's building, shift the car into park, step out, and flip my seatback forward.

"Out you get," I say to Wendy. "And make it snappy."

"I'll take however much time I want to, thankyouverymuch."

I hold a hand out to her, and at first she ignores it, but when she struggles to climb out of the backseat without flashing me or anyone else who might be looking, she reluctantly lets me help her. When she's finally on her feet outside the car, I cup her face, lean down, and kiss her nose. She tosses me a mock glare and flounces away from me.

"Remember ... snappy," I say.

She flips me the bird without turning around, and I chuckle.

"You two ...," Leslie says from the sidewalk. She shakes her head and then follows Wendy into the building without finishing her statement.

thirty-six

· · ·

Wendy

"You kissed Randall Hamilton," Leslie says as soon as the door to my apartment building closes behind her.

I try and fail to stifle a grin. "I did."

"And …?"

I know what she's asking, and I press the elevator button while saying, "I only thought about Tammy before and after, not during."

We step into the elevator. "That's a good start, I guess. Is that why you did it—why you asked him to kiss you? So you could see how you'd react?"

"Yes. I knew I needed to find out if I could deal with the kissing issue before letting him back into my heart. I didn't want to spend the whole weekend wondering, so I went for it. I honestly wasn't sure he'd say yes. I would have felt like a gigantic fool if he'd said no."

"There was zero chance that man was going to say no to kissing you."

We're quiet until we're in my apartment. Leslie sits on my bed while I change into comfier clothes.

"Does it bother you that you thought about Tammy at all," she asks, "even if not during the kiss?"

"It does, but I think that'll fade with time." I pull a tank top on. "At least I hope so. I *really* hope so. Because if not, …" I don't want to finish that thought.

"Yeah." She gives me a sad smile.

"But the man can kiss, I'll give him that." Oh, can he kiss. Although I don't want to think about what it took for him to learn how to kiss like that.

She chuckles. "That's good to hear, but please don't give me details."

"I won't. I may kiss and tell, but the details are private."

We head downstairs with my bags, and Randall loads them in the trunk.

"You sure you're only going for the weekend?" he asks. "I wouldn't take this much stuff for a month-long trip."

"You're such a man."

"You say that as if it's something I should be ashamed of." He puffs out his chest and pounds on it like a caveman. "Methinks you're glad I'm a man."

I ignore him and climb back into the car, which is much easier now that I'm wearing shorts instead of a skirt.

"Leslie's bags will have to go on your lap," he tells me as he slides back into his seat and pulls onto the street for the three-block drive to Leslie's apartment.

"As if there's room," I scoff. "Next weekend we're trading this car in for something more comfortable."

"Oh, *we* are trading in *my* car?"

I cross my arms over my chest, even though he can't see that part of me in the mirror. "We are."

"Personally, I think this car is extremely comfortable." He pats his seat. "It's like being wrapped in a leather hug. What do you think, Leslie?"

"Will you two stop it?" she says.

"Why?" Randall responds. "It's fun. I told you she likes it."

"You sound like an old married couple. I feel like I'm listening to my parents bicker."

"Then I'm glad we make you feel right at home."

Leslie groans, and I giggle. I do love the bickering. It's almost as fun as the bantering. Randall and I continue quibbling about the car until we pull up in front of Leslie's building. She jumps out before we come to a full stop and slams the door before I can tell her I want to go with her.

"Let me out," I order Randall.

"Nope. You're staying here with me."

"I am not."

I push on the passenger seat and try to reach the door handle, but the interior of this car is so confining and my arms are so short I'm unable to reach it. Randall simply watches and laughs at me.

"Let. Me. Out." I punch the back of his seat on each word.

"Huh-uh."

"Then I'm crawling up there to let myself out."

"Go ahead. Try it," he challenges.

"Oh, you'd better believe I'll do more than try."

I maneuver onto my knees on the back seat—not without some difficulty—and poke my head between the front seats. "Here I come. Don't you try to stop me."

Randall's lips twitch, but he doesn't let himself smile. "I wouldn't dare."

I succeed in getting my top half between the seats, but when it comes to my hips, no matter which way I turn, I can't get them through. I curse the curves I inherited from my mother, and Randall laughs at me again.

"Where'd you learn to talk like that?" he asks.

"Wouldn't you like to know?"

I finally manage to wriggle my hips through the gap, but then I'm not sure what to do. I turn so I'm sitting on the console facing backward and give Randall the strongest glare I can muster.

"You need some help?" he asks.

"No."

His gaze travels along the half of my body he can see, and I tug up the neckline of my tank top, which was riding low after my struggle.

"I think you do," he says, lips twitching again.

"I do not."

"Then come on up."

I try to figure out how to move myself into the passenger seat without falling and hitting my head or kneeing Randall in the face. When I realize I can't manage it, I settle myself back down on the console.

"If anyone looks into this car," Randall says, "they're going to wonder what on earth we're getting up to."

"We're not getting up to anything."

He wiggles his eyebrows. "Maybe we should."

"Stop wiggling your eyebrows. You might think it's sexy, but I think it's creepy."

"No, you don't."

I sigh.

"Do you at least need some help getting back into your seat?" he asks. "You look incredibly uncomfortable."

"No."

"Fine, then. Stay stuck."

"I'm not stuck." I cross my arms over my chest, elbowing Randall in the process, but not caring. "I'm taking a break."

"All right." He runs a finger across my bottom lip, and my body erupts with goosebumps, which he notices with a grin. "But while you take that break, I can think of something fun we can do since you're right here with your mouth so close to mine."

I suck in a breath, and my gaze dips to his mouth. "Banter?"

"Nope." He licks his lips very slowly.

"Bicker?"

"Wrong again. Now, will you please, *please* shut up and kiss me before Leslie comes back?"

My mouth is on his before he has time to react. When he recovers from the initial shock, one of his hands cups the back of my head while the other snakes around my body to hold me in place. My current position isn't exactly comfortable, but I'm not about to complain when he's doing magical things to my mouth.

I don't hear the car door open, and my body jerks when Leslie says, "Ugh, get a room."

Randall unlatches his lips from mine but doesn't let me go as he calmly says to her, "We might need a little help getting her back into her seat."

Leslie sighs. "Fine. I'll do that while you put my bag in the trunk. And before you say it won't fit, it will. I'm a much lighter packer than your kissing buddy."

Randall gives me another quick kiss on the lips and says, "Kissing buddies. I like that new title."

I roll my eyes, but I also can't help but grin at him.

"Any day now," Leslie says.

He kisses me one more time.

thirty-seven

. . .

Randall

"I f I don't land you at least half of your joint assets plus sizable alimony payments in the divorce settlement, I won't charge you a penny for my services," the divorce lawyer tells my mother.

Mom, dressed to kill in a burgundy skirt suit and string of pearls, sits up straight in her chair and replies, "I appreciate the gesture, Samuel, but that's unnecessary."

"It's absolutely necessary. Walter deserves nothing after the way he's treated your entire family, and we'll make him pay. And if the fee is on the line, my team will work that much harder for you."

Mom, Ash, Samuel Bernard, and I are sitting in a conference room in an office building owned by one of Samuel's friends. We decided a neutral location was best, as we didn't want anyone seeing Mom and Samuel together and potentially tipping Dad off to what's coming. We need to get all our ducks in a row before he gets wind of anything.

"We'll get a private investigator onto him this weekend," Samuel says, "since you think he's with the secretary again. We'll do our best to get photographic proof of the affair over the course of the next few weeks before we file."

Mom says, "I don't want to see the photos."

"You probably won't have to," he assures her.

"Good. Now, about the house," Mom says. "Ash told me I shouldn't move out, or I lose power in negotiating, right?"

"Yes. And unfortunately, you can't kick Walter out, since his name is on the deed. You're going to have to keep living with him for the time being, because I can guarantee he won't move out, either, for the same reason."

"What if I have proof of verbal abuse and threats?"

"What?" Ash and I say in unison.

"Calm down, boys." Mom flaps her hand at us.

"I'm not going to calm down," I say. "Dad threatened you? When? How?"

"I'm going to kill him," Ash says.

"I'll pretend I didn't hear that," Samuel tells my brother with a wry look.

"He has never actually hit me," Mom explains, "although he's come close a few times, and threats have become a regular occurrence."

"You've gotta be kidding me," Ash mutters.

"You say you have proof of these threats?" Samuel asks.

Mom reaches into her purse, pulls out a mini cassette of the type found in answering machines, and slides it across the table to Samuel.

"Dad was dumb enough to threaten you on tape?" I say. "He must be slipping."

"He was drunk. When I got home from dinner with you boys last week, I had a message from him on my private line at home. He demanded to know why I wasn't home and answering my phone, and he said if he found out I'd been with you two, there'd be hell to pay. And he described exactly what that would be." She looks at Samuel. "Does it matter that he was drunk when he said it? Does that invalidate it?"

"If anything, it could make things worse for him." Samuel sticks the tape into his briefcase. "I'll make a copy of this for you, in case this one disappears."

"Will that be enough to get him out of the house?" Mom asks.

"Yes. We'll file an Order of Protection. He'll fight it, but with this tape, we'll win that battle."

Is it bad that I'm happy something good will come of my father's threats?

Mom says, "The last thing I need us to discuss today is Sonya. She won't be eighteen until February."

"We may still be dealing with all this then," Samuel says, "but if it gets settled more quickly than I think it might, do you think he'll fight for custody?"

"He's never shown much interest in the girls, but he'll probably fight for her just to be contrary."

"The threats against you should help here, too. Add to that the fact that mothers typically win custody cases, and you'll be fine."

"Today's meeting went better than expected," I say to Ash over dinner. Since we can't go to McConnell's anymore, and because I've given up drinking for now, we're at Pat's Diner, where Wendy and I had ice cream last week.

"Mostly thanks to a drunken mistake," Ash says.

His words hit me hard, even though that's not the way he meant them. "This apple doesn't fall far from the tree, does it?"

Ash closes his eyes. "Randall—"

"I know, I know." I wave my fork in the air. "I'm nothing like him, and so on and so forth."

"You're not. I'll tell you that every day if I need to."

"I don't think that'll be necessary."

"I might do it anyway."

I shrug. "Fine. Stroke my ego on a daily basis. See how well that works out for you."

"You make an excellent point."

We eat in silence for a few minutes.

"What do you think the women are up to?" I ask him.

"Something girly."

"Painting their nails? Watching sappy movies? Talking about us? Having a pillow fight?"

Ash shoots me a wry grin. "I don't think girls really have pillow fights."

I snort. "How would you know?"

"Two of the people I'm closest to are teenage girls. I think I know more than you."

"I could imagine Wendy having a pillow fight."

"You just want to imagine her in pajamas."

Now he gets a grin from me. "I don't have to imagine that. I can remember it." And I do. Often.

"Oh." He blushes. "Yeah. What's the latest with you and her?"

"She kissed me," I say as nonchalantly as possible, as if I haven't been replaying our kisses in my mind all day.

Ash's fork halts on the way to his mouth. "What?"

"Before we left work to go pick up your car, she came into my office and asked me to kiss her. Said she needed to know if she'd think about Tammy while kissing me, and we couldn't move forward until she found out. So we kissed."

"And …?"

"She didn't think about Tammy."

"She said that?"

"She didn't need to." I give him a cocky smirk.

"Wow. Okay. So you're dating again?"

I stab some green beans with my fork. "I don't know."

"You didn't discuss that?"

"We didn't really have time."

"Hmm."

"Hmm, what?" I stick the green beans into my mouth.

"I think if she considers the two of you to be dating now, she would have said so. That would have taken her all of five seconds. There was time."

I swallow and glare at him. "Sometimes I don't like you very much."

He shrugs.

"You should be nice to me," I say. "I gave you a home."

"I can afford my own home. I moved in with you because you couldn't afford that fancy two-bedroom apartment on your new salary."

That shuts me up. Even though I assumed that was the case, he hasn't said it before.

"I'm sorry," he says. "I shouldn't have said that."

"It's true," I finally admit. "And you didn't have to do that for me."

"I know, but there was also no reason for both of us to be uprooted from our homes because of Dad. Plus, it was partly self-ish. I wasn't all that interested in signing a year-long lease, since I was hoping there'd be another person involved in my housing decisions before the year is up."

It takes me a second to figure out what he's talking about, but when I do, I grin at him. "When *are* you going to pop the question? I get that you didn't want to talk about it with our sisters, but now it's just me, and I need to know."

"Why do you need to know?"

"Because I'm your best friend, that's why."

He sighs. "I guess that's a good enough reason. And the answer is I don't know. I don't want to do it too soon. It's not even been two months since she came back into my life."

"But she's the one. It's obvious to anyone with eyes and a brain who's around you for more than five seconds. And the two of you have already dealt with more drama together than most couples do in a decade. If you were going to break up, it would have happened by now. Frankly, since she's willing to put up with our family's mess, you need to stick a ring on her finger pronto."

"I have to buy one first."

"We'll do it tomorrow," I declare.

"We're spending tomorrow with Mom," he reminds me.

"I'm sure she'd love nothing more than to go ring shopping with us."

"She can't be seen with us in public yet."

"Oh, yeah." I tap my fingers on the tabletop. "We'll do it soon, though."

"Why do you need to be there?"

"Because I can't let you accidentally buy her a cubic zirconia. That's totally something you would do."

"No." He shakes his head. "That's something *you* would do."

thirty-eight

· · ·

Wendy

"So," the older of Randall's sisters says to me as we're all lounging on the couches and eating popcorn at the lake house Friday night, "what's going on between you and our brother?"

Before I consider how much to tell her, I take a second to remember this one is Tonya. Since the girls' names are so similar, I had to come up with a way to remember which of them is which. Tonya-with-a-T is taller and older. Sonya-with-an-S is shorter and younger.

"We're spending some time together." I know it's a vague answer, but Randall and I didn't talk about whether we're officially dating again yet, so I can't tell the girls we are. Plus, I don't know what he might have told them about us.

Sonya rolls her eyes. "That's what he said. What I really want to know is if this 'spending time together' includes kissing."

The heat rushing from my neck up my face reveals the answer I didn't want to give, and Tonya tosses a piece of popcorn at me.

"Ha!" she says. "I knew Randall was holding out on us. You two are totally dating."

Leslie sends me a shrewd look. We had this conversation in the car on the way to pick up the girls, so she knows I'm still not sure about the nature of the relationship. I'm also not about to tell his sisters what he did to make me question it.

"He and I have been friends for a while," I finally say, "so we're taking things slow."

Sonya nods. "That makes sense."

Tonya smacks her sister's arm. "It does not. If anything, since they already know each other, that should help speed things along."

"Think about it," Sonya says to her. "Not only are Randall and Wendy friends, but his brother and her best friend are dating each other. If they don't take it slow, they risk ruining their friendships not only with each other but also with Leslie and Ash. And Wendy has the most to lose, because if it came down to Leslie and Ash needing to pick sides, they'd have to go with Randall, since he's family."

I feel sick thinking about that possibility. Leslie has stuck with me so far, but we've only known each other all of two months, and she's almost certainly going to marry Randall's brother.

Leslie jumps in. "You're partly right, Sonya, but not completely. I wouldn't automatically pick Randall. Yes, he might be my family someday, but Wendy is like family to me, and I'm not going to drop her if things don't work out with her and Randall. She's my best friend, and no man is going to change that."

The pressure in my chest eases with Leslie's words, and I give her a grateful smile.

Tonya says, "Good for you, and to be honest, he's the most likely one to mess things up anyway. If he did, I'd take Wendy's side, too."

Sonya's eyes widen. "You wouldn't."

"Um, excuse me," Tonya says, "but you're offending the woman sitting right here in front of us who is also graciously giving up her weekend for us. If Randall hurts her—and let's be honest, that's not a far-fetched idea—I'm not siding with him only because he's our brother."

Sonya's face drops, and she looks at me. "I'm sorry, Wendy."

"Don't be sorry about having family loyalty," I tell her, and then I look at Tonya. "And I wouldn't expect you to choose one of us over the other. If something happened between Randall and me that meant we wouldn't be friends anymore, you could still be supportive of both of us if you wanted to. Of course, you'd probably rarely see me if that happened, but I'd never want you to feel like you needed to pick sides. If you did, though, I'd tell you to choose Randall every time, no matter what."

"Even if he ends up being as terrible as Dad?" Tonya says.

"Tonya!" Sonya admonishes while tossing an entire handful of popcorn at her sister. "He'd never!"

Tonya buries her head in her hands. "I know. I was trying to make a point."

"That was an awful way to make it. Randall is a *good* man, and you know it."

Tonya looks back up at us. "I'm sorry. Please forgive me, everyone. Can we talk about something else now?"

"Have you spent much time with Mr. and Mrs. Hamilton?" Leslie asks Melissa.

It's Saturday afternoon, and the three of us are laying out in the sun on the small beach drinking margaritas while Tonya and Sonya ride the WaveRunners on the lake. I'm surprised Leslie brought up the topic, since we're not supposed to mention the divorce, and this conversation could lead to speculation on Melissa's part.

"Not a whole lot," Melissa says. "I saw them at church and at school events when I was a kid, but I paid little attention to them. My general impression was that Mr. Hamilton was pompous and fake, and Mrs. Hamilton was a good woman but wasn't to be trifled with. I've only seen them once since I moved back," she gives Leslie a wry look, "when my parents and I had dinner at their house last month. Mrs. Hamilton was the most friendly and animated I've ever seen her while trying to get Ash and me to fall for each other. Mr. Hamilton spoke to nobody but my dad and occasionally his wife, and that was mostly to complain to her about something or to order her around."

"Did she do what he said?" I can't help but ask.

"No, but she didn't make a big deal out of it. She simply brushed his comments off and started up a new conversation."

To keep *this* conversation from moving further into the topic of the Hamilton marriage, I say, "Melissa, thanks again for being my shoulder to cry on after the Randall debacle."

"Not a problem," she replies. "I was glad I could be there for you. How have things been with him the past couple weeks?"

After I give her the update, I ask, "Do you think I'm getting over what he did too soon?"

"I'll admit, I'm a little surprised, but it's not up to me to decide when and how you should forgive him and move past what happened. If this feels right to you, it doesn't matter what anyone other than you and Randall think about it."

"It does feel right," I say. "I don't want to hold a grudge with him simply because I'm scared I might be moving too fast. I want to move on as best we can and hope I can eventually not think about Tammy at all when I'm with him."

Melissa nods. "That makes sense. I hope you're able to make it work."

"Thanks."

Leslie asks Melissa, "Is there anyone you have your eye on? Any handsome men at work?"

"There's plenty of good-looking men on the team," she replies. "You've seen them. You *work* with one of them."

Leslie laughs. "Yes, Diego Sanchez is quite easy on the eyes."

"Would you want to date a professional athlete?" I ask Melissa.

"It wouldn't be ideal. He'd be gone so much of the time, and it would be hard to raise a family. From the interactions I've had with players' wives since I've been with the organization, I've seen and heard firsthand how difficult it can be. The women support each other, but they all know that at any time their husband could be traded, and then they're off to a new place to start all over again."

I say, "Anybody in the front office you're interested in, then?"

"Not really. I'm not sure I want to date someone I work with every day." She cuts a glance at me. "That could get awkward if things don't work out."

"Hear, hear." I raise my glass to her.

"What about Bobby Jacobs?" Leslie asks. "Could anything happen there?"

Melissa shakes her head. "I don't think he likes me very much. Whenever he's in the office, he gives me one of those man-nods and rarely speaks." She shrugs. "He also seems like he really gets around, and he's like twice my age."

"No, he's not," Leslie says. "He's thirty-five."

My eyebrows shoot up. "Really? I figured he's much older than that, considering his success and reputation."

"Is a ten-year difference too much?" Leslie asks Melissa.

"I don't know, but it's a moot point with him. He's not interested, and I've overheard him on the phone with more than one woman. When he's around, he'll sometimes use the empty office next to mine to make phone calls. It's hard not to overhear."

I wrinkle my nose. "Yeah, if he has multiple women in his life, you don't want any part of that."

thirty-nine

. . .

Randall

"You're driving me crazy," Ash says. "Please get out of this apartment and go do something."

We spent most of the day yesterday with Mom, and now it's late Sunday afternoon and I'm anxiously awaiting the women's return from the lake later today. I don't know whether to expect Wendy to call me or want to see me tonight.

"I don't have anybody to do anything with," I say as I flip through the TV channels for the seventeenth time in the past hour.

"You need to find some more friends."

"I know. But how? I've never had to go out and find new friends before."

It's true. At school, it was easy, because I was constantly around groups of people with similar interests to me. And when I moved back to Chicago after law school, I reconnected with a few childhood friends and was absorbed into their group. They honestly weren't my favorite people in the world, but they were mostly fun, until one of them slept with my girlfriend. I'm not all that sad to not have them in my life anymore, but I'm lonely.

Ash snorts. "I feel so sorry for you."

"Come on, man. Help me out here."

"Well, there's Bobby."

"Yeah, and it turns out I like him, but he's only here part of the time, so that's not exactly helpful."

"Anybody at Carter-Jenkins? What about Brian? He's a good dude."

I narrow my eyes at him. "If he's such a 'good dude,' why aren't you friends with him? You worked with him for two years."

"I don't need as many people around me as you do."

He's right again. He can get by with a couple of close friends, but I thrive in a group.

Ash adds, "Ask Wendy what she thinks about Brian. She'll know if the two of you would hit it off as friends."

I shrug. "Okay. I can do that. But it doesn't help me right now."

"What will help *me* is for you to stop changing the channel every three seconds. It's nice outside for a change. Go out on the balcony and read your book."

Much to his surprise, I push myself off the couch, drop the remote on his chest, and do what he says.

When the phone rings several hours later, pulling my focus from my book, I hope it's Wendy, but I'm pretty sure it'll be Leslie calling for Ash. My heart races as I wait to find out, but when my brother doesn't come out to get me within thirty seconds, I give up hoping and start reading again.

"I'm heading over to Leslie's," he says through the balcony screen door a few minutes later.

I close my book and pull my feet off the small patio table they were resting on. "Did she say how things went?"

"Sounds like they had a good time."

I hold my hands palm up. "That's all you've got? They had a good time?"

"We didn't have a full conversation because I'm going over there."

"But I want details now."

He shrugs. "Tough. I'll see you later." Then he's gone.

I head back into the apartment in search of something to eat.

There's not much in the fridge, but I'm not about to leave to get something, because I don't want to miss a potential call from Wendy. Of course, I could call her, but I'm not sure she'd want me to. I'm trying to let her set the pace, and I don't want to move too fast.

An hour later, when I haven't heard from her, I can't take it anymore. I pick up the phone and punch in her number, but I stop before hitting the last digit and hang up again. I do this two more times before smacking myself on the back of the head and dialing her entire number. I groan when the busy signal beeps in my ear, and I hang the phone back up.

Ten long minutes later I'm about to try again when it rings.

I grab it up. "Hello?"

"Hi."

My smile is so big it hurts. "Did you have a good weekend?"

"I did. Um …"

"Yeah?" I prompt.

"Do you want to come over?"

My heart leaps into my throat. "I'll be there soon. Have you eaten dinner?"

"No."

"Hungry?"

"Famished."

"How about I pick up a pizza on the way?"

"Sounds perfect. Thank you."

"What toppings do you want?"

"Ham and pineapple."

"Say it ain't so."

Wendy giggles. "It's so."

"I hope you realize that's a travesty."

"Travesty or not, it's what I like. You can get whatever you like on your half."

"My half? I think I'll be eating more than half. I'm a lot bigger than you."

"You get half. If you attempt to deprive me of one ounce of my half of that pizza, there will be hell to pay."

"Noted."

Wendy laughs when she spies the two pizza boxes in my hands as she opens her door.

"Didn't want to test me?" she teases.

"Didn't want any pineapple juice on one ounce of my half of the pizza," I reply as I enter and set the boxes on the table, where plates and drinks await us.

She giggles, and when I turn back around to her, she's only a foot away. I'm dying to kiss her, but there's not a chance I'm making the first move. We gaze at each other for a few seconds, and then she steps forward, wraps her arms around me, and rests her cheek against my chest.

"I missed you," she whispers.

I fold my arms around her and hold her tight. "Same here."

It feels so right to hold her again, but I can't help the tiny pang of disappointment that she didn't kiss me. I hope she doesn't regret her choice to kiss me on Friday, and if she doesn't, I hope it wasn't a one-time thing.

After a few seconds, she leans her head back so she can look up at me. "Just so you know, I want to kiss you, but I also want to talk to you. I'm pretty sure if we kiss now, we'll never get to the talking *or* the eating, and I'm starving."

"I'm starving for you, but I'll settle for pizza." I lean down and press my lips to her forehead before letting go of her and pulling out her chair. "Your dinner awaits, my lady."

She sits. "Why thank you, kind sir."

I push her chair in and take a seat around the corner of the table from her. My leg bumps into her knee, and when she doesn't move her leg away, neither do I. "Are we conversing in Austen speak again?"

"Indeed." She inclines her head toward me. "And you shall serve me."

I chuckle as I open her pizza box and slide two pieces onto her plate. "As you wish."

We eat the first few bites of our pizza in companionable silence, and then I say, "Would you care to regale me with tales of your adventures with my female relations?"

She smiles. "Yes, but I can't do it in Austen speak. It takes more energy than I have at the moment."

"My sisters wore you out, huh?"

"They have a lot more energy than this old lady, I'll tell you that."

"You're not an old lady," I gently chastise her.

"Much older than them."

"True, but not old."

She nods. "We had a really good time. I enjoyed getting to know them better. They're a lot alike in many ways, but very different in others."

"Yeah, they're an interesting pair. Tonya often acts more like the youngest child than Sonya does. She's more impulsive and adventurous, while Sonya is more steady and introspective, though not nearly on the scale Ash is. But when they're together, Sonya feeds off Tonya and is spunkier."

"Don't take offense at this," she says, "but it seems like you and Ash are kind of like that, too."

"Yeah, he seems more like the oldest, more responsible child who was born to be a leader, while I've always been more irresponsible and less likely to take the lead in anything other than getting into trouble and screwing things up."

forty

. . .

Wendy

"Is that really how you feel about yourself?" I ask Randall. "Do you think you're an irresponsible screwup who's not a good leader?"

"Sometimes," he readily admits.

"I disagree."

His hand halts as he reaches into the pizza box for another piece. "You do?"

My heart goes out to him. It's no wonder he doubts himself, considering the way his father has always treated him. "I do."

He finally grabs his slice of pizza, and he doesn't look at me when he says, "Even after what I did?"

"Yes. Have you made irresponsible decisions? Of course. We all do. But that's not who you are. You aren't an irresponsible person—you simply sometimes do things that are irresponsible."

He chews a bite of pizza as he thinks about what I said. "That's an interesting way of looking at it."

"It's the right way of looking at it. You wouldn't have made it through an elite prep school, college, and law school if you were irresponsible. George wouldn't have hired you if he thought you were irresponsible. You're not who your father has led you to believe you are, Randall. You're a smart, strong, caring man."

With a quick glance at me he says somewhat accusingly, "But you said Ash is more like the older brother."

"I did, but I didn't mean it in the way you took it. Ash is more structured and controlled and focused on achievement, like oldest children typically are, whereas you're more social, adventurous, and charming. Neither is better than the other. The two of you are simply the opposite of most sibling pairs. That's all I was saying."

"Oh."

I reach over and take his free hand in mine. "As for your leadership abilities, I saw them when we were working on the proposal for the Diego Sanchez Foundation. It seemed like Ash took the lead on that, and in the most obvious ways he did, but you had a knack for making suggestions and observations that gently steered us in the right direction at the right time. I don't think you realized you were doing it. I know Ash didn't realize it, but I think George did. I've also seen you doing it at Carter-Jenkins, and I believe that's the sign of a true leader—guiding people where they need to go without them knowing it."

"And without me knowing it either, apparently." He shoots me a wry grin. "Thank you for helping me see that."

"You're welcome." I squeeze his hand and let go of it.

He tilts his chair onto its back legs. "How'd you learn so much about all this stuff?"

"I work in PR. It's my job to understand how people tick and why they do what they do, and to pinpoint the things that make them unique and attractive to others. And I'm not talking about physical attractiveness."

Randall smirks at me. "But if you were going to talk about my physical attractiveness …"

I roll my eyes at him.

"Come on, now," he prompts. "Don't hold out on me."

"Are you seriously fishing for more compliments from me?"

"How about if I start?" He links his hands behind his head.

"Start what? Complimenting yourself?"

He shakes his head. "Start by talking about *your* exquisite physical attractiveness."

Randall doesn't miss the blush that starts on my chest and quickly moves upward to my face. He closely watches its progression with a satisfied grin.

"I'm thinking you need to learn how to take a compliment, Glinda."

I swallow hard but don't reply. He's right. I have a hard time receiving compliments, especially from men. I never believe they're sincere.

"First," he says, "I love your curves."

The temperature of my skin increases a few more degrees as his eyes take me in, and I squirm in my seat as he peruses me for so long I'm not sure he's going to say anything else.

He finally continues, "I can tell you don't love your body, but I think it's perfect." The heat in his gaze assures me he's one hundred percent sincere.

"Thank you," I murmur.

"Your hair is magnificent. Running my fingers through those fiery waves is one of my absolute favorite things in the world."

I shiver. It's one of my favorite things, too.

His chair legs hit the floor, and he reaches out to caress my cheek with the back of his hand, triggering goosebumps over my entire body. "Your skin is so soft and pure. I know you don't love this creamy tone, since it seems to be every woman's goal to be as tan as possible these days, but it suits you to a T. I don't want it to be marred by the sun or a tanning bed. I love being able to tell when I'm making you blush, like you are now. And this sprinkling of freckles across your nose and cheeks has been driving me crazy for weeks." His fingertips dance across my skin. "I want to kiss each and every one of them."

I'm now breathing heavily and not at all ashamed of it.

"Would you like me to go on?" he asks with a soft smile as he moves his hand back to the table.

I nod while staring intently at his hand, as if that will make it reach out to touch me again.

"While I could rave about your physical beauty for days, the thing I find most stunning about you is your heart."

My gaze jumps back to his eyes, which are pinning me with a look so tender I feel a pricking behind my eyes, and my belly fills with heat.

He continues, "You're kind and thoughtful, and you find so

much joy in helping people and showing them the strength and beauty and potential in themselves. I love watching it, but being on the receiving end of it is life altering."

My eyes are now filled with tears. "Do you mean it?"

"I mean all of it. More than you know."

I stand on trembling legs and hold my hand out to him. "Come with me."

He rises to his feet and takes my hand in his, and I guide him to the couch, where he takes a seat and helps me climb onto his lap. I curl against him as I usually do, but instead of resting my head on his shoulder, I tilt my face to his. He brushes a tear off my cheek with his thumb and then keeps stroking my cheek as he stares into my eyes.

"Kiss me, Randall." I grip the front of his shirt. "Kiss me like you've never kissed anyone before."

forty-one

. . .

Randall

I have never felt like I do in this moment with Wendy—this moment before I kiss her because she desperately wants me to, not because she's hoping she can move past my mistakes. In the past I've told women I loved them, and I truly believed I did, but now I realize I was sorely mistaken. What I felt for them was lust mixed with a dose of affection. What I'm feeling now is love, pure and simple.

"Please, Randall." Wendy's hand slides into my hair and her fingernails lightly scrape my scalp. "Don't make me wait any longer."

I close the distance between us and kiss her gently, slowly, trying to communicate my feelings without words. I know she can't handle the words yet, so I'll wait to say them, but I want her to feel them. She melts into me, savoring the kiss along with me.

Wendy asked me to kiss her like I've never kissed anyone before, but what's happening between us is unlike anything I've ever imagined. I never knew kissing could be like this—so sweet yet intimate and soul-connecting. This kiss isn't a gateway to more. It *is* more.

When her lips make their way to my neck and along my collar, I suck in a breath and am reminded why I wouldn't let her do this before. My hands slide into her hair, and I gently guide her mouth back to mine before we pass the point of no return. I can't imagine she's ready for anything beyond kissing, so I save her from the regrets that would surely come.

We take only brief breaks to catch our breaths and smile at each other before losing ourselves again. Eventually my legs go numb and I pull away from her mouth and shift her in my arms.

"You okay?" she asks.

"Better than I've ever been … except I can't feel my legs."

"Oh! Let me get off you, then."

"I want to argue with you, but I currently feel like a floating torso, so it's probably for the best if you do."

She giggles and slides off me. Then she sits cross-legged next to me so she's facing my side with her knees touching my leg. When she grins at me with a twinkle in her eye, I wonder what she's about to do. Then she starts karate-chopping my leg with her tiny hands, and I burst into laughter.

"Can you feel it yet?" she asks, hands chopping up and down my thigh.

"It's starting to tingle."

While she pounds the life back into my leg, I lift my hand to her head and run my fingers through her hair over and over, reveling in the silky feel of it sliding across my skin.

She closes her eyes. "Mmm, keep doing that."

"Does it make you tingle?" I tease.

"Maybe." She opens her eyes back up and smirks. "Is the feeling back in your leg?"

It's been back for a while, but I say, "Almost."

She doubles down on the chopping, making me laugh again. "All right, that one's good," I state. "On to the other one, Daniel-san."

"Nope," she says. "Now I want to see you try to walk with one numb leg, Mr. Miyagi."

"Why am I Mr. Miyagi? At least I should be the handsome blonde dude." It's been a few years since I took my college girl-friend to see *The Karate Kid*, and I can't remember the guy's name.

"Johnny? He's a bully! You're not a bully." She pokes my chest.

"You're a wise old man deep down in this heart, just like Mr. Miyagi."

I capture her hand in mine and bring her finger to my lips for a kiss. "How did I ever find someone like you?"

"You didn't find me," she says matter-of-factly and pushes up onto her knees so she can kiss my cheek. "I found you."

"Ooo, cocky much?" I wrap an arm around her waist so she can't sit back down.

"Only when I'm with you. Is the feeling back in your other leg?"

"Yes." I kiss her nose.

"Good. Now you can spoon me. It's been two and a half weeks since I've gotten a good spooning from you, and I'm really feeling the negative effects."

I chuckle as I maneuver us into position. "And what would those effects be?"

She settles in against me and sighs. "Oh, a little of this and a little of that. You know: gout, indigestion, sciatica, bunions, the usual."

"I didn't realize a lack of spooning could trigger such severe side effects."

She rubs her bare foot along my leg. "Feel those bunions? It's been a rough eighteen days."

"Ah, so you've been counting the days, then?" I smile into her hair.

"Every single one," she says softly.

I pull her more closely to me. "I'm sorry it's my fault it's been so long. I know you don't want me to apologize any more, and I promise this will be the last time, but I'm so sorry, Wendy." I pull her more tightly into me. "So sorry."

"I know," she whispers.

Wendy's breaths soon even out, which fills me with hope for our future. If she can so easily fall asleep in my arms, she's on her way back to trusting me.

I startle awake when Wendy slides out of my embrace. "Where you going?" I mumble.

"Little girls' room," she whispers. "Go back to sleep."

"I should go home."

"You're welcome to stay there on the couch, though you'd probably be more comfortable at home."

Even in my groggy state, I catch onto the fact that she didn't invite me to sleep in her bed again, and I slowly sit up and stretch. "Yeah, I'd better go."

"Okay, let me go to the bathroom, and I'll be right back to say goodnight." She scampers off.

By the time she returns, I'm mostly awake and leaning against the wall by the door. She slips her arms around me, and I lean down to kiss the top of her head. I'm not going to kiss her on the mouth before I go, partly because I'm in dire need of mouthwash after our three-hour late-night nap, and partly because I'm afraid if we start kissing again, I won't leave.

"You didn't kiss each and every one of my freckles tonight," Wendy says.

I chuckle. "We'll save that for next time."

"And the time after that," she adds.

"Deal." I press my lips to her head again and then set her away from me. "I'll see you at work in a few short hours."

She smiles. "Thanks for coming over."

"Thanks for inviting me."

As I start to open the door, she hesitatingly says, "Randall?"

I turn back to her. "Yes?"

"I forgive you. You know that, right?"

I nod, although I'm still a bit in awe of that reality.

"I also want us to officially date again, but I'm not ready to let you back into my bed, even for an innocent sleepover. I'll get there, but I can't do it yet. Okay?"

"Yeah. I understand."

"Thanks for not pressuring me."

"I'd never pressure you, Wendy. That's not who I am."

"I know." She wrings her hands. "I'm not used to that, is all."

I gather her back into my arms. "I'm sorry you're not used to it, but you need to get used to it, because I'll never do that to you. Please believe that."

She nods against me. "I do."

forty-two

. . .

Wendy

Randall and I soon settle into a rhythm. We eat lunch together at least once a week, and we spend time together three or four nights a week. A few times, we've taken his sisters out to eat or to a movie when their dad's not around. And we've continued the pattern of not kissing when we first see each other, to ensure we spend time talking first.

It's not uncommon for us to fall asleep together on my couch, but I still haven't invited him to stay over again. True to his word, he hasn't complained about going home in the middle of the night, but I know he's disappointed each time it happens. I also know I need to move forward on this issue, but every time I'm tempted to ask him to crawl into my bed with me, I ultimately can't do it.

On a Tuesday night a few weeks after the lake weekend, I finally summon up the nerve. Randall comes by late, after going out with Brian and a few other guys from work, and as soon as we hit the couch, I ask, "Will you stay with me all night tonight?"

Randall smooths a lock of hair behind my ear. "You know I will, but are you sure?"

I place my hand over his heart. "I am."

"To be clear, you're talking about me sleeping here, right? Not anything else?"

"Sleeping. One step at a time. Is that okay?"

"Of course it's okay. But as soon as you're ready to take that next step, you let me know."

He gives me a wink, and I giggle.

"Just so you know," I say, "my body has been ready for a long time, but my heart still isn't quite there."

I've determined that until I know with absolute certainty that I love him and he loves me back, I won't take that final step with him. Although I care much more for him than any other man I've ever been with, I'm holding myself back precisely because of those feelings. I know I won't be able to bear the pain if I take that last intimate leap with him and then he shatters me again.

He kisses my forehead. "Your heart matters most, so I'm glad that's what you're listening to."

That very heart melts at his words, which makes it a little more ready.

He asks, "What's our topic of conversation for tonight?"

Each time we're together, we pick a different topic to discuss. Sometimes it's serious, and other times it's silly. One night we ranked our favorite Muppets, gave detailed explanations for each, and critiqued the other person's obviously wrong choices. But tonight it's time to be serious, which is the primary reason I want him to stay with me.

"There's two topics tonight. First is me visiting Andrea," I say.

"Ah. You got your flights?"

"Yes, Leslie and I are flying to Arkansas a week from Friday. We'll take off work that day, and then we'll fly back on Sunday." I pause. "And we're staying with Shannon."

Randall nods. "Sounds like a good plan."

I search his eyes. "You're okay with the Shannon thing?"

He cups my cheek with one hand. "I don't love it. You know that. But I trust you, and I trust Leslie's judgment, and I'm choosing to trust Shannon, too, even though I don't know him very well."

"Thank you. I know this isn't easy for you, but I'm glad you trust me. Now for the other topic: the divorce."

He drops his hand from my face and leans his head back against the couch cushion. "Mom's filing next week."

"Everything's in order?"

"The lawyer needs to do a few last-minute things, and then the Order of Protection will be filed and Dad will be served."

"How do you feel about that?"

"Honestly, I have mixed feelings. I want Mom and the girls to get away from him, so I'm glad for their sakes. I'm also looking forward to the lawyer taking Dad down, which I'm fairly certain will happen, with the evidence we have against him when it comes to his mistresses and his threats against Mom."

When he doesn't tell me the other side of what he's feeling, I prompt, "But …"

"But my parents are getting divorced. I know I'm an adult, and it's been a long time coming, and it's what needs to happen, but it's still hard, you know?"

My eyes mist up, and I nod.

"I'm also afraid of what he'll do to retaliate against all of us. And I can't help but believe Ash and I set all this into motion when we left the firm. I feel a sense of responsibility for it."

I sit up straight, look him directly in the eye, and smooth my hand down the side of his face. "None of what is happening with your dad is your fault. *None of it.* He's the one who chose to treat his family like dirt—not you. And you should be proud of your mom for finally having the courage to get out of an abusive marriage."

"I am, but how did I not know he was emotionally and verbally abusing her and physically threatening her? I should have known, considering the way he's always treated me."

"It wasn't your responsibility to see it or do anything about it. You were a kid the last time you lived in their house full-time, and I'm sure he hid it well. Most abusers do." A tear slides down his cheek and I kiss it away. "I hate that you're having to deal with this."

We're both silent for a while and then he says, "Will you hold me? You know I love being the cuddler, while you're the cuddlee, but can we switch it up tonight?"

"We can, and we will."

I readjust my position so I can wrap my arms around him and

hold him tightly in my embrace. He rests his head against mine and strokes my hair without saying a word. We stay in this position until well after I feel all the tension leave his body. Then I stand and hold my hand out to him. "Come on. Let's get ready for bed."

We brush our teeth side by side, and he leaves me to change into my armadillo pajamas he loves so much. When I come back out, he's lying in my bed in my brother's sweatpants. The sight of him shirtless in my bed is nearly my undoing, but this is not the night to do more than sleep.

I turn off the light, climb in next to him, and curl against his side with my head resting on his shoulder and my arm wrapped securely around his middle. He pulls the sheet over us as I try not to think about the fact that my cheek and arm are touching his warm, bare skin.

"You okay?" I ask him.

"I will be."

I tilt my head up to look at him in the darkness. "Anything else I can do to help?"

He pulls me a little closer against him. "You're doing exactly what I need you to do."

forty-three

. . .

Randall

Wendy and I didn't kiss at all tonight, but shockingly I don't care. We took a giant step forward in our relationship, and that's more important than any amount of kissing. The woman I love is sleeping soundly in my arms in her bed, which would have been unimaginable to either of us a short time ago.

Wendy snorts lightly, and I smile. Even her sleeping noises are adorable.

"You're really here?" she mumbles. "Not a dream?"

"I'm here." I caress her arm with my thumb. "Go back to sleep."

"Mmmm." Her fingers flex into my chest, and her breathing immediately evens out again.

I doze off and on all night, waking every time Wendy moves or makes a noise, but I don't mind. Someday, Lord willing, I'll be used to her sleeping against me, but for now I want to enjoy every second of it.

When her clock radio alarm goes off, Rick Astley is singing "Never Gonna Give You Up," which makes me smile through my morning haze. I should despise this song, since I've let Wendy down and made her cry. But it's also a reminder that I plan to do everything I can to not hurt her again, and I definitely never intend to give her up.

"Off," Wendy demands. "Turn it off."

"But I like this song," I protest, making no move to disentangle us from each other and shut off the alarm.

"Don't care if I never hear it again. Annoying song."

I chuckle. "Your spider-monkey ways have rendered my limbs useless, so you're going to have to turn it off yourself."

"Don't wanna let go." Her moving lips tickle my chest. "I like being a monkey."

"Then you're going to have to put up with Rick."

"Fine."

After a few seconds, I say, "It's driving you crazy, isn't it?"

"Mmhm."

"There's an easy way to fix that problem."

She groans and pulls herself off me, but as soon as she hits the snooze button, she's back.

I sift my fingers through her hair. "We need to get up."

"No."

"The next time I stay over, I'm turning Patrick's picture around to face the wall. I feel like he's staring at us."

Wendy giggles. "He's our chaperone."

"He's a pretty good one. I'm not about to do anything inappropriate with him watching. Now, if you don't get off me—and particularly if you don't stop pressing your elbow into my gut—you're going to have to change your sheets."

"Why?" When I don't answer, she says, "Oh. Little boys' room. Got it." She rolls off me again.

While I'm in the bathroom, I change back into my clothes and brush my teeth, so I can kiss her before I leave. As soon as I open the door, Wendy darts in.

"You woke up fast," I state.

"Want to kiss you before you go," she says as she loads toothpaste onto her toothbrush.

I lean against the doorframe and watch her brush her teeth.

"You're so weird," she says after she rinses her mouth.

I cross my arms over my chest. "Why do you say that?"

"Because you watched me brush my teeth like a psycho, like you did in the mirror last night."

"I didn't realize that was one of the hallmarks of a psychopath."

"It's the main one." She tugs my arms down and then reaches up to my neck to pull my head down to hers. "Now kiss me."

"She finally let you stay the night again, huh?" Ash says as he stands in our kitchen eating a bowl of cereal.

"Yup."

"That's all I get?"

I stick a piece of bread in the toaster. "Yup."

"No other details you'd like to share?"

"We slept. End of story."

"Gotcha. That's a big step, though."

"Yup."

He rinses his bowl and spoon and loads them in the dishwasher. "As much as I've enjoyed this scintillating conversation, I need to get to work. See you tonight?"

"Maybe." I'm hoping not, because that will likely mean I'm with Wendy again.

"All righty then." Ash shrugs. "I guess I'll see you sometime."

I watch him leave while wondering why I wouldn't talk to him. I honestly have no idea, unless it's because I'm tired from lack of sleep. No point worrying about it, though. Ash won't be offended that I wasn't talkative.

A couple minutes later, the intercom by the front door buzzes, startling me so much I drop my freshly buttered toast. I pick it up, blow on it, and take a bite while I cross to the door and press the button to talk to the doorman. "What's up, Jeff?"

"Wendy O'Halloran is here for you."

My eyebrows raise. "Send her up."

I open the door and stand in the doorway with an eye on the elevator at the end of the hall, munching on my toast while praying Wendy's here for a good reason and isn't having some sort of crisis. The elevator doors finally open, revealing an absolute vision in a green skirt suit. Wendy's mouth curves into a smile when she spots me, and she rushes down the hall without ever taking her eyes off mine.

"Everything okay?" I ask when she approaches.

Instead of answering, she pushes me inside, slams the door, tosses the rest of my toast to the side, yanks my head down to hers, and kisses me like we've been apart for weeks, not an hour. Without breaking the connection, I walk us over to the couch and sit down on the arm so our faces are on the same level and she can stand between my legs. Though I'm itching to run my fingers through her hair, I refrain, as I don't want to thoroughly mess it up, because we both need to be at work soon.

I let her continue to control the pace, which borders on frantic at first but then evens out into a slower, more sensual kiss. After a few minutes, her mouth draws away from mine, but she leaves her arms looped around my neck.

"What was that for?" I ask breathlessly.

"Making up for not kissing you last night."

"You did a pretty good job of that earlier this morning."

She smirks at me. "I did, didn't I?"

"Indeed. How'd you know I'd still be home?" I ask as I rearrange a few strands of her hair.

"I took a chance. I was waiting for the bus when I decided I needed to kiss you again, so I walked over here."

"What if Ash was in here when you marched in and mauled my face?"

She traces my lips with her fingers, making me want to pull her fully onto the couch with me.

"He's a big boy. He could have handled it. But I knew he wasn't here, because I saw his car pull out of the garage," she explains.

"Ah. Everything worked out just right for you, then."

"It did. And I'm also getting a ride to work from my boyfriend." Now she's tracing my jawline.

This is the first time she has referred to me as her boyfriend, which makes my chest swell. "Oh, you are?"

She nods. "Uh-huh."

"Even though I refused to trade in the car you hate?" I plan to replace it with something more practical and affordable, but I haven't told her that yet. It's more fun to listen to her complain about it.

"I don't hate it."

I cock my head to the side, momentarily disrupting her finger tracing. "Pretty sure you do."

"I hate the backseat, not the entire car."

"Backseats can be fun." I wiggle my eyebrows at her, but she pinches them between her fingers to keep them from moving.

"Not your backseat. You'd never fit in there by yourself, much less both of us together."

"We could always try. It would make for a great story."

She giggles. "I'd rather make out with you on the couch."

"Who said anything about making out?"

She swats my chest. "You're a bad, bad man."

"What are you talking about? Backseats are an excellent place for a conversation."

"Funny guy." She takes a step back and tugs at my hand. "Let's go, or we'll be late."

"Yes, ma'am."

forty-four

. . .

Wendy

"What's our topic for tonight?" Randall asks me on Saturday night. A cold front came through earlier today, dropping the temperature to a bearable level with low humidity, so we walked over to the lake, where a brisk breeze is blowing and whipping up waves. I'm sitting between his legs with his arms draped around me.

"Church," I say.

"Church?"

"Drop those eyebrows back down," I say.

"How did you know they were up?"

"From the tone of your voice."

His arms tighten around me. "I love that you know that."

I smile and twist slightly so I can look at him. "Me, too." I give him a quick peck on the cheek before facing the lake again.

"What about church?" he asks.

"I want to go tomorrow."

"Do you usually go to church? Is this something I've completely failed to learn about you?"

I shake my head. "No. I went as a kid, and I go when I'm visiting my family, but I've never gone here."

"But you want to go now?"

"Uh-huh. With you, if you're willing."

"Why? I mean, why the sudden urge to go to church, not why go with me. And of course I'll go with you."

"I miss it."

My hair blows up with a gust of wind, and Randall gathers it in his hands and tucks it down the back of my shirt.

"What do you miss about it?"

"The routine, the tradition, the feelings I get when I'm there."

"What kinds of feelings?"

"Peace, mostly."

"I know what you mean. I miss those same things."

"I also want to raise my kids in church," I add, hoping the statement won't make him run for the hills. I've not felt comfortable talking to him about children yet, but we need to.

He's silent for a moment before asking carefully, "You want kids?"

I nod. "I want three."

"Me, too," he whispers.

I breathe a silent sigh of relief. "I don't want to get pregnant tomorrow or anything," I add, "but I also don't want to wait long to have kids once I'm married. I'll be thirty-one in a few weeks. I don't have all the time in the world."

When he doesn't say anything, my heart inches up into my throat, but then I realize he probably doesn't know what's appropriate to say, since we haven't talked about a hypothetical marriage either.

I ask him, "Would you want to wait long to have kids after you get married?"

"I'd be okay with it either way," he says. "Sooner or later, doesn't matter."

We're both quiet for a while, and he rests his chin on my head as we watch the waves roll in.

"You'll be an amazing mom," he finally says.

"Yeah?"

"You'll be so patient with them and so loving and supportive, like you are with me." He presses a kiss to the top of my head as warmth fills my chest at his words.

"And you'll be a great dad," I say.

"I'm not so sure about that."

I twist in his arms so I can look at him. "Why do you say that?"

"I didn't have the best role model, did I? What do I know about being a good dad?"

My heart aches for him. I fully turn to face him, and I grip his hands in mine.

"That has nothing to do with how good of a dad you'll be. First of all, your father taught you all the things to not do or say to your kids. Second, I've seen how you interact with your sisters, which tells me most of what I need to know. And finally, I know how you treat me and care for me, and if you put even half as much effort into being a good parent, you'll be knocking it out of the park with your future kids." I almost said, "our future kids," but I caught myself in time.

He gives me a shaky smile. "That may all be true, but I'm terrified I'll mess them up."

"Oh, baby," I shift closer and wrap my arms around him, "you won't mess them up. You won't always know what to do. Nobody does. But you'll love them with all your heart, and I have no doubt you'll do everything you can to raise your children up to be good, kind people. Don't you ever believe you won't be a good dad. Don't let your father or anyone or anything else make you believe such an absurd thing." I lean back so I can look him in the eye. "Promise me."

"Why are you so good to me?" he asks.

"Promise me."

"I promise."

I nod. "And I'm good to you because I care about you—*so much.*"

I wish I could tell him I love him, but I'm scared to death to fully admit it to him. I rarely think about him kissing Tammy anymore, but a tiny part of me is still terrified of being hurt again. I realize I'm being contradictory after what I said to him, but I can't quite believe a relationship is actually going to work out for me, though I want to believe it so badly.

Randall cups my face in his hands and gives me the sweetest, softest kiss. He doesn't draw it out, likely because we're in public, but after his mouth pulls away from mine, he turns me around and tucks me back against him. He now holds me tightly, possessively, and I'm feeling more cherished than I ever dreamed I could.

"Do you have a church picked out for tomorrow?" he asks.

"The place Leslie and Ash go to isn't too far away from our apartments. It's close enough to walk there."

Randall's body tenses in shock. "Ash goes to church?"

"He's been going with Leslie."

"How did I not know that?"

"You're apparently not very observant on Sunday mornings. Plus, your brother is a man of many mysteries."

"You're not wrong there."

"Leslie says it's a causal type of place. You don't need to wear a suit or anything. Just khakis and a Polo."

"That could be one reason I didn't know my brother became a churchgoer," he muses. "If he walked out of the apartment in a suit on a Sunday, I think I'd notice."

"Tell yourself whatever makes you feel better about your lack of knowledge of your brother's comings and goings," I tease.

"Speaking of comings and goings, how are you feeling about going to meet Andrea next weekend?"

"Good. I'm excited to meet her and Emily."

"She decided for sure that you'll meet Emily?"

"First it'll be the two of us meeting for dinner on Friday evening, and then if that goes well, I'll meet Emily on Saturday."

"She sounds like a good mom."

"Yeah, I like that she's being careful with her daughter's heart, even though I'm dying to meet my niece."

"You'll meet her. There's absolutely no way Andrea won't fall in love with you." He tilts my head so he can kiss my temple. "You sure you don't want me to go with you?"

"I'd love to have you with me, but you need to be here for your mom and sisters in case things go poorly with your dad."

My body moves with his chest as he takes a few deep breaths, and I feel his heart pound against my back.

"Things had better not go poorly," he grits out between clenched teeth.

"I hope not, and I wish I could promise you things will be fine, but you need to be prepared for the worst, for the girls' sake."

"I don't want to think about what the worst would be."

"Be ready to get them out of that house if you need to. I know your mom is determined not to leave, but you need to protect your sisters in any way possible—not only from physical harm but also from additional emotional harm. Do you know exactly when your dad will be served the papers?"

"The current plan is Thursday at one o'clock."

"You're taking the day off work, right?" I ask.

"Yes. Ash and I both are."

"Okay, that morning, after you know your dad has left for work, go get the girls and take them to your apartment. Keep them there for as long as you need to—overnight or for a few nights if necessary. They don't need to witness what happens at home."

I feel him nodding. "I like that idea, but I can't leave them alone, and I don't want Mom to be alone, either."

"Then you stay with them and let Ash be with your mom."

"I think that might work."

"Tomorrow you're telling your sisters what's happening?"

"Mom is bringing them to our place tomorrow evening, and we'll tell them together. They're going to be mad we didn't tell them before now, but we couldn't risk them letting something slip in front of Dad or to any of their friends. It's still a little risky, but they'll never forgive us if we wait until Thursday to tell them."

"If they need someone who's not family to talk to about it afterward, bring them to me."

He squeezes me. "I told you you'll be an amazing mom. You're already proving it with the way you care for my sisters."

forty-five

. . .

Randall

"Do you want us to put off our trip to Arkansas so we'll be here for you next weekend?" Wendy asks Ash and me. We're eating lunch at Pat's Diner after church while discussing the logistics for the week.

"No," I say, and Ash shakes his head in agreement with me. "You need to do this. You're ready to meet your sister and niece, and I don't want our family's mess to keep you from meeting your own family. You're going."

"Okay." She places her hand on my arm. "Thank you."

I know she feels bad about the timing, but if she doesn't go this weekend, she won't have another chance for at least another six weeks, due to scheduling issues. I'm not letting her make that sacrifice for me.

Leslie looks at Wendy with a question in her eyes, and Wendy nods.

"I can stay, though," Leslie says. "I can be here for the girls if both of you need to be with your mom."

"No," Ash now says. "Wendy needs you with her, and you haven't seen Shannon in a couple months. Randall and I talked earlier this morning about bringing Melissa in on what's happening. We're going to tell her what's going on and see if she can spend time with the girls if needed next weekend."

"Oh, that's a great plan," Wendy says. "Your sisters had a blast with her at the lake."

"Yeah, Melissa's a lot of fun," Leslie says. "I didn't realize it until we spent an extended time with her. I think it helped that it was only women, and as more time passes since her engagement ended, the happier and more lighthearted she seems."

"Agreed. Melissa will be great for them next weekend," Wendy says, and then she looks back and forth between Ash and me. "But tonight, or any other night before we leave for Arkansas, if your sisters need women around them, bring them to one of us."

"We will," I say. "Thanks."

Ash thanks them as well and then asks Wendy, "Are you going to be able to meet Leslie's parents while you're there, or will you be with your family the whole time?"

"I'll be able to meet them on Friday."

"Yes," Leslie says, "Mom's planning to drive into the city to pick us up from the airport and take us to Shannon's, so he won't need to take off work to do that. Then Dad and my little sister Cynthia will drive in from Oakville after work to meet Wendy before she goes out to dinner with Andrea."

Wendy grins at Ash. "Are you jealous I'll get to meet her parents before you do?"

"A little," he admits with a smile. "But I'll get to meet them when they come here in a few weeks."

I try not to smile, knowing Ash plans on proposing to Leslie while they're here. Mom is going with us to help pick out a ring next week.

"I want to say I'll hate you all forever," Tonya says, "but that's not true. I'll probably only hate you for tonight. How could you keep this from us?"

True to form, Tonya is livid, while Sonya is sobbing in my arms on the love seat.

"We didn't want you to be upset or worried about it any longer than you had to be," Mom explains from her spot next to Tonya on the couch.

"We're already upset and worried because Dad's such a tyrant and treats you like you're lower than the deep end of the pool," Tonya retorts. "How did you think us knowing about the divorce would make things worse? In the long run, it'll make things ever so much better." She folds her arms over her chest. "I don't appreciate being treated like a baby."

"Tonya, stop it," Sonya chokes out. "They were only trying to protect us."

Tonya ignores her. "Do Leslie and Wendy know?"

"They do," Ash says.

She narrows her eyes at him. "Did they know when we went to the lake? Is that why they took us out of town—so you could plan this divorce without us around?"

Ash sighs, knowing he can't lie to her. "Yes."

"I cannot believe you did this to us, and I can't believe they betrayed us like that, either. I thought they were our friends!"

"They are," Sonya says, pulling away from me and wiping her face with a tissue. "They love us."

"When people love you, they don't keep things like this from you."

"They do," Sonya replies, sitting up straight and glaring at our sister. "They protect you from things that will hurt you. They give up their entire weekends to spend time with you. Don't you dare say Leslie and Wendy aren't our friends. They *are.*"

"Okay, fine. They're our friends. But I'm still mad." Tonya pouts, and I try to hide my smile, but she spots it and points at me, "And don't you laugh at me. You don't get to laugh."

I hold my hands up. "Not laughing. There's nothing funny about any of this."

"Kids," Mom says, "let's stop arguing about whether it was right or wrong for us to not tell you girls about this earlier. What's done is done. Now we need to focus on what's going to happen this week."

We lay out the plan for Thursday, and of course Tonya has something to say about it.

"We don't need Randall to babysit us. We need to be at home with Mom, supporting her."

"I'll be supporting Mom," Ash says. "You need to stay away."

"We don't." If Tonya were standing, she would undoubtedly have stomped her foot.

"You do," I say. "Dad has damaged us all enough. We're not letting him anywhere near you two after he finds out about this. You'll stay here for as long as we think is necessary to keep you safe."

Sonya turns her anxious gaze on me. "You think he'll hurt us? Like physically?"

"There's no telling what he'll do." We don't want to tell them about his threats against Mom if we don't have to.

"He'd never hit us," Tonya says. "That's not his style. He's never acted like he'd do that."

Mom, Ash, and I exchange looks, and Mom says, "He has with me."

Both girls gasp.

"He hits you?" Tonya says, eyes wide.

"No, but he has threatened to."

Sonya rushes over to Mom's side and throws her arms around her. "Mom! How could you not tell us? Why didn't you leave him before now?"

Tonya embraces Mom from the other side. "We would have *made* you leave him if we knew. I'm so sorry we didn't see what was happening."

"It's all right, girls," Mom says as she pats their legs, since there's nothing else she can do with the two of them basically wrapped around her. "It wasn't your job to see. And telling your children such a thing isn't anything most parents want to do."

Tonya lets go of Mom, takes a deep breath, and says, "Okay, we'll stay here with Randall on Thursday. But only because we don't want you three to worry about us, not because we can't handle Dad."

Ash says, "Good. Now, there's another secret I've been

keeping from you, but this is one you're going to love, and I'll need your help with it."

Sonya beams and claps her hands together. "You and Leslie are getting engaged!"

He chuckles. "I hope we are, but you have to promise not to let anything slip to Leslie about it."

"We promise!" Tonya says, bouncing in her seat. Much like Ash, she's not one to hold a grudge. "What do you need help with?"

"I need you girls to find out her ring size. Think you can manage that without her knowing what you're up to? You can let Wendy in on it if needed." He shoots a quick glance at me, and I nod. I know what he's doing—giving the girls a distraction from the divorce—and it seems to be working.

"Psh." Tonya flicks her wrist at us. "Child's play. We're on it."

forty-six

. . .

Wendy

I'm reading a book on my couch, trying not to wonder how things are going at Randall and Ash's apartment, when my phone rings.

"Hello?" I say into the receiver.

"It's me," Leslie says. "Ash is picking me up in a couple minutes. He'll have the girls with him, and he's dropping all three of us at your place. We'll be there soon."

"Sounds good. Did he say how things went?"

"He didn't say much, but he said it was better than he anticipated."

"That's good. I'll see you in a few minutes."

While I wait, I set out some snacks in case the girls are hungry. Soon, I'm buzzing them up, and a minute later they burst into my apartment. Well, Tonya and Sonya burst in. Leslie calmly enters behind them and gives me a wide-eyed look. I force myself not to giggle.

The sisters both take their shoes off inside the door, give me enthusiastic hugs, and then descend upon the snacks. They load up their plates, plop down on the couch, and kick their bare feet up onto the coffee table, making themselves right at home.

"What's happening here?" I whisper to Leslie as I pour us each a glass of wine.

"Beats me. I thought they'd be upset, but they seem the opposite."

I take a seat by the girls and let Leslie claim the easy chair.

"So," I say, "do you ladies want to talk about what's happening?"

"No," Tonya says.

"Yes, we do," Sonya counters. "We can't talk to anyone else about this until after Thursday, and we can't say much about it then."

"Yeah," Tonya adds, suddenly ready to talk, "we can't tell anyone any details, because we don't want Dad to hear about it and turn it against Mom somehow. We gotta keep our mouths shut."

"Except with you two," Sonya says.

"So how are you feeling about it?" I ask them.

"Mad," Tonya says.

"Sad," Sonya adds.

Tonya nods. "Yeah, that, too."

"Let's start with the anger," Leslie says. "Why are you mad?"

"Because Dad's an even bigger jackwad than we thought," Tonya says. "Did you know he threatened Mom?"

Wendy and I both nod.

"I don't know how she stood him all these years. I feel so bad for her. But I'm mad at her, too, because she didn't leave sooner and get us out of there."

I say, "It can be really hard to leave a situation like that, especially when you rely on the other person to provide for you and your children."

Tonya crosses her arms over her chest. "We don't need his money."

She would definitely miss it if it weren't there, but now's not the time to point that out.

"Okay," Leslie says, "but I think your mom maybe also didn't want to disrupt your lives. This is going to cause a lot of changes for all of you. They're not all bad changes, but even good change can be hard and stressful."

I turn sideways on the couch so I can see both girls. "Maybe focus on the fact that your mom has the courage to leave your dad now, and don't wonder what might have happened if she had done it years ago. There's nothing you can do to change that."

"Yeah, we need to support her." Sonya pokes Tonya's leg. "Not be mad at her."

"I'll be mad at her if I want to be mad at her, while also supporting her," Tonya retorts. "I'm also mad that Mom, our brothers, and you two," she points at Leslie and me, "have known about this for weeks and didn't tell us."

I wondered if that would be an issue. "I'm sorry we couldn't tell you, but it wasn't our information to tell, and your mom and brothers were trying to protect you as much as they could from what's coming. There was no need for you to have to worry about it for that long."

"But Ash and Randall had to worry about it," Sonya says, tears filling her eyes. "I'm sad they had to go through all the preparation without us being there to support them."

I take her hand in mine. "They had us, honey. Not that they wouldn't have loved your support, too, but we're not as close to the situation as you are. We've been able to be strong for them while they figured out how to create the best outcome for you two and your mom. And we're here for you, too. Whenever you need us—to talk to you, to cry with you, to distract you—we're here." I pause. "Well, except this weekend, when we'll be in Arkansas. But you'll have Melissa then, and you can still call us if you need to."

"Definitely," Leslie says. "I'll give you my brother's phone number."

"You shouldn't have to deal with our family's dysfunction," Tonya says. "That makes me mad, too. It's not just us who Dad's affected with his awfulness. You've had to deal with it, too, and that's not fair to you."

"We're happy go through this with you," Leslie says, "because we love all of you. We might not be family, but we'll support you like family."

"You're not family *yet*," Tonya says, her expression quickly changing from irritated to gleeful.

"*Tonya.*" Sonya pokes her again.

"What?" her sister replies. "They're dating our brothers, who are ridiculously in love with them. They'll be family." She nods with certainty.

I freeze at her words. Is Randall ridiculously in love with me? I know he's guarding his feelings toward me to some extent, due to not wanting to rush or spook me, but does he truly care for me enough that his sisters can tell?

"Does anybody need more snacks?" Leslie says as she gets to her feet, obviously choosing not to engage in the change of topic.

"I'll take some more cookies," Tonya says, "and a soda. Thanks."

"Coming right up, after I make a pit stop in the bathroom," Leslie tells her.

As soon as Leslie's out of sight, the girls hold a whispered conversation that includes a lot of giggling. Then they stop and both look at me.

"We know you can keep a secret," Tonya whispers to me, "so we're going to tell you one, but you can't tell Leslie."

"You gotta pinky swear," Sonya adds, also in a whisper, holding her finger out.

I curl my pinky around hers, and Tonya reaches over to add hers to the mix.

"I pinky swear," I say as solemnly as I can.

"Whisper!" Tonya whisper-shouts as we unlink our fingers.

I lower my voice. "Oops, sorry."

Tonya cuts a glance in the direction of the bathroom and says so quietly I can barely hear her, "Ash is going to propose to Leslie and wants us to find out her ring size!"

I clap my hand over my mouth so I don't shriek in excitement at the news, even though it's not surprising.

"You need me to help with that?" I murmur.

"Yes," Sonya says with a glare at Tonya, "because *she's* going to give it away if she tries. She's not exactly subtle."

Tonya glares right back at her. "If we didn't need to whisper, I'd be yelling at you for that."

Sonya shrugs. "It's true."

"Leave it with me," I say. "I'll find out and let you know." I could just tell Ash directly, but I don't want the girls to feel left out, and I know he doesn't either.

Suddenly, Tonya sits up straight. "Leslie, can you bring Sonya another cookie, too, please?"

"Sure thing."

Leslie must have turned the other way, because Tonya blows out a long breath and mouths, "That was close."

When Leslie rejoins us, it takes every ounce of strength I have to not grin at her like a fool. I now know why the girls were in such a strange mood when they arrived. Ash took a big chance telling them. I'm guessing he did so to give them something positive to think about this week, but it'll be a miracle if they don't spill the beans to Leslie before he has time to pop the question.

forty-seven

. . .

Randall

"Stop pacing," Tonya orders me. "You're driving us bananas. You're supposed to be helping us, not making us nervous."

I make another turn and stride across my living room again. "I can't stop. I want to know what's happening." It's now three o'clock on Thursday afternoon, and Dad was supposed to be served the papers at one. We should have heard something by now about how he's responding.

Sonya gets off the couch and wraps her arms around me when I pass her again, which finally forces me to stop. "Please, Randall. Sit down."

"Do we need to call Wendy?" Tonya asks me with narrowed eyes.

"No!"

"Ha!" Tonya points at me. "You're scared of her."

I peel Sonya's arms off me and move to the couch. "I'm not scared of her."

"But you don't want her to know you're acting like this, do you?"

No, because she'd be disappointed in me. I drop my head into my hands, and Sonya sits next to me and rubs circles on my back.

She says, "I think you need our support as much as we need yours today. Tell us what you're feeling."

I pound my fist into my knee. "I'm feeling like I should have insisted I be the one to stay with Mom. I'm the oldest. That should be my responsibility. And Ash knows you girls so much better than I do. He'd know what to do to make you feel better. Instead, I'm making everything worse."

Tonya sits on my other side and wraps an arm around me. "You're not."

"But you just said—"

"What I said was stupid," Tonya says. "They're your parents, too. You have as much right to be upset about what's happening as we are. You don't have to be strong for us all the time, Randall. If you're anxious or scared, you can say it. We can handle it. We're not little kids anymore. Let us help you, too."

I suck in a few deep breaths as I consider what she said, and I determine she's right. Plus, anything I'm thinking or feeling, they're probably thinking or feeling, too.

"Okay," I say, "the biggest thing is I'm scared Dad is going to carry out his threats and hurt Mom. Physically, I mean. He's already hurt her plenty in every other conceivable way."

"He won't hurt her," Sonya says. "Ash won't let him."

"What if he does?"

"He won't. Ash is practically a giant. Dad can't hurt Mom if Ash is there, no matter how hard he tries. You know that."

"But it should be me there. If Ash gets hurt because I wasn't man enough to be there, I'll never forgive myself."

"Randall," Tonya says, "you were man enough to insist your little sisters not witness whatever is happening between our parents today and to ignore your desire to be there in order to be here with us. That's as important as what Ash is doing."

"She's right," Sonya agrees. "I can't tell you how glad I am that I'm not there. Yes, I want to know what's happening, too, but I would've been a basket case if I'd been there, and then the rest of you would've been focused on me instead of Mom and whatever Dad was doing. All three of us are exactly where we need to be— right here, together."

Brrrring!

I jump up and grab the phone off the end table, my heart beating wildly. "Hello?"

"It's me," Wendy says. "I'm dying over here, wondering how you're doing. Leslie is, too."

"We haven't heard anything yet." I glance at my sisters, who both relax back against the couch with the knowledge it's not Ash or Mom on the phone.

"Do you think that's a good thing or a bad thing?"

"I don't know."

"Are you okay? Do you need me to leave work early and come over?"

While I would love her to be here, I realize this is something I need to do with my sisters. I need them to know I trust them to support me. "No," I say. "We're all good here. The girls are keeping me in line." I smile at them, and they both grin back.

"Let me know if you change your mind," Wendy says. "Call me later, okay?"

"You know I will. Thanks for checking on us."

"You're welcome, baby. I'll talk to you soon."

The term of endearment hits me right in the heart, and I can barely choke out my goodbye. When I hang up the phone, Sonya pats my vacated spot on the couch, inviting me back. I move the phone to the coffee table, take a seat, and put my arms around both of my sisters. They snuggle up against me, and we sit quietly, waiting for the call.

Twenty silent minutes later, the phone rings again. This time, I don't panic. I carefully remove my arms from my sisters and calmly pick up the phone.

It's Ash, and he sounds like he's been through the wringer.

"He reacted about like you'd expect," he explains. "He yelled. He cursed. He threw things. He broke things."

"Did he ...?" I can't say the words.

"No, he didn't try to hit her, if that's what you're asking, but I'm certain he would have if I weren't here. He wouldn't dare to do it with an audience."

I sigh in relief, and my sisters clutch my arms.

"Is Mom okay?" Tonya whispers.

I nod, and then Sonya moves around me so she can hold on to Tonya.

"I didn't let him in the house," Ash says. "With the Protection Order in place, he had no right to come in, as you know, although he tried."

My heart drops. "Ash …"

"I'm okay. I'll have some bruises, but his actions will help us in the long run. I'll give a statement, and we'll take pictures."

"I'm sorry. I should have been there."

"No, you shouldn't have. You're exactly where you needed to be. I can't imagine the trauma it would have caused the girls if they'd been here."

"I can't believe he was so dumb," I say.

"Me, neither, but I'm glad he was. I've never seen him that angry."

"How did you get him to leave?"

"I had Harold call the cops."

"Harold was there?" Harold has been our full-time handyman on the property for as long as I can remember. He must be at least seventy by now, but he has no intention of retiring.

"He was, even though we sent all the staff home. He refused to leave, because he knew something was up. He's still here, and he's determined to stay the night to help protect Mom."

I smile at the old man's loyalty to Mom. "Good ol' Harold."

"Anyway," Ash says, "Dad knew he'd be in trouble if he didn't leave before the police arrived. Mom packed one bag for him and had it waiting out front, so he threw it in the car and peeled out while he had the chance."

"Mom packed him a bag?"

"Filled with nothing but underwear and Ritz crackers—not in the package."

I burst into laughter. Dad always said Ritz was the poor man's cracker and wouldn't allow them in the house.

"Oh, I love that woman," I say. "How's she doing?"

"She's hanging in there. Dad said some terrible things to her, and I know his words had to cut her like a knife, but she stood tall and didn't retaliate. I was proud of her."

"Is she there with you now?" I ask. "Can I talk to her?"

"No, she's taking a bubble bath."

"Good for her."

"Are you staying there tonight?"

"Yes. Diego told me to take the day off tomorrow, too, so I can be here with her. Keep the girls there with you for tonight, in case Dad tries to do anything here. But I know they're going to want to see Mom tomorrow, so we'll bring them over for a while. I'm not sure about them staying overnight here, though. We'll have to play that by ear."

forty-eight

. . .

Wendy

"I s it okay if Leslie and I come over, or would you three rather be by yourselves?" I ask Randall on the phone, after he gives me a brief rundown of what happened.

"Please come," he says. "We're about to drive each other crazy over here."

"Do you need food?"

"Yes, please. The girls like Chinese, so why don't you grab some takeout? Get a variety of stuff. I'll pay you back."

"You won't pay us back, and we'll get enough so you'll have leftovers if you need something for lunch tomorrow." George let him take another day off work so he can tend to his family.

"You're too good to me," he says.

"I'm exactly the right amount of good," I counter. "You deserve all the amounts of goodness anyway."

When he doesn't respond, I ask, "You doing okay?"

"I'm mentally exhausted. Trying to wrap my brain around everything."

"It's a lot to process. I'll help you with it later. I'll make sure we get some time alone."

"Promise?"

"Promise."

"Now tell me how you're really doing," I tell Randall as I lie curled up against him on his bed.

"I wish I could be there with Mom and Ash tonight." He trails his fingers through my hair. "I want to see Mom and make sure she's okay. And I want to be there in case Dad tries anything else."

I prop myself up on my elbow so I can look him in the eye. "Then go. Leslie and I will stay here with your sisters. Go. Seriously."

"But you're flying to Arkansas first thing in the morning."

"We'll stay here. This is more important. We need to take care of your family."

He shakes his head. "You can't do that for us."

"We can."

"No. Our family is not more important than yours or Leslie's. You need to meet your sister and niece. Leslie needs to spend time with her siblings and parents. I'll hate myself forever if I don't make you go."

I poke him in the chest. "You can't make either of us do anything, just so you know, but I understand what you're saying." I smooth my hand over the spot I poked. "How about this? You go up to the house in a little bit. Spend an hour or two with your mom, and if you still feel like you need to stay overnight, then stay, get up early, and be back here before Leslie and I need to leave for the airport. We both already packed, so we'll run home and get our bags tonight and be prepared to spend the night and head out from here in the morning."

"No. I can't leave you women here alone overnight."

I fight against the anger bubbling inside me at his words because I know his intentions are pure and he doesn't need me going off on a feminist rant, but I can't fully let it go.

"Randall," I say in an even tone, "we are four strong women who do not need a man here to protect us. Your dad is not about to try to hurt us, especially after what he pulled at the house. If you're truly afraid he might try to come here to confront you, tell the doorman to not let him up and to call the police if he tries to defy that order."

"Okay. This is all such a mess, isn't it? I wish we could all be together tonight—Mom, my siblings, me, *and* you and Leslie."

"I know you want that, and I do, too." I reach up to smooth the wrinkles forming on his forehead. "But that's not possible, so we need to do the next best thing. Which, in case you've forgotten, is for you to go be with your mom and Ash, while Leslie and I stay here with your sisters."

He shifts us so we're facing each other on our sides. "How do you always know exactly what to do?" He tucks my hair behind my ear and then lets his fingers linger on my face.

I chuckle. "That is very much not the case."

"It is," he says. "You're so wise."

One corner of my mouth tilts up. "It's because I'm so much older than you."

He smirks at me. "I knew that would come in handy someday."

I poke him in the belly, and he responds by tickling me mercilessly, which turns into kissing. By the time we come up for air, I'm on my back, and he's hovering above me, braced on his forearms so he won't crush me. Our faces are so close our heavy breaths mingle together.

"Wendy," he breathes into me, his lips barely brushing mine, his pupils so dilated I can barely detect any blue. "I want …"

He doesn't finish his thought, but I know what he wants. I can't move, though my entire body is trembling beneath his. But we can't do this—not with his sisters on the other side of the wall, not with all the emotions surrounding this night. This is neither the time nor the place for what our bodies are practically insisting we do. I finally give a slight shake of my head and his eyes close. Then he lets out a soft groan and rolls off me.

"I'm sorry." He flings his arm over his eyes. "I know you're not ready for that, and I promised not to pressure you. I'm the worst boyfriend ever."

I turn toward him again and place my hand on his chest. "No, you're not." I tug his arm off his face and push myself up so we can look at each other, but his eyes are still closed. "Randall, look at me."

He slowly opens his eyes and turns his head toward me, his eyes full of sorrow.

"You didn't do anything wrong," I insist. "You didn't pressure me. When I said no, you listened. And I *am* ready. I'm sure of that now, and oh, how I wish I could comfort you in that way. But this isn't how we want our first time to happen—when you're stressed and upset, and we'd be rushed and trying to keep your sisters from hearing what we're doing. That's not the memory I want for us."

His eyes close again and I gently press my lips to each of his eyelids. Then I take a deep breath and say, "I don't want memory that for us … because I love you."

forty-nine

. . .

Randall

My heart stops. My lungs stop. My brain tries to process what it just heard but is incapable of doing so. Surely Wendy didn't tell me she loves me. Or if she did, she didn't mean it.

"I love you, Randall Hamilton," she says again with certainty.

My body begins to function again, my eyes pop open, and my mouth curves into a smile. "You do?" I can hear the awe in my voice.

Wendy nods and smiles back at me. "So much."

I quickly sit up with my back against the headboard and haul her onto my lap. "I love you, too, Wendy O'Halloran." My smile grows bigger. "So much."

"I know," she says with a cheeky grin. "Your sisters told me."

I laugh. "How did they know? I didn't say a word."

She shrugs. "Sibling intuition, I guess."

"They've had plenty of time to intuit."

Her eyes widen. "Oh, yeah?"

"I knew I loved you that night we first kissed on your couch."

She thinks for a moment. "Even though I didn't let you stay the night?"

"Yes. Should I get a trophy for that?"

"You get a nose kiss for that." She gives me a quick peck.

I smile and kiss her forehead. "It was fun when we couldn't kiss on the lips."

"Maybe for you."

I kiss both of her cheeks. "Not for you?"

"I wanted to kiss you so badly."

I tilt her head down so I can kiss the top of it. "I know you did. You made that very clear."

She laughs. "You wanted to kiss me, too."

"I wanted to do more than kiss you." I kiss her nose. "But I'm glad we waited. Made it ever so much better when we did finally lock lips."

"Speaking of waiting," she says. "It's been a good three minutes since I told you I love you, and you have yet to lock these lips onto mine." She outlines my lips with her finger.

"Patience is a virtue, my love." I tap her nose. "Before I claim your luscious lips, I have one question."

"What's that?"

"How much is 'so much'?"

"More much than you can imagine."

"It can't be more much than my 'so much.'"

She pouts. "Can so."

"How about we both love each other the most much?"

"Nope. I insist I love you so much more. Now stop stalling, and kiss me," she taps her lips, "right here."

"He didn't say a word about Sonya," Mom says. "That might be the thing I'm most angry about."

"What did you want him to say?" I ask.

She picks at a loose thread on the arm of her chair in her sitting room. "I don't want him to have any contact with her, obviously, and I'd spirit her away to Antarctica if he tried to fight for custody. But I hoped he'd at least remember we still have a minor child at home and maybe he'd have a small desire to spend some time with her. All he cared about was his money and this house and my betrayal." She barks out a laugh. "As if I'm the betrayer in this family."

"I get what you're saying, but are you surprised by any of it?"

"No, but a tiny part of me hoped he'd act like a civilized human being for once."

I nod, because a tiny part of me still hopes for the same thing. "Have you told any of your friends yet?"

"I called Elizabeth Teague a little while ago. Since I knew you boys already told Melissa, I figured I'd let her mom know, too. We've gotten close over the past few months since we had them over for dinner. She and William will take my side instead of your father's."

"That's going to be tough, isn't it?" I ask. "Your friends having to take sides."

"Yes, and to be honest, I think many of them will publicly side with your dad, although most of them despise him. Even if I end up with half of our assets, he'll still be a very rich and powerful man. A lot of people will be scared to cross him."

"But not the Teagues?"

"No, they're old money and better connected than he is. They have no fear of your father."

"Good. Are you going to be okay, Mom?" I reach over and cover her hand with my own. "Ash told me Dad said some pretty nasty things to you today."

"It was no worse than some of the things he's said in the past. I'll get over it."

She turns her hand over, squeezes mine, and then slides it away.

"You shouldn't have to get over it," I say, "because he shouldn't have said it. I wish I'd known the extent of how he treated you so I could've done something about it."

"There was nothing you could've done. And I'm the one who should've done something, because I knew he treated you and Ash terribly. I begged him to stop, but that wasn't enough. I should've done more."

"Were you scared of what he'd do if you tried?"

Her eyes glitter with unshed tears as she nods. "I was afraid he would hit me—or worse, hit you boys." She gives me a sharp look. "He never touched you, did he?"

"No, and it was rare that he even yelled at me. It was his disappointment in me that hurt the most."

"I'm sorry, Randall. I should have protected you from him."

"*He* should have protected me," I say vehemently. "That was supposed to be his job."

"It was, and he failed miserably. But you, my son, are doing an excellent job of protecting your family. Thank you for shielding your sisters from what happened here today, and thank you for being here with me now."

I nod, because if I speak, I'm afraid I'll start crying.

"And I'll also be thanking Wendy and Leslie for all they've done for us, especially for the girls."

"They've gone above and beyond," I choke out.

Mom gives me an appraising look. "Do you love her? Is she the one?"

My face breaks into a smile. "Yes, and yes."

She smiles back at me. "Have you told her?"

"Tonight she told me she loves me, and I said it back."

Her eyes open wide. "Yet you came here to me instead of staying with her?"

"She kind of made me."

Mom laughs. "Of course she did. And it proves she truly loves you—and our family."

"She's so amazing, Mom. And it's not that I didn't want to come here. I wanted to be here all day, and it drove me crazy that I wasn't. But the girls helped me understand what I was doing for them was as important as what Ash was doing here."

"They were right."

"Yes, but once I knew they were going to be fine, I needed to see with my own eyes that you're all right."

"I will be. And you don't have to stay the night. Go back to your girlfriend."

"I'd be tempted to do that, if she wasn't asleep in my bed … with Leslie."

She laughs again. "Yes, that would be a little awkward, wouldn't it?"

fifty

. . .

Wendy

"Are you feeling okay?" I ask Leslie as we get ready in Randall's bathroom early Friday morning. She's not quite her usual self today, though granted I'm not used to seeing her so early in the morning.

"I'm tired," she responds while applying eyeshadow, "and a little nauseous. With all the stress of yesterday and being in an unfamiliar bed, I didn't sleep very well, which always makes me feel a little sick."

"Probably didn't help that I kept trying to snuggle up to you in my sleep." I grin at her in the mirror.

"I'll admit I panicked a couple times when I woke up to someone draped halfway across me."

I shrug. "It's what I do. Thankfully Randall doesn't mind it."

Leslie smiles at me. "Because he loves you."

"He does." My smile is so big it hurts.

"And you love him."

"I do." I stick my lipstick into my pocket. There's no point in putting it on until after I kiss my man goodbye.

"I can't believe you let him go last night."

"I had to. He was so upset all day that he couldn't be with his mom. I made him go."

"And now you have to leave him for two and a half days."

"We'll live." I look at my watch. "Speaking of Randall, he'll be here in a few minutes, and our taxi will arrive in ten. You ready?"

"Just need to spray my hair, but I'm waiting for you to leave so I don't make you choke."

"I appreciate that."

I pack my toiletry bag into my suitcase and then carry it into the living room as Randall enters the apartment. Our eyes lock, and I drop the bag at my feet as he quickly strides across the room to me. He lifts me up, and I wrap my legs around his middle as our mouths crash together. The kiss doesn't last nearly as long as I'd like, but when Leslie enters the room and clears her throat, Randall reluctantly releases my mouth and slides me back down to the floor.

"I'll be in the kitchen for a minute," Leslie says, giving us a smile as she disappears into the small galley kitchen, leaving us to say our goodbyes.

Randall cups my face in his hands. "I love you so much. Don't you ever forget it."

"I never will." I rest my hands on his chest. "And don't you forget I love you so much more. I wish I could be here with you, but if you need me, I'll be a phone call away. Leslie left Shannon's number for you."

"Call me tonight after you get back from dinner with Andrea. I want to know how it goes, okay?"

I nod. "I'll tell you every detail. And I'll want to know how everything goes here today. I'm glad your mom is doing all right and nothing crazy happened overnight. I feel better about leaving you, knowing everything seems to be okay." Ash called earlier to give us an update and let us know Randall would be back by the time we needed to leave.

"Me, too. Now, kiss me one more time before Leslie comes back to ruin our fun once again."

"Leslie, we have to go home," I say. "You can't get on a plane like this."

"I'll be fine. We have to go." Her voice is so weak, I can barely hear her.

I stand from my seat in the boarding area for our flight. "You're not fine, and we're not going. Nobody wants to see, hear, or smell you using a barf bag on the plane."

She tugs me back down. "There's nothing left inside me, so I'll be fine."

"You won't be, and we don't know if this is something contagious." My eyes widen and I grab her hand. "Wait. You're not pregnant, are you?"

She stares at me with wide eyes before shaking her head. "No."

"You're sure?"

Leslie nods. "Positive."

"Okay," I say. "I'm calling Randall to tell him to come pick us up."

"No," she says in a stronger voice. "Well, he can come get me," she concedes, "but not you. You have to go meet Andrea and Emily. I can't be the person responsible for that not happening."

"I can't go without you," I say. "I need to stay here and make sure you're okay since Ash can't. And Randall won't be happy if I go and stay with Shannon by myself."

Leslie shakes her head vehemently. "You're not staying here to be my nurse. And you could get a hotel room in Little Rock, but I hope you won't. My brother isn't going to do anything to you except be kind and drive you wherever you need to go. Randall needs to be able to deal with that and trust you."

She's right. "Okay. I'll go and stay with Shannon, and you'll go home."

I head to the nearest pay phone to make the call. Unsurprisingly, Randall is shocked to hear my voice.

"What's wrong?" he demands.

"Leslie's sick. You need to come to the airport and pick her up."

"Okay, but what—"

"Bring your sisters with you if you don't want to leave them alone. In fact, it might work out best to bring them, because they can stay with the car while you come to the gate to get Leslie. There's no way she'll be able to walk out of here on her own, and I can't help her or I'll miss the flight. We start boarding any minute."

"You'll be okay going by yourself?"

"I'll be fine. Shannon will take good care of me—as a friend and nothing more. You need to trust me on that, Randall."

"I do trust you," he says softly.

"I love you." I can't help but smile when I say it.

"I love you so much more. Tell Leslie I'll be there as soon as I can."

Although I've not met Leslie's mom, I've seen photos of her, and I have no trouble spotting her at the airport. When I wave and catch her eye, she beams at me and then draws me into a hug when I reach her.

"It's so nice to meet you, Wendy. And I'm so sorry about Leslie. She caught me on the phone before I left home to let me know what happened."

I give her a sad smile. "I'm the one who should be saying, 'I'm sorry about Leslie,' to you. You're not going to get to see her now. Instead you get to drive a stranger around."

"You're not a stranger. You're my daughter's best friend, and I've heard a lot about you."

"All good, I hope."

"Of course. Now, let's get you out of here and grab some lunch before I take you to Shannon's to get settled in." She starts walking toward baggage claim, and I fall into step beside her. "Unless you'd be more comfortable staying at our house, since Leslie's not here? I know it's not convenient because we live so far out of the city, but we'd be glad to have you and to drive you wherever you need to go."

"Thank you so much for the offer, but I'll be fine with Shannon. I don't want to put you out."

"Well, the offer stands, so if you change your mind, let me know."

The two of us make small talk as we wait for my suitcase and then drive to a locally owned soup and sandwich shop for lunch.

"This place is lovely," I say. "It feels so homey." The small dining area is set up more like a dining room in a home than a restaurant. It holds six tables of various sizes and styles, but they all complement each other.

"It's my favorite place. I always eat here when I come to the city." She chuckles. "I bet it sounds funny to you for me to call Little Rock a city, considering it's about twenty times smaller than Chicago."

I smile. "It's more like a big town to me, but it's much larger than your town, right?"

"Yes, Oakville's population is just under two thousand. And we live in the country, so our population is two—or three this summer since Cynthia's home from college."

"And she's coming into the city this evening, too, right?"

"Yes, she has a part-time summer job at the Oakville newspaper, and she'll drive in with her father after work."

"I bet she's sad she won't get to see her sister."

"She doesn't know yet."

My eyebrows arch. "No?"

"No, I'm not going to tell her until she gets here, or I'm afraid she won't come. Not that she wouldn't want to meet you, but her sister was the real draw."

"I get that. I wouldn't be all that excited about driving forty minutes to meet my little brothers' friends, if my brothers weren't going to be there. But will she be mad when she finds out you could have told her but didn't?"

"She'll be fine. She loves spending time with Shannon, and I want her to meet you. From what Leslie has said, there's a chance you could be extended family someday." She gives me a sly grin.

"Oh, she said that, did she?"

"Granted, she didn't say much other than you're dating Ash's brother. But she was excited about the prospect of the two of you maybe being sisters-in-law someday, in addition to being best friends."

"I think there's a good chance we will be," I admit with a smile.

"Yes?" She claps her hands. "I'm hearing lots of wedding bells in my future!"

fifty-one

. . .

"**D**ad's fighting the Order of Protection," Ash says to me over the phone. I took the call in my bedroom so our sisters won't hear anything we don't want them to. I'm hoping they're not listening in on the living room phone.

"Of course he is," I say. "Did you expect any different?"

"No. He's also demanding to be let into the house to get some of his things today."

I stand from my bed and pace. "And you're letting him?"

"We have to, but Mom can't be here."

I run my fingers through my hair. "Then I'm coming up there."

"You'll leave the girls?"

"Mom can come here, and I'll go there. Since we know Dad will be at the house, he can't also be here harassing them. It'll be fine. Then when we know he's gone, Mom can go back to the house and take the girls if we think that'll be okay."

"We'll see what we think about that after he comes to the house."

"What time will he be there?"

"Two."

I look at the clock. It's eleven-thirty now. "All right, I'll be there by one, in case he shows up early, which wouldn't surprise me. Send Mom here whenever you want."

"Will you stop by and check on Leslie before you come up here?"

"I will. Our sisters have already insisted they're making her some soup."

"They'd better get a move on, then."

"It's a can of Campbell's. You know those girls can't cook. Won't take long."

When I arrive at the house, I pull into the circle drive out front like I always used to do, but Ash pokes his head out the door and tells me to go to the garage.

"Don't want Dad to damage my car, do you?" I ask when I enter the house a minute later.

"Nope. Also, I talked to Samuel, and he's coming over, too."

"Ah, that'll be good. Surely Dad won't go ballistic if Mom's lawyer is here."

"How was Leslie?"

I take a seat on the couch in the den. "Pretty weak. Said she threw up again. I left her the soup and some Gatorade, but I doubt she'll be able to keep it down."

"I should be there for her. I hate that I can't be." He drops down into a recliner, and I notice how exhausted he looks.

"After Dad leaves, you need to go. You haven't seen her since Wednesday, and you need to, for both of your sakes. We'll figure out how to make things work here without you for a while. Take a few hours for yourself and go take care of her."

"I will. Thanks."

"I hope what she has isn't contagious. The last thing we need is for us all to get sick."

"Right," he says. "I hope Wendy doesn't get sick while she's gone."

"Me, too."

He cranks up the feet on the recliner. "Are you okay with her staying at Shannon's without Leslie?"

"I guess I have to be, because it's what's happening. Logically, I know things will be fine, and I completely trust her. But there's still this little part of me that's nervous about it because of Colleen."

Ash shakes his head. "Wendy is not Colleen."

"I know she's not. Like I said, I know I don't have anything to worry about with Wendy, but I guess I've not quite moved on from what Colleen did to me. Her betrayal still hurts, even though I know she wasn't right for me, and Wendy is exactly right for me."

"She really is perfect for you. And I don't know if it's her influence, or simply you making the decision to change, but you're so much more yourself than you've been in a long time."

"You think so?"

"I know so."

I cock my head to the side. "What … what is it that makes you say that? What's different about me?"

"You've stopped acting."

One of my eyebrows lifts. "Acting?"

"Yeah. You used to act cocky about things you had no clue about, while at the same time you acted like you were a dumb, selfish, screw-up. But now you admit when you don't know what you're doing, and you're letting yourself be who you truly are: a smart, kind, generous man who thinks about putting others' needs before his own. I'm proud of you."

My chest feels light, because it means more than I could say that my little brother is proud of me.

"You're gonna make me cry over here, man."

He rolls his eyes. "Shut up. I'm trying to be nice."

"You are being nice. Thank you."

"You're welcome. Now, keep your trap shut so I can take a short nap before Hurricane Walter makes landfall."

My dad arrives at two o'clock with his own divorce attorney in tow, and he says exactly zero words to us, likely per his lawyer's instruction. However, he glares at us whenever possible, which is pretty much the entire time he's at the house, since we ensure at least one of us keeps him within sight at all times. We're not about to give him a chance to raid the safe or any other secret hiding places he may have around the house.

While Dad packs up some clothes and a few items from his office, his lawyer uses a video camera to take inventory of the valuables in the house. Ash and I, with Samuel's help, convince him to not record in our sisters' rooms, to protect their privacy, but he insists on checking for any expensive jewelry or artwork in their space.

Within an hour, they're gone, and Samuel leaves shortly thereafter.

"Go to Leslie's," I tell my brother as I herd him toward the garage door, "and stay all night. We'll be fine here. It seems like Dad's going to behave himself for now. I'll stay here with Mom and the girls tonight, and we'll talk in the morning to figure out what we'll do for the rest of the weekend."

He turns to me before entering the garage. "Thanks for all you've done. We couldn't have made it through this week without you."

"You don't have to thank me, because I was happy to do all of it. And thank you for everything, too. It took a team effort, and we did it."

He gives me a half smile. "Yeah, we did."

Then I do something I haven't done since we were kids and wrap my arms around him. After a couple seconds of him standing as rigid as a tree, he circles his arms around me and hugs me back for longer than I thought he would. When his hold loosens, I let him go. He clasps my shoulder and nods before heading out the door, his eyes glistening.

fifty-two

. . .

Wendy

"You have my number," Shannon says as he pulls up to the restaurant where I'm meeting Andrea. "Call me when you're ready for me to pick you up, even if that's in ten minutes when you discover your long-lost sister is actually a lizard in disguise."

I chuckle. "But I don't want to interrupt your meal with your family."

"We're eating at my house for exactly that reason—so you can get ahold of me when you're ready to go, whenever that might be. It doesn't matter if that's fifteen minutes from now or four hours. Leslie can't be here for you, but I am."

I open the door. "Thanks, Shannon."

"No 'Sexy Shannon' anymore?" he teases.

I smile. "I doubt Randall would appreciate that."

"Nor would my kinda-sorta new girlfriend."

My eyebrows shoot up. "Oh?"

"Yeah, I'll tell you about her later. Go meet your sister."

I flip the sun visor down to give my hair and makeup one last check in the mirror, but Shannon flips it back up. "You look gorgeous. Go."

His comment would have unnerved me if he hadn't told me he has a girlfriend, but since he did, I know his only intention is to give me confidence. "Yes, sir."

When I step up to the hostess stand, the girl does a double-take, and I laugh. "Did someone who looks like me come in here recently?"

"Yeah, like three minutes ago," she says with wide eyes.

"That's my sister." I feel giddy that I can actually say that. *I have a sister.*

"I'll take you to her, then." As she leads me across the restaurant, she says, "Are you twins?"

"No, we're a couple years apart."

Then I spot Andrea, and I burst out laughing again, as does she. She rises from her seat and steps toward me as I approach. We spread our arms out at the same time and hug each other tightly.

"I love your outfit," she says, referring to my short-sleeve light-green button up shirt and cream-colored pants that match hers almost exactly.

"You have excellent style," I reply.

We take our seats and grin at each other for longer than would normally be comfortable, but we're both in awe of being here.

"What do we talk about first?" she finally asks.

"I don't know! I want to know everything I don't yet know about you *and* Emily."

"Let's start with Emily."

"That's what I was hoping you'd say."

"Are you still upset with your mom?" I ask Andrea a few hours later. We've eaten appetizers, the main meal, and dessert, and now she's drinking a decaf coffee and I'm nursing a glass of wine, extending our time as long as we can without irritating our waitress too much. We've already determined we'll leave her a sizable tip since we've monopolized the table all evening.

"I'm not," she says. "I knew from the beginning I'd eventually get over what she did. As a single mom myself, I know how tricky it can be to talk to your kid about their absent dad. It's hard to know the right thing to do. What about you? You and your mom okay?"

"Yeah, we're good, and she's very excited I'm meeting you. She threatened to come down here, too, but I made Dad promise he wouldn't let her. I didn't want to overwhelm you and Emily."

"I would love to meet her someday," she says. "I'm glad she doesn't resent me."

"My mom would never resent you. None of this is your fault. She doesn't resent your mom, either, for that matter. It was all such a long time ago, and it's Jack she was mad at, not your mom. He was the one who cheated."

"She sounds like a great mom."

"The best."

"I like to think mine is the best, so maybe we'll say they're a tie."

"I can deal with that."

"So about tomorrow …"

"Yeah?" I hold my breath as I wait for her to tell me if I get to meet Emily.

"How about you meet us at a park near our apartment around nine? We'll let Emily play for a while to wear her out, and then there's a diner nearby where we can have brunch."

I beam at her. "Sounds perfect."

Andrea gives me a ride back to Shannon's, and as soon as I arrive, he gives me some privacy so I can call Randall from the kitchen phone. Then I get ready for bed and join him in the living room, where he's watching Johnny Carson and drinking a Coors from the bottle. He turns the volume down as I settle onto the couch.

"Everything go well with the sister?"

"Amazingly well. It's like we were … well, separated at birth, which we were, in a way."

"I guess you're right. That's great you get along so well. So does that mean you passed the test to get to meet the niece?"

I tell him about our plans for the next day. "If you can take me to the park, Andrea says she can bring me back here afterward, since we don't know what time that will be."

"Works for me."

"Great. Thanks for being my chauffeur."

"It's my pleasure."

"So tell me about this kinda-sorta girlfriend you mentioned earlier."

"Her name is Christi—with an I, mind you—and she's an interior designer. Her office is in the same building as the engineering firm where I work."

I raise an eyebrow. "Why does it matter that her name ends in an I?"

"She likes everyone to know that, for some reason, so I thought I'd pass along that little nugget of information."

"Sounds to me like you're making fun of her."

"Maybe a little."

I laugh. "So this isn't a serious thing?"

"Not yet. Like I told you before, I've never been serious with anyone, because I never had the desire to be until recently. Is Christi the one? Eh, maybe so, but probably not. We've gone out four times now, and I'm not any fonder of her than I was at the beginning, so that probably means something."

"Could be, but you never know. If there's nobody else you're interested in, there's no harm in dating her for a while longer to see if you do grow more fond of her. Just be honest with her about your feelings and your intentions, whatever they may be."

"Thank you for the advice, wise one." He tilts his bottle toward me, and I tilt an imaginary bottle back at him in a "cheers" motion. "What about you and Randall? Is that serious?"

I try to stifle my smile, but I can't. "It is."

His eyebrows raise. "I see that smile. Do you love him?"

I nod. "Yeah."

"Is he the one?"

"I think so." I press my lips together and then say. "Shannon, I have to tell you, when I was talking to you a couple months ago, I was also kind of seeing him. It wasn't anything official, but we were spending quite a bit of time together. I should have told you that."

He shakes his head. "You didn't need to tell me. We weren't dating."

"I know. But I still feel bad."

"Don't. It doesn't matter. And you've found the man you love. That's what matters."

"Thank you."

"No need to thank me. No hard feelings here. It wasn't meant to be with you and me. I'll find my one someday."

fifty-three

. . .

Randall

"**R**andall, wake up!" Mom shakes my shoulder and says my name again.

For a few seconds I can't figure out where I am, but then I remember I'm in my childhood bedroom. I sit straight up when I register the look of shock on my mother's face in the dim light from the hallway, along with her wild hair and apparently hastily donned robe, as one side hangs much lower than the other.

"Mom? What's wrong?" I reach out for her.

"Your father's dead."

My hand freezes, inches from hers. "What?"

"He was in a car accident," she says in a monotone voice.

I rotate my body so I'm sitting on the side of the bed, and I carefully pull her down beside me and wrap my arm around her.

"Okay, tell me what happened."

"The doorbell rang and woke me up," she says, "and it scared me, since it's so early."

I glance at the clock to see it's a little past five, and with a pang I realize I heard the doorbell, but I thought it was a dream. I should have been more alert, considering my job for the night was to protect my family.

"Mom, why didn't you wake me up?" It could have been Dad, but I can't say that now.

"I don't know. I wasn't thinking because I woke from a dead sleep. I'm sorry. I should have gotten you."

"It's okay." I rub my hand up and down her arm. "Tell me what happened."

"It was the police. They asked if I'm Walter Hamilton's wife, and I said yes, because I still am. Then they said he was in an accident, and he didn't make it. That's all I know so far. They're still downstairs. They say I need to go identify the body."

My heart squeezes. "You are not going to identify the body. I'll do that." It's the last thing I want to do, but I'm not about to let my mother go through that torture.

"Will you come downstairs and talk to them with me?" she asks in a small voice, much unlike her usual confident tone.

"You better believe I will. Let me throw some clothes on. Stay right there."

I grab a pair of shorts and a shirt out of my duffel and head into my bathroom to put them on and brush my teeth. A minute later I'm back, and Mom hasn't moved a muscle.

I gently take her arm and help her stand. She's still in a state of shock, so I straighten her robe and smooth down her hair. Then I take her hand and guide her out of my room and downstairs to the foyer, where two uniformed police officers stand waiting for us. I introduce myself, usher them into the sitting room, and help Mom into her chair.

"Ma'am," the female officer says to Mom, "would you like something to drink? Some water, maybe?" She shoots me a look that demands, "Get your mother a drink."

"That's a good idea, Mom," I say. "I'll be right back."

I rush to the kitchen and pour her a glass of ice water. I also grab two cookies from the cookie jar, since I know she hasn't eaten anything and could probably use a sugar boost. The officer nods in approval when I hand Mom the glass and set the cookies on the small table beside her.

"Officers," I say, "what can you tell us about what happened?"

"We're still gathering information," the male officer says, "but it was a single-car accident on Lake Shore Drive. The car appears to have hit the median at a high rate of speed and then flipped over multiple times. We're hoping to find some witnesses who can tell us more." He clears his throat. "There was also a passenger."

"A young woman?" Mom asks. It's the first thing she's said since we left my room.

"Uh, yes. A Bridget Anderson. Is she family?"

The female officer winces at his carelessness. She knows exactly who the woman is.

"She's his secretary," Mom says, "and girlfriend."

Both officers are stunned into silence at her admission.

"We're—we were—getting a divorce," Mom explains. "Did she make it?"

"No, ma'am."

Mom's hand goes to her chest. "Oh, no. Her poor parents."

"What time did this happen?" I ask, to change the subject from my dad's much younger mistress.

"Around two o'clock. They appeared to be on their way home from a fancy event. He was wearing a tuxedo."

Mom nods. "Last night was the lung cancer benefit gala."

"What do you need from us?" I ask the officers.

"We'll need someone to formally identify the body."

"That would be me," I say.

"Good." She gives me another nod of approval. "Then we'll have you come by the station afterward, and we'll have some more questions and information for you."

I stand. "Thank you, officers." I get the address of the morgue and police station and escort them out, with a promise to head downtown as soon as possible.

When I return to the sitting room, Mom is staring at the fireplace. I kneel by her chair and take her hand in mine. "Tell me what you're feeling."

"Numb. Shocked. Sad. Relieved. Guilty for feeling relieved."

"You have the right to feel all of those things, and more."

"How am I going to tell your sisters?"

"We'll tell them together, but first I need to call Ash."

Melissa went with me to identify the body and talk to the police, so everyone else could stay together at the house once Ash arrived.

As we're heading back to the car from the police station, she says, "I guess Wendy will be coming home early from Arkansas?"

I pause before admitting, "I haven't told her."

She stops walking. "You *what?* Tell me I heard that wrong."

"I can't tell her. If I do, she'll insist on coming home, but she's meeting her niece today. I can't let her miss that."

"Randall, you have to tell her."

"I'm not going to ruin her weekend with her new family."

Melissa puts her hand on my arm. "Listen to me, Randall Hamilton. She'll be furious with you if you don't tell her this. Plus, you need her. I know you do. You need comfort and support, too, as much as anyone else in your family does, and none of us can give you what she can."

"But—"

"Since you don't want her to come home, you go to her. Go to the airport, get on a plane, and fly to Arkansas."

I shake my head. "I can't leave my family. I can't let them deal with all this without me."

"You can, and every last one of them will tell you to go." She starts walking, faster than before. "We're going to your apartment, where you'll call your family, call Leslie's brother, and pack your bag. Then we'll get you to the airport, and we'll pray hard that you'll be able to catch a direct flight to Little Rock this morning." She looks at her watch. "It's only eight-thirty. We're going to make this happen."

When I arrive in Little Rock at noon, I search the gate area for Shannon, hoping he's here. Miraculously, a direct flight to Little Rock was leaving twenty-five minutes after I arrived at the ticket counter, and I had barely enough time to make a quick stop at a pay phone to leave a message on Shannon's answering machine letting him know my flight number and arrival time. Considering my first call to him from my place also resulted in me leaving a message on his machine, I'm not certain he knows I'm here.

My heart plummets when I don't spot him, and I follow the crowd toward baggage claim and the exit, keeping my eyes peeled for a pay phone so I can try calling him yet again.

"Randall!" a voice calls as I'm about to drop my quarter into the slot on a phone.

I hang up the receiver as Shannon lopes toward me. "I'm sorry," he says, "I only got your messages twenty minutes ago. After I dropped Wendy off at the park, I ran some errands before going back home."

"No need to be sorry."

I clap my hand on his shoulder in greeting, but he pulls me into a hug. "I'm sorry about your dad, though," he says. "I know things weren't great there, but still, I'm sure it's not easy."

"Thanks. I appreciate it."

When I pull away, I expect an awkward moment, but there's not one. Shannon starts walking, and I fall into step beside him.

"How do you want to do this?" he says. "I don't know where she is or when she'll be home. All I know is they were eating brunch at a diner near the park where I dropped her off, but then they were going to play it by ear. They could be anywhere in the city by now, and I have no idea where Andrea lives, what her phone number is, or what her car looks like." He gives me a quick glance. "Sorry, man."

"Again, nothing to be sorry for. I guess we go back to your house and see if we can find Andrea's number and address in the phone book, or we can call information, but I'm guessing they're not at her house anyway. So we'll wait."

fifty-four

. . .

Wendy

I can honestly say Emily is my favorite child ever. She reminds me so much of myself when I was little. Not only does she look like me—and her mother—but she's smart, spunky, and funny. Her goal for the day seems to be entertaining me as much as possible, and she's succeeding.

"Aunt Wendy," she says, while grabbing onto my hand and absolutely melting my heart, "come see the giraffes. They're my favorite!"

After we had brunch, we decided to head to the zoo for a few hours, since Andrea and Emily hold season passes. Emily knows exactly where everything is, and she wants me to see it all.

As we watch the giraffes amble around their enclosure, Andrea says to me, "I'm pretty sure she's a fan not only of the giraffes but also of her aunt."

I smile at her. "I think so, too." I put an arm around my sister. "I can't believe we're here and that we're all getting along so well. This is a dream come true, but I wish you didn't live so far from me."

"I know," she says. "I'm so glad we have more family now— and that it's *you*—but I wish we lived closer, too. I'm hoping we can come visit you a couple times a year. It should be easier in the summers when I'm only working part-time."

"And I'll come here, too. And we'll call and write letters and maybe go on trips together sometimes?"

"I'd like that." My sister smiles. "But it sounds like maybe you'll soon have another person to include in your travel planning, so don't get too far ahead of yourself here."

I feel the blush heating my neck and face. "I hope you're right, but that doesn't mean I'm not going to see my sister and niece every chance I get, even if there might be another person with me sometimes."

"I'm looking forward to getting to know Randall better," she says. "Maybe at the wedding?"

I whip my head toward her. "Don't jinx it!"

She laughs. "I'm not jinxing anything. But I wasn't talking about *your* wedding. Don't you think your friend and Randall's brother will get married here in Arkansas, since this is where she's from?"

"Oh, yeah, I guess you're right," I say. "But I don't know when that will be. I hope you'll be able to see Randall again before then."

"Me, too." She leans around me to speak to her daughter. "Let's go, kiddo. Time for us to take Aunt Wendy to her friend's house and then go home and rest for a while. Then we'll see if your aunt can meet us again later tonight or in the morning before she flies back home to Chicago." She raises an eyebrow at me.

I squeeze Emily's hand. "Definitely."

I knock and then open Shannon's unlocked front door without waiting for him to answer it. When my gaze lands on him, I say, "Oh, my goodness, Emily is so ..." I halt, and I feel all the blood drain from my head as I spy my boyfriend slowly standing from the couch with a look of heartbreaking grief on his face.

I cast a frantic look at Shannon, who nods toward Randall and heads down the hall, and then I hurtle across the room and launch myself into Randall's arms.

"What happened, baby?" I ask. "Why are you here?"

"My dad …" His voice breaks along with my heart.

"What about your dad?" I tilt my head up to look at his face. "What did he do?"

"There was a car accident. He … he didn't make it." Tears begin to stream down his face.

"Oh, Randall," I breathe out. "Here, sit down." I guide him back down onto the couch, grab some tissues from the end table, climb onto his lap, and hold him tightly.

"I don't know why I'm crying." He sniffles and swipes a tissue across his face. "I didn't cry before."

"You're crying because your dad died, honey, that's why. And I think you probably didn't cry earlier because you were in shock and you needed to be strong for your family. But now it's just you and me, and you can cry all you want, because I can be the strong one now."

"But I shouldn't cry for him. He was a terrible person."

"I know, but that doesn't make this any less traumatizing."

He takes a halting breath. "I identified his body. It was awful."

My heart hurts for him so badly I can't stand it. "I'm so sorry you had to go through that."

"I didn't want to, but I couldn't let anyone else do it."

I squeeze him more tightly. "I know. And I love you for that."

He leans his head against mine. "I love *you*."

I slide one arm out from around him and press it against his heart. "I'm glad you came to me."

"I needed you, and I knew if I called to tell you what happened, you'd come straight home, but I didn't want you to miss out on meeting Emily."

I love this selfless man more than I could have ever imagined. "You're right. I would have gone to you. Do we need to head back home tonight?"

"No. I'm going back first thing in the morning. There are more seats left on that flight if you want to change your flight to go with me."

"Of course I do. I'm not going to leave your side for the next few days. I'll call and do that in a little bit."

"I got a hotel room for tonight." He pauses. "Will you stay there with me?"

My heart rate increases with the knowledge of what that will mean for us. "Yes."

"We don't have to—"

I put my hand over his mouth. "I want to."

He removes my hand. "We'll see."

"We'll do more than see, mister." I poke his chest. "We're taking advantage of that hotel room."

He chuckles, and my heart soars at the sound.

"If you insist," he says.

"I do. And you can take advantage of the fact that my lips are inches from yours right now and kiss me."

He does, but we keep it brief, considering where we are. Then we hold each other in silence for a few minutes.

"Did you make plans with Andrea for tonight?" he finally asks.

"We loosely made dinner plans, but before finalizing them, I wanted to check with Shannon about whether he could drive me, and she's going to see if her mom can join us. I told her I'd call her in about an hour and we'd figure it out."

"Okay. Shannon said he can drive us to the hotel when we're ready. Maybe they can meet us at the hotel restaurant or another place nearby we can walk to. That is, if you're okay with me joining you."

"Of course I am. Andrea was saying she wants to get to know you, and I want you to meet Emily. And I'm ready to go to the hotel now."

"Oh, are you?" He wiggles his eyebrows, and I roll my eyes.

"I am. We need time to talk through what happened today and what the next few days will look like. Then we'll go to an early dinner with Andrea and her mom and Emily. And then we'll go back to the room and enjoy each other without worrying about anyone needing us or waiting for us or anything else."

fifty-five

. . .

Randall

"Tell me how you're feeling about your dad right now."
Wendy holds one hand out to me, and I grasp it and rest
our joined hands on my knee.

We're in our hotel room, which has a small living area, and
we're sitting facing each other on the love seat. We have a half
hour before we need to leave to meet Andrea, Emily, and
Andrea's mom for dinner.

"I'm angry," I say.

"What are you angry about?"

I rub my free hand across my forehead. "I'm angry at myself
for being both sad and relieved. I don't want to be either of those
things. I shouldn't be sad about the death of someone who treated
me and the rest of my family so badly. And I'm mad that I'm
relieved by someone's death, no matter how awful he was. I
thought I was better than that. And it's driving me crazy to feel all
these contradictory emotions at the same time."

"Grief rarely makes sense, so don't try to make it make sense.
And don't let today's feelings inform how you view yourself.
You're having to deal with so much right now. Let yourself feel
what you feel, and don't judge yourself for it."

I nod. "I'll try. And here's another thing I'm mad about, even
though it's illogical. If this was going to happen, why not before

Thursday, so we wouldn't have needed to go through everything that led up to and happened that day?"

She thinks about my question for a few moments. "I understand what you're saying, but maybe think about it from a different perspective. You and your mom and siblings now have a much stronger bond with each other due to what you experienced together earlier this week. You discovered you can lean on each other and count on each other and sacrifice for each other. I don't know that you had that kind of relationship before. Did you?"

I shake my head. "Not really. We loved each other, obviously, but we'd never gone through something so intense and so personal together." I sigh. "I hate to admit you're right."

Wendy cocks her head to the side. "Why do you hate to admit it?" Interestingly, she's curious, not irritated by my statement.

"Because you're always the one who makes things make sense. You have the good ideas, the right answers, and know exactly what to do. I feel like I don't bring anything to this relationship. You give, and I take."

"Baby, that's so not true. Look at where we are right now." She sweeps her hand out to encompass the room. "We're in Arkansas together because you came here. I didn't tell you to do that. That was all you."

I hang my head. "That was actually Melissa."

"This was her idea?" Again, she's simply curious.

"Yeah. She went with me to the morgue and police station so Ash could stay at home with Mom and the girls, and she set me straight when she found out I hadn't told you what happened yet. I told her I couldn't mess up your weekend, and she said if I didn't want you to give up your plans for me, then I needed to go to you."

Wendy reaches up to stroke my cheek. "Regardless of whose idea it was, you willingly gave up your plans for me. I'm sure there are many things you could be doing at home right now, but instead you came here for me."

"Yeah," I say, "and my family is having to pick up the slack at home because of it."

"Did any of them tell you not to come?"

"No," I reluctantly admit. "When I told them I wanted to come here but didn't want to leave them to handle things without me, they all said they'd be upset if I didn't come to you."

"See?" She caresses my hand with her thumb. "This isn't a contest. It's not about who gives the most. But you give me so much, even if you don't realize it. You give me comfort and peace and stability, and you even provide me with entertainment sometimes." She grins at me.

I smile back. "I can be pretty funny."

"Yes, but please don't ignore the rest of what I said. You're not just a funny guy who goes with the flow. Maybe you used to be, but you're not now. You're not when you're with me. You're not when you're with your sisters or Ash or your mom."

"I know I'm different than I was, and I like who I am now, but it's not necessarily easy. I'm not used to being this responsible person who has people depending on me. I'm afraid I'm going to fail and let everybody down."

"You will fail at times. Everybody does. But then you make things right as best you can and move forward, and you don't do it alone. You do it with the love and support of the very people you failed. That's the way family is supposed to work. You stick together even when you screw up or you're scared or you don't know what to do."

"I can see what you're saying, but that's not the way my family has worked in the past, so it doesn't come naturally to me. I don't automatically know these things. I'm going to need you to teach me."

"I will. But I don't always get it right, either. I haven't gotten everything right with you."

My forehead wrinkles. "What are you talking about? You've done everything right."

"I haven't. I should have told you I love you weeks ago, but I was terrified. At first I was scared to fully trust you again, and then I was afraid you didn't feel the same way and you wouldn't say it back, so I refused to admit it. But you loved me all along. I know you didn't tell me so because you were letting me move at my own pace due to my insecurities, and I'm sorry I put you through that."

"It wasn't a hardship to love you without knowing for sure when or if you would love me back," I say.

"Maybe not, but if I had trusted myself and trusted you, I could have given you more of myself this week when you needed what I was afraid to give."

"You've given me everything I've needed this week." I lean forward and softly kiss her forehead and then her lips. "Please don't regret not doing some things sooner. I don't, and I never will. If you didn't feel right telling me you loved me earlier, you shouldn't have, no matter the reason. I was prepared to quietly love you for as long as it took for you to be ready."

fifty-six

. . .

Wendy

"Are you going to be my uncle?" Emily asks Randall at dinner.

I feel my face heat as Andrea's mom stifles a laugh and Randall's eyes widen.

"Emily," her mother chastises, "that's not a polite question to ask."

"But why not? They love each other, so that means they'll get married, and then he'll be my uncle, and then they'll have babies, and I'll be their big cousin!"

"That's not always the way it works, honey," Andrea says, shooting Randall and me an apologetic look.

Emily gets on her knees on her chair and puts her hand on Randall's shoulder, which is easy for her to do since she insisted on sitting next to him. "But don't you want to marry Aunt Wendy? She's really great. She's the best aunt I've ever had."

I smile at her statement, even though I'm the only aunt she's ever had.

"She's the best aunt anybody will ever have," Randall says as he covers her tiny hand with his own, making my heart stutter. "And she's greater than great. As for whether I'm going to marry her, that's something she and I need to talk about before we tell you about it."

"Okay." Emily looks back and forth between Randall and me. "You can talk about it now."

He laughs and ruffles her hair. "I think we'll talk about it later when it's just the two of us. But if we decide we're going to get married, I promise you'll be one of the first people we tell. Okay?"

She nods and removes her hand from his shoulder.

"But for now I'll tell you a secret," he says. "Do you want to know what it is?"

Emily's eyes go wide as she nods again.

"I have a nickname for Aunt Wendy that only I use, but I'll let you use it, too, if you want. But only you can use it—not your mom or your grandma or anybody else."

"Okay," she says breathlessly. "What is it?"

"Glinda."

Her little nose wrinkles. "Glinda? Why do you call her Glinda?"

"Have you ever seen *The Wizard of Oz?*" he asks.

"Yep." I can tell she's trying to connect the dots. "Oh! The good witch! Her name is Glinda!" She claps her little hands. "That's the best nickname for Aunt Wendy ... I mean Aunt Glinda." She beams at me.

Randall also smiles at me. If it were possible for an entire reproductive system to explode, mine would be doing so at this exact moment.

As soon as the hotel elevator doors close behind us, Randall's mouth is on mine. When the doors open on our floor, he doesn't stop kissing me but instead hoists me up so he can carry me down the hall.

"Put me down," I say against his mouth.

"Not a chance."

I pull my lips slightly away from his. "What if somebody sees us?"

"Why do you care? I thought you were secretly an exhibitionist."

I giggle. "I guess I don't care."

And he's kissing me again. When we get to our door, he fumbles in his pocket for the key, which is difficult with me in his arms and our mouths locked together. He finally lets us into the room and drops the key on the floor as the door slams shut. Then he presses my back against the door. His lips pull away and his forehead rests against mine as he says, "You're sure this is what you want?"

"Mmmhm." I press my lips to his again, but he doesn't kiss me back.

"I need you to say yes if you're sure," he says.

"Yes. Stop talking."

Some time later, we order an ice cream sundae from room service and sit on the bed feeding it to each other. The experience ends up being more entertaining than romantic, considering Randall decides to use his left hand again, which results in him getting more ice cream on my face and robe than in my mouth.

He leans forward to lick a drop of ice cream off my chin, and I giggle.

"Do you want to talk about what Emily asked me?" he asks.

I go still. "You want to talk about getting married?"

He nods. "I think we should. Is that where you see us potentially heading?" He feeds me another bite of sundae before I can respond and adds, "Because that's my goal."

"It's your *goal?*" I mumble around the ice cream.

His face goes slack. "It's not yours?"

I swallow quickly. "Baby, that's not what I'm saying." I place my hand on his knee. "Yes, that's where I see us potentially heading. But you said it as if you're checking us off a list of life goals. College, check." I make a check mark in the air with my other hand. "Law school, check. Job, check. Marriage, check."

He captures my hand in his when I make the last check. "You know that's not what I mean."

"Do I?" I take a deep breath. "I'm not trying to start an argument here, and I don't doubt your love for me. But I don't want you to see our relationship as an achievement or the next thing you need to accomplish in life."

"It's not. I promise. I want to marry you because you're *you*," he kisses the back of my hand, "not because I think it's the next thing I need to do."

When I register the lack of the word "potentially" in his statement this time, my heart rate picks up along with my breath rate. He can't mean it, can he? And if he does, can I allow myself to believe it?

"Is this conversation making you anxious?" he asks me.

"A little," I admit.

"Why?" He kisses my hand again.

"Because we're moving really fast all of a sudden. It's been an emotional week. I don't want us to get ahead of ourselves here." I look down. "I'm afraid this is all too good to be true, and you're going to wake up in a few days and wonder what you've managed to get yourself into."

He puts a finger under my chin and tilts my head up until I'm looking at him. "Babe, don't let your fears steal this from you. There's no one else I want to spend my life with, and I need you to believe that. I'm not going anywhere without you. You can trust me to be here for you always."

Tears fill my eyes. "You really mean it?"

"I do. I'm not asking you to marry me right now. But I'm telling you that's my intention someday, and that day will come sooner rather than later. Does that work for you?"

I swallow the lump in my throat and nod. "Yes. I love you so much, Ponyboy."

"I love you so much more, my gorgeous Glinda."

fifty-seven

. . .

Randall

"I don't want to go back to the real world," Wendy says against my chest, where she's draped in her usual spider-monkey fashion.

"I know, babe. I don't either." I smooth my hand over her hip. "But we have to."

"That was by far the best night of my life."

I can't stop my grin. "Oh, yeah?"

"Best sleep I've ever gotten," she teases.

"I don't recall you doing much sleeping."

She lifts her head to peer at me through a curtain of red hair. "Sleep is overrated."

"It definitely was last night." I move her hair out of the way so I can see her beautiful face, and then I turn my head to check the alarm clock. "All right, enough stalling. We can't miss our plane. I've got a lot of stuff to help Ash get done this afternoon."

I push myself up into a sitting position, thinking she'll remove herself from me in the process, but she doesn't. "What do you think you're doing?"

"I told you I wasn't going to leave your side the next few days." She wraps her arms more tightly around my neck. "I meant that literally."

"This should be fun, then." I swing my legs over the side of the bed and stand, but I don't hold onto her, so she quickly grapples for a hold on me but is unsuccessful at everything other than scratching the back of my neck. I grab her before she hits the floor and set her solidly on her feet.

She fists her hands on her hips. "You were going to let me fall?"

"Um, no. I caught you, remember? It happened five seconds ago?"

"Whatever."

She stomps off to the bathroom, and I follow in her wake.

"You gonna watch me brush my teeth again, like the psycho you are?" she asks as she squeezes toothpaste onto her brush.

I circle my arms around her from behind, set my chin on the top of her head, and gaze at her in the mirror. "I intend to watch you brush your teeth as often as I possibly can for the rest of my life."

We go directly to my parents' house from the airport. When we enter the front door, my sisters pounce on Wendy and drag her off to who knows where.

My brother claps his hand on my shoulder and gives me a knowing look. "I hope you had your fun, because we have a few days of not-so-fun tasks ahead of us."

"Best fun I've ever had, and I'm ready for whatever you throw at me. Let's get to it."

As he leads the way to Dad's office, I ask him how Leslie's doing.

"Better. Still not fully back to herself, but she should be okay tomorrow. The girls spent the morning at her place while Mom and I went to the funeral home to make the arrangements. None of the rest of us got sick, so we figured it would be safe for them to spend some time with her."

While he pulls some files out of a drawer, I ask him, "Would you be upset if Wendy and I get married before you and Leslie do?"

The file folders fall to the floor, papers scattering everywhere, but my usually meticulous brother pays no attention to them.

"Are you serious?" he asks.

"More than I've ever been. Would you be mad? Or would Leslie?"

"I'd prefer you to lock Wendy down as soon as possible before she comes to her senses."

"You're hilarious. So you don't care, but what about Leslie?"

"She'll love it. She was plotting for you two to get married before we knew you were spending time together."

"She truly won't be mad?"

"I'm pretty sure she won't be, but feel free to ask her. You're really planning to do this soon?"

"I'm hoping we'll be married before the end of the year."

He lets out a long whistle. "Have you two talked about it, or are you planning to spring it on her?"

"We talked about it." To an extent.

"Good. Then go for it. If you're both sure, then get it done and start making little redheaded babies for Mom to dote on."

"'Dote on'? Who are you?"

He shrugs. "No idea where that came from. Any other significant life decisions you need my input on before we get down to business?"

"Nope."

"So your dad didn't disinherit you and Ash after all?" Wendy asks.

It's the night before Dad's funeral, and we're on her couch for the first time in over a week. If I had to explain how at home I feel right here with her in my arms, I couldn't do it.

"No, he couldn't without Mom's permission. And she admitted that her refusal to do so is why he was making the recent threats against her."

"I love your mom."

I lean my head against hers. "Me, too. She's been through a lot more than I ever imagined. And I'm so glad she's now free of him."

"You're free of him, too, and I'm glad of that. And I hope you always remember you're not the man he said you were."

"Babe?" I run my fingers through her hair.

"Yeah?"

"When do you think you'll be ready to marry me?"

I expected her to freeze at the question, but she doesn't.

"Soon," she says.

My breath hitches in my throat. "How soon is soon?"

"As soon as you're ready to ask me for real."

My eyes widen. "Then—"

She claps her hand over my mouth. "I'm not done."

I lick her fingers, so she pinches my lips together instead.

"And when you have a ring," she adds. "I don't want a diamond, by the way. I want an emerald."

I remove her hand. "How about an emerald *and* diamonds?"

Her eyes sparkle. "I think I could make do with that."

"Want to make it even easier on me and tell me your ring size?"

"Four."

I kiss her nose. "This might be the quickest engagement planning session in the history of the world."

"Oh, there'd better be more than a ring, buddy."

"Um, okay. What else do you want?" I ask.

"That's up to you. I'm not doing everything for you. My only rule is it can have nothing to do with sports."

"Got it. I'll call Harry Caray tomorrow."

"Harry who?"

I chuckle. "Never mind. It's cute you don't get my sports jokes, even though ninety percent of the people in Chicago would've gotten that one."

"Don't make fun of my lack of sports knowledge if you want me to accept your emerald-and-diamonds ring."

I give her a serious nod. "Duly noted."

"You're spending the night, right?"

I cup her face in my hands. "I'm spending every single night with you for the rest of my life."

She raises an eyebrow. "That might be a little excessive. How about ninety-nine-point-nine-nine percent of nights?"

"I can work with that, but I'll miss you dreadfully on the other point-zero-one percent of nights."

"I'll miss you more."

"I'll miss you so much more."

epilogue

. . .

Milwaukee, November 1988

Wendy

"Aunt Glinda, is it time yet?"

My niece races toward me in a tiny replica of my wedding dress. Leslie catches her and swings her up into her arms before she can either knock me over or mess up my dress, at the risk of wrinkling both of their dresses.

"It's almost time, kiddo." I lean over and kiss her cheek. "Thank you for being my flower girl."

"I'm the mini bride, *not* the flower girl."

I force my smile down. "Oh, sorry," I say seriously. "Thank you for being my mini bride … who will toss flower petals down the aisle in front of me."

"You're welcome. I saw Uncle Randall a little bit ago," she announces. "He looks sooooo handsome. If you weren't going to marry him, I would."

The rest of us chuckle at her pronouncement.

"I'm glad you like him that much," I say.

"I don't like him." She dramatically places her hand over her heart. "I *love* him."

"What a coincidence. So do I!" I shoot her a silly grin, and she giggles before wriggling out of Leslie's arms and running back out of the room.

"Stay close!" Andrea yells after her. She turns to me, "It'll be just our luck if we can't find her when it's time for the ceremony."

"I'm pretty sure she won't miss her big moment."

My sister leans against the vanity while Melissa stands behind me, fussing with my hair.

"I saw you two eyeing my brother earlier," Leslie says to my other bridesmaids.

"Who, me?" Andrea says with an innocent look. "Why would I be eyeing up the most attractive man I've ever seen?"

I giggle while Leslie rolls her eyes.

Melissa adds with a sigh, "Too bad he has a girlfriend. I'd fight Andrea to the death over him if he didn't."

"Come on," Andrea says, "at least let me live long enough to be jealous of you. Plus, I think I have the advantage here, considering he and I live in the same city."

I ignore their continuing banter and ask Leslie, "How serious do you think Shannon is with Christi-with-an-I?"

"Pretty serious," she says. "They had a slow start, but they've been together five months now, which beats his previous record by four months."

My mother and Randall's mother enter the room together, talking animatedly. They're already the best of friends.

"Almost ready?" Mom asks and leans in to gently brush her lips against my cheek without messing up my makeup.

I grasp her hand. "I'm ready. You can send Dad in anytime."

"Even though I didn't know you when you were a baby, you'll always be my baby girl," my dad says as we wait for the church sanctuary doors to open. "You know that, right?"

I nod with tear-filled eyes. "I know. Now stop saying sappy things so I don't ruin my makeup."

"One more sappy thing," he says. "I'm proud of you for inviting Jack. I know that wasn't easy for you."

I swipe my finger under my eye to catch a tear before it falls. "It wasn't, but it was the right thing to do. Randall helped me see I need to give Jack a chance to show me he's not the same man who left me behind when he was still only a kid himself. Randall will never get an opportunity to see if his father can become a better man, but I can."

"He's a wise man—your almost-husband, I mean. I doubt I'll ever say those words about Jack."

I give him a soft smile. "I love you, Daddy."

"Love you more."

The opening bars of Pachelbel's *Canon in D* reach our ears, and the sanctuary doors swing open in front of us, revealing a room full of people who love me. But the only person I focus on is the man standing at the end of the aisle—the one who loves me so much more than all the rest.

Have you read
Leslie and Ash's story?

Paperbacks available at most online retailers

Ebooks available only on Amazon

IF YOU ENJOYED THIS BOOK, JOIN AUTHOR DANA WILKERSON'S ROMANCE MAILING LIST!

When you join the list, you receive bonus scenes, writing updates, sneak peeks of upcoming books, the potential of joining an upcoming launch team, book recommendations, and much more. Come join the fun!

To join, go to danawilkerson.com and click "Sign Up."

About the Author

Dana Wilkerson is the author of the Throwback RomComs series. She has been a professional writer and editor for almost two decades and was the collaborative writer of two non-fiction *New York Times* best sellers: *The Vow: The True Events That Inspired the Movie* (Kim and Krickitt Carpenter) and *Balancing It All* (Candace Cameron Bure).

She is also the author of the Totally 80s Mysteries cozy mystery series as D.A. Wilkerson.

Dana lives in Oklahoma and enjoys traveling, reading, being an aunt, binge-watching crime shows, and attending Oklahoma City Thunder basketball games.

Find Dana Online

Facebook and Instagram: @danawilkersonbooks

Website: danawilkerson.com

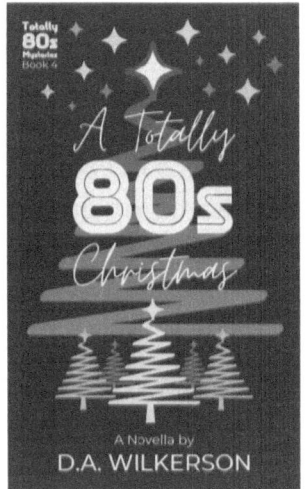

Totally 80s Mysteries

Available on Amazon